Throwaway Boy

by

J. E. Mooney

Acknowledgments

I want to thank my content editor, Mary Ann De Stefano, who set me on the right course corrections for nearly every aspect of this book.

Thanks to my copy editor Beth Mansbridge who was steadfast and excruciatingly detailed, making sure I sent nothing to publishers that wasn't as right as could be possible.

Thanks to Sam and Regina Christiansen who contributed in substantive ways to this endeavor with cover ideas, plot twists and general encouragement.

I want to thank my editor at Taylor and Seale, Veronica H. Hart, for recognizing the unique story and storytelling of Throwaway Boy and for her support of the book overall.

Finally, thanks to my wife, Robyn Lynn Mooney, to whom this book is dedicated, for trusting me to tell a story that belongs to her and for her belief in me, despite all I do to convince her differently.

This book is dedicated to Robyn Lynn Mooney, in memory of Christopher Skiner.

PART 1

Tina and Ricky

1

Christina Gets the News

When her office phone rang, Christina Spear cradled the receiver between her shoulder and chin. "Spearhead Design," she answered, "Tina speaking."

"I just thought you should know, Christina …."

The voice of Ricky Plyer's grandmother was unmistakable. "Hello, Ruthann," Tina said, sighing into the phone. "Thought I should know what, exactly?"

"Ricky's killed hisself. He's dead. Happened yesterday up in Dahlonega, Georgia."

Tina could barely move. Tears brimmed, then overflowed down her cheeks. "That … no, no. It can't be, Ruthann! Ricky was doing so, so well!" She grabbed a tissue from the box on her desk.

"'Fraid so. I know how close you was to Ricky an' all. He always said how much he wanted to be like you, all successful and confident."

A guttural sob burst from Tina, and the phone receiver fell from her chin to her desk. She was trembling when she picked it up, upside down. She screamed as she righted the phone. Her assistant, Dale, rushed into the office, but Tina stopped him with a traffic-cop stiff arm. He stood frozen, looking frightened.

"I-I can't believe this, Ruthann. … I can't believe Ricky would do such a thing. He just graduated from high school.

… He was counseling his friends from juvenile detention. He … he had a girlfriend. Jesus Christ, Ricky had his life on track! This makes no sense!" She sniffed her runny nose as more tears came.

"I know. I know. But Ricky's had a hard life. You know well, as most. Momma all drugged and in prison. Daddy never in the picture. No wonder he was stealin' and fightin' at such an early age. You did what you could. But demons is demons. Couple years a gettin' better don't erase nuthin'."

Tina's mind raced. When she'd met Ricky over three years ago, he was her first "project," after she volunteered to help young people acclimatize to life outside of juvenile detention. She recalled the carrot-topped, round-faced boy, stocky and sullen—mean, even—sitting in his grandmother's home a few days after his release. Tina compared her early memory to the young man she had taken to lunch only five weeks ago: smiling, brimming with plans, and surrounded by friends. He could not have, would not have taken his own life when the promise of that life was tangible and growing. Tina's body shook.

"Anyways, I just want to let you know," Ruthann said.

Tina looked at the receiver as if it were melting. Holding it at arm's length, she said, "Ruthann, I need to know everything. Where was he? At his brother's? What changed between last month and now. I want to—"

The dial tone buzzed in her ear. Tina raised the phone above her head as if to throw it, but eventually placed it back on its cradle.

Dale stuttered, "Tina, I …. Is there anything … what can I do?"

Tina looked at him with a plea surging in her eyes. She shook her head. "Nothing right now, Dale. Thank you."

"Ah … Okay. Look. You holler if you need anything. And I mean anything."

"I will. Thank you."

Dale was dismissed.

Tina turned in her chair and picked up a framed photo from the credenza. She and Ricky were posing in bright sunlight, with a parked F-16 fighter jet behind them. The photo been taken at the Naval Air Station Jacksonville Air Show, Ricky's first outing after leaving "juvy." She touched the glass on the picture, and then held the photo, arms outstretched as if a better vantage point might reveal something new, a clue as to why this bright, troubled boy would take his own life. She saw only the opening of a new life. What could have happened to that promise?

Tina felt a shudder rip through her body. She stood, put both hands on her desk, and took a few deep breaths. When she returned to normal, her questions had been supplanted with determination. Something terrible must have changed in Ricky's life to make him want to end it. She had to understand what forced such an about-face. She needed to know why he had not reached out to Tina when he needed her most.

"Dale," she called out, "could you come here, please?"

Her number two made a quick, stumbling appearance at her doorway. "Sure, Tina. Tell me what's going—I mean, tell me what you need."

"You remember Ricky Plyer, the young man I mentored when he was probationally released from juvenile detention three years ago? I just got word of his death." Seeing Dale's mouth gape open, she said, "I know." Tina wiped her nose again as her eyes watered. "I need time to get with the family and see how I can help." She shook her head. "I'm going to take some time off. We've got three requests for quotes for office space and deliverables for our two big projects. Please take the lead on these. I don't know how much time I'll need, but I'll stay in touch."

"I've got this, Tina. We've got this. We're a well-oiled machine, don't cha know."

Dale's normally endearing Minnesota expression only intruded on Tina at this moment. "That's all for now. Thanks, Dale."

Inside her Audi Cabriolet, she pounded her fists on the steering wheel, turned on the engine, and sat still. Aloud, she said, "My God, Ricky. How the hell could you do this? How in the name of God could this happen!"

2

Release?

Three years earlier, there was a late-afternoon rain typical of most July days in St. Augustine, Florida. It steamed back into the air, off the asphalt and concrete in Ruthann Plyer's neighborhood, The Pines. The queen palms and pin oaks blocked the sun more than the clouds themselves.

Rhonda Kingswood drove through the dense moisture with autopilot ease. To her passenger, new juvenile mentor Tina Spear, she said, "The Plyers live two blocks ahead."

"It may be a low-income neighborhood," Tina observed, swiveling her head, "but all the homes and yards seem well maintained."

"Hold that thought," Rhonda said.

She pulled up along the curb in front of 223 Pine Knob Court. The driveway looked as though a town sanitation truck had dumped half its cargo the full length of broken pavement and dirt. Three trash cans, two on their sides and one upside down, lay among the clutter. Tina drew a quick breath and opened the passenger door. The evaporating rain formed a fog over the yard. It clung like mold to the piles of household items and waste. Grass and weeds grew knee-high. An old refrigerator without a door perched on cinder blocks at the end of the driveway. A path emerged, on which Rhonda led Tina, to the back porch. Its screen door was ajar.

Rhonda knocked.

No answer.

She knocked again, twice, and called, "Ruthann? Ricky? It's Rhonda Kingswood. I'm here with Ricky's out-placement mentor. May we please come in?"

A rumbling sound came from inside the house. An interior door opened, through which poured a cacophony of rap music, television, and a barking dog. The smell of stale cigarette smoke made Tina gag. She tried to clear her throat. A woman stood at the threshold.

"Cole, shut that mutt of yours up, will ya?" Ruthann Plyer said, over her shoulder, as she stepped onto the porch. She stopped at the screen door, took a drag on her cigarette, and observed, "Well, don't you two look all nice an' prim. Come on in, come on in. It ain't still rainin', is it?"

Rhonda preceded Tina onto the porch, where three bicycles, with five wheels among them, lay together, pocked with rust. A worn sofa with torn cushions was covered with animal hair and newspapers.

"The rains have stopped," Rhonda answered, as if Ruthann had expected a response.

The interior door led into the kitchen, where the air was heavy and dank. Pots and dishes from days before awaited cleaning. The trio walked through to the living room. On a dining room chair in a corner by a window, sat a boy playing on a game device. He didn't look up. A man wearing dungarees and a sleeveless undershirt emerged from the back room. He held on to a mixed-breed dog about the size of a German shepherd. The dog leapt, all four legs into the air, but the fast-held leash grounded him instantly. The man snarled at the dog to stay down.

Standing in the center of the room, Rhonda asserted control. "Ruthann, would you mind switching off the television for a few moments? I want to introduce Ms. Spear to the family."

Ruthann obliged with a shrug. "Cole, turn off your music, will ya?"

"Ms. Spear is the volunteer mentor with Project Uplift. As you know, part of Ricky's court-ordered release from Seminole Forks requires that he be teamed with a mentor. As I'm sure you recall, Ruthann, a mentor is a guide and go-to adult, not a probation officer like myself."

Ruthann nodded.

Rhonda looked over at Ricky. "Ricky, will you please come over and meet Ms. Spear?"

Tina and Rhonda could have been steamed broccoli, for all the attention the boy gave the two women. He continued playing his game.

A gesture from Rhonda to Ruthann caused the latter to scratch her head. As an understanding of sorts rose in Ruthann, she pointed to the man holding the dog in the doorway. "This here's Cole Hart. He's Ricky's ex-stepdad. Been staying with us till he gets settled."

Cole brushed a few long strands of hair off his face and took a step toward the visitors. His dog jumped up, and Cole hit it on the head with a closed fist. "Get the fuck down!"

The dog lay down with a whimper.

Cole offered his hand, saying, "Pleased to meet you."

The women looked at each other and, in turn, tentatively shook Cole's hand. Without thinking they both wiped their hand on their slacks.

"We're here," Rhonda repeated, "to introduce Ms. Spear and Ricky to each other and to … hopefully …"—Rhonda inhaled to stifle the sigh in her voice—"set a time when the two of you—you, Ricky, and you, Ms. Spear, can meet."

Tina took a step forward. "If I could, Rhonda … Ricky, I'd like it if you would please call me Tina. Okay?"

Still nothing from Ricky. She walked over to him and squatted next to his seat.

Ricky turned his back to her and moved to the end of the couch.

"Ricky, look. Please. I want you to have a person you can say anything to. That's me. I'm a grown-up, so it will probably be hard at first. But here's the thing. I've got thr— two boys, myself. They're in their twenties now, but they were once fourteen, like you. They told me almost everything and what they didn't tell me, I always found out. And maybe you can meet them someday." She paused. "I'm not afraid of you, Ricky, and you have no reason to be afraid of me."

"Not afraid of no woman."

"Well, there's a start."

Rhonda walked over and stood behind Tina, still hunched down. "Ricky, we know you don't want to go back to detention. Right?"

Ricky shook his head.

"So, to help make sure you don't, you and Ms. Spear need to see each other from time to time."

"Why?" Ricky burst out. "What's she gonna do, anyway?"

Tina wobbled on her bended legs, eventually standing up. Rhonda started to answer, but Tina stopped her with a wave of her hand.

"Because, Ricky, I'm an adult who will be your friend. Not because I have to. Because I want to. I asked if I could be your friend."

Ricky looked at Tina from the corners of his eyes. He looked back at his game, but he had stopped playing.

"I'll tell you what. Today's Monday. I'll come by here on Wednesday, and we'll go somewhere for lunch, okay? Just you and me. Tell me what you'd like to have for lunch, and we'll go there."

"Micky D's."

Tina looked at Rhonda.

"McDonald's," Rhonda explained.

Tina Spear hadn't eaten fast food in fifteen years. "I'd love to have lunch with you at McDonald's, Ricky. My treat. How about I pick you up here at twelve thirty on Wednesday? Is that okay, Ruthann?"

She shrugged. "Suits me fine. We'll see if the boy's ready."

After Rhonda reiterated the ground rules for mentors, mentees, and their families, the two professional women walked back to Rhonda's car and left The Pines.

Tina's thoughts rushed into her voice as they rode back into town. "What the hell kind of environment is that for a young man? Or for anyone? No wonder he's been in juvenile detention. And is there any information on the whereabouts of his real parents? I'm having trouble picturing Ruthann as a grandmother, let alone a mother!"

Rhonda kept her eyes on the road. "As far as anyone knows, his biological mother has been either in rehab or prison in Georgia for years. I'm sure you recall this from Ricky's file."

Tina nodded.

"What the file didn't tell you was she's in prison now for her third possession with intent to sell, for prostitution, and assault, which was knocked down from attempted murder."

"What the…! Jesus. How awful."

"His father was never in the picture. I doubt even the mother knows who the father is. Ricky's birth certificate has the father listed as unknown."

"This boy never had a chance, did he?"

"Hard to say for sure. His older brother, by fifteen or so years, made it into the army. He's been in the military nine or ten years, I believe."

"Does Ricky have any relationship with this brother? Could that be a starting place for finding him a decent male role model?"

"If you can get it out of Ricky. Ruthann may know something, but she can be difficult to ... interpret."

"Wow," Tina said, staring forward. "I have my work cut out for me, don't I?"

"Yes, ma'am. Yes, you do. I know this isn't easy and you're a volunteer. But I've seen good volunteers change the lives of some of these kids. That's a tall order and may not be possible here, but it's damn sure worth the try."

Tina smiled and looked at Rhonda.

Rhonda returned her smile, still staring at the road. "Though I don't know you, I'm going to go out on a limb here. You're a business owner, right? A successful one, I understand. Say you take that energy, that grit it took you to build a business, and you apply it to this boy and his development. You could do some real good here. Think of that."

"Great pep talk, Rhonda. You don't have to worry about me. I've got a feeling about Ricky. A good feeling."

"Hold that thought," Rhonda said.

* * *

Two days later it seemed odd and a bit appropriate to Tina that the trip to the Plyer's home in the middle of a sunny day had the same feeling as the journey during a rainy evening two days prior. Little sunlight penetrated the palm, pine, and oak canopy. When she got out of her car, the air clung to her like a rag from a washing machine.

She knocked on the back porch door and called, "Ricky? Ruthann? It's Tina Spear."

After a few seconds she knocked and called again. "I'm here to take Ricky to lunch."

When another thirty seconds passed, Tina knocked louder and opened the screen door and the interior door. She crossed the threshold and stopped.

"Ricky? Ricky Plyer. It's your friend, Tina."

Silence. She walked through the kitchen, observing the unchanged décor, into the living room. Ricky was on the couch, wearing jeans and a T-shirt identical to the ones he had on two nights ago. Today he also sported a pair of earphones plugged into his Game Boy, on which he was actively tapping.

Tina's heart suddenly doubled its pace. He looked so much like her middle son, Max. Totally absorbed in a minute digital dimension, headphones or earbuds blocking out the rest of the world. She didn't try to suppress the surge of sadness welling up in her throat.

Ricky looked up and stared at the grown-up in front of him.

She held out her hand. "Come on, young man. You and I are going to lunch."

When Ricky didn't move, Tina slowly moved her hands up to Ricky's head. He leaned away from her, but not fast or far enough to keep Tina from grabbing hold of the earphones and lifting them quickly from Ricky's ears.

"Hey!" he yelled. He grabbed at the headphones, but Tina had moved a few steps back. Ricky started to rise but sat back down as he pursed his lips. "Those are mine!"

"I know, and I'll give them back to you in a second. But you and I are going to lunch now, remember? And by the way, where is your grandmother?"

"She went out."

"And your ex-stepdad?"

"He went out."

"So, it's just you and me, right?"

Ricky shrugged.

"How about you and I go to lunch? Come on. Up, up!" She again extended her hand.

Ricky didn't move.

"You are hungry, aren't you?"

Another shrug.

"Say we go to Micky D's and get some burgers. I'll bring you back here safe and sound, I promise. And you'll get your headphones back."

Ricky rose, did not take Tina's hand, and headed out through the kitchen. She caught up to him at the screen door.

Tina hesitated. "Should we lock the back door here, Ricky?"

"Nope."

"Nope? Ricky, the house needs to be secured when no one is home."

"Bedrooms' locked up. 'S all anyone cares about. 'Sides, no lock for this door."

Tina nodded, then shook her head. "All righty, then! Off we go. I'm pretty hungry."

Ricky came up to the passenger side of Tina's car and stared, wide-eyed, as if it was a spaceship. Tina opened the door for him, and he got in. She took her seat and looked over at Ricky.

"Buckle up!" she ordered.

"Why, you a bad driver?"

"Very funny. As a matter of fact, I'm an excellent driver, but lots of other people are not. Please put your seatbelt on."

Ricky stared straight ahead.

"If you are even a bit hungry and you want to get out and do something a bit more fun than sitting in your grandmother's house all day long, then please buckle your seat belt so we can get going. Please."

Sloth-like, Ricky took hold of the strap behind him, fumbling as he tried to pull it forward. Tina bent across to help him. Ricky recoiled, fending Tina off with his elbow. Hands back in her lap, Tina said, "I couldn't figure these out for the longest time, either. But I learned eventually. May I show you what I learned, Ricky?"

He nodded and allowed Tina to show him how to buckle himself up in her car.

"You're welcome, my friend." She drove out of the neighborhood.

Though she had never been inside the McDonald's on Ponce de Leon Boulevard, Tina had seen the steady line of cars most weekdays. Reasoning that it was going to be a long wait, she asked Ricky if he wanted to go in and sit down.

"Don't wanna go in," he answered. "Too many assholes."

"Fine with me." She smiled.

At the window, she ordered a fish sandwich, hold the mayo, and a cup of water. For Ricky she ordered a Big Mac, fries, and a chocolate shake. Back on the road the silence between them felt like a chasm, as Ricky ate and Tina thought better of trying to gobble down a lunch she didn't want. She turned down a side street and made a right onto San Marco, heading to downtown St. Augustine. When they were coming around a corner, Ricky pointed to the Castillo de San Marcos, the imposing Spanish fort that had survived since the late 1600s.

"Holy shit!" He pointed. "What's that?"

"That, young man, is the first masonry fort ever constructed in the US, built by Pedro Menendez in 1665. Well, it was started in 1665. It took the Spanish thirty years to complete."

"Why so long?" Ricky asked with his mouth full.

"Those were brutal times, Ricky. They built everything from scratch. The Spanish, the French, and the British were all at war with each other. Money ran out. It took amazing courage and force of will, in those times, just to hang on to life, you know."

Ricky swallowed. "Makes no sense."

Tina tilted her head. "Why would you say such a thing?"

"Thirty years to build a fort? Why didn't they go somewhere else?"

"They couldn't go anywhere else. They were trying to make a home here."

Ricky shrugged and shook his head as he took a big bite of his sandwich.

Tina shook her head as well. So much like Max and so not like Max at all.

3

Saying Goodbye

Tina was relieved her husband Walter wouldn't make the drive with her to pay his respects in Dahlonega. For too long now, extended car rides together had been tense silences, unwanted remorse, and arguing.

Waiting for Walter at the door, she was ready to leave at six, wearing jeans, a gray knit top, and a Spearhead design baseball cap. In her bag she had two changes of clothes, a toiletry kit, and her laptop.

"Planning to put the top down?" Walter asked in a monotone, pointing to her head and handing her a travel mug of fresh black coffee.

Tina tried to chuckle, took hold of the mug, and tiptoed, offering her cheek for her lanky husband to kiss. "Thanks. Only on the back roads and only if it's cool enough. Hopefully, the Georgia mountain air will accommodate me."

"Please be careful. And try not to ask too many questions."

"Walter, please. I'm only there to pay my respects and hear about Ricky from those who knew him. It will be difficult enough without my prying."

"You know what I mean. I know you, Christina Spear. You can't live with all the uncertainty you've conjured about his death."

She narrowed her eyes. "I haven't conjured anything. But I haven't a shred of information how this might have happened. And yes, a big part of why I want to attend his service is to learn what happened."

Silence filled the foyer.

"Please give me the benefit of the doubt here," she said. "I know you think I've projected Max into Ricky, this ... what did you call him early on? ... undeserving hoodlum. But he needed a special kind of care to grow past the hand he'd been dealt. Oh, Walter, this is another old conversation. I have to go."

He lowered his head. "Okay. I didn't mean to hurt you. I didn't. I only want you to get some distance from this before you get hurt even more. God knows, there's enough pain in this household without mining the pain of others."

"That's a ridiculous thing to say."

"Jesus Christ, Tina. You don't know these people. I'm just asking that you be patient. You know how you get." He instantly regretted his choice of words.

"How I get? You can be such an ass. I'm leaving now." She pushed by him, through the doorway.

"I'm sorry," he said, and she stopped at those words.

He continued. "That came out wrong. I meant you are so strong-willed, so certain of yourself and your hunches, that you can overwhelm people. You know that's true. I'm only asking that you keep a low profile. That's all. Please just tone down the probing."

She turned to face him. "Ricky's suicide makes no sense. And I can't find any information about him. No phone, no address. Nothing. Ruthann has pretty much disappeared. The last time I saw Ricky, he had just returned from his brother's, and he seemed quite happy to have reconnected with him."

"Are you even sure there is a service for Ricky tomorrow?"

J. E. Mooney / 17

"I'm not, and that's the very reason why I have to go now. I'll be safe, Walter."

"Right. Keep me posted. No looking behind the curtains, okay?"

"Really, Walter. Sometimes you worry just to worry."

A smile like a sneer crossed his lips before he planted a kiss on Tina's cheek. He put his hands on her shoulders. "These last six years have been brutal: We both need time together without any noise. You know. Time that's only ours."

She stepped back so that his arms fell away. "We try. We give up. We try again. My God, it makes me so weary."

"Dr. Arnau believes we can break this cycle."

"I need to finish this business about Ricky. Then we can make some space to sort 'us' out."

She turned and walked quickly to her car before Walter could answer, the wind twirling her ponytail like a pinwheel. Walter stood in the threshold, arms folded. He waved as the Cabriolet turned out of the driveway and sped away. Tina didn't wave back.

Dahlonega, 65 miles north of Atlanta, was a seven-hour drive for Tina. Her plan was to get there no later than midafternoon and go straight to the police department to find out where Ricky's body had been taken and when his service would take place. Ruthann would be no help getting information. The woman never answered her phone when Tina called her. Never.

The early-morning traffic up I-95 was easy into Jacksonville, where she diverted to I-10 and then to I-75 for Atlanta. She tuned her satellite radio to a news and commentary program she listened to regularly. Today she found it difficult to follow the reported events and the quirky analysis. She sipped the coffee and let tears roll down her cheeks as she revisited her time with Ricky. A laugh sprang unexpectedly with a memory of Ricky's high school graduation. After the ceremony he ran toward Tina with a big smile and tripped on the long red graduation gown, hurtling dervish-like, flailing arms barely keeping his balance and laughing the whole time. When he finally stopped, in control and out of breath, Ricky stood awkwardly in front of Tina, expectant and shy. She had put her arms around him and hugged him for the second time in three years.

An Amber Alert squawked like a prehistoric bird over the radio, shattering her reverie. Another lost child somewhere. A little girl had possibly become the victim of a depraved person who lured her close enough to ensnare her and commit something unthinkable. Or maybe she had just wandered off. Maybe her parents or the authorities would find her in the coming days, scared yet safe in some forest or park. Maybe it would turn out to be another exception to the missing child outcomes.

Traffic through Atlanta was never easy unless it was in the early morning before the rush of commuters. Tina sought to calm herself with some classical music. Mussorgsky's *Night on Bald Mountain* was playing. It was a piece she liked, energetic and evocative. But there was already too much frenzy on the highway, so she turned off her radio. Around I-285, the Atlanta perimeter, she exited to Route 19 and Alpharetta, and continued north until she saw the signs for Dahlonega.

The Lumpkin County Sheriff's Department was part of the recently built municipal complex. Most of the offices of the town government were housed there. Not sure whom to ask for nor for what, Tina approached the day officer's window. There was no line, but all of the ten chairs in the narrow corridor were occupied.

When the day officer finally noticed her, Tina said, "I need your help, please. A young man committed suicide two days ago here, and I was hoping the police would know where his body was taken and when the funeral might be."

"What's your relationship to the deceased, ma'am?" asked the officer, without looking up from her computer.

"I was one of his counselors and a mentor to him."

The day officer swiveled her head toward Tina. "What's the boy's name?"

"The *young man's* name is … was Richard Plyer. He was known as Ricky. I understand his brother, Jacob Plyer, has been living here since his discharge from the military."

The officer nodded and typed again on the computer keyboard. She stared at the screen, eventually crossing her arms across her lap and nodding some more. "And your name, ma'am?"

"Christina Spear."

"As you are not related to the boy, Ms. Spear, I can't release any information to you. You'll have to go the family and perhaps they can help."

"But the family is my problem, Officer. They have been … in a bad way before and after Ricky's death. They don't communicate well."

"I'm unable to help you at this time, Ms. Spear."

Tina wasn't surprised. "Where can I find Ricky's brother, Jacob Plyer, Officer?"

"Phone book or internet would be your best bet."

Tina took out her iPhone and saw she had no signal in the building. "Is there a library nearby?" she asked.

"Lumpkin County Library is out the door you came through, take a right and your second left. Not five minutes' walk."

Tina thanked the officer and left. She was going to find Ricky's service if she had to visit every church in the county.

On her way to the library Tina noticed her cell service had been restored. She stopped near a sidewalk and punched in: Jacob Plyer Lumpkin County Georgia. Her search engine came back with paid people-finder services and finally the White Pages. There was no listing for anyone named Plyer, so she continued to the library.

Tina noted how full of light the library was, particularly compared to the police department. Past the security gate, she hurried to where two young women were in conversation behind a check-out counter. One of them greeted Tina. The young woman directed her to a directory area where she could get on the internet and find other local reference materials. She gave Tina a temporary password.

Her search was inconclusive for about ten minutes, until she looked at the online version of the local paper and turned up Ricky's obituary.

"Richard Plyer, 18, formerly of St. Augustine, Florida, and resident of Auraria, Georgia, died Thursday at his home. He is survived by his brother Jacob Plyer, also of Auraria."

This stark, cryptic notice brought the tears back to Tina. Nowhere was there any indication of Ricky's trajectory, the struggles he had endured and overcome, the life he was building. She wiped her eyes and looked for more. There was nothing. Not even a mention of a service. And since when had Ricky become a "resident" of Auraria?

"So strange," she said out loud. "Auraria. Where is that?" She thought she recalled seeing a sign for Auraria before she entered Dahlonega. Some additional searching turned up references to the old gold rush town south of Dahlonega. Today, apparently, it was considered a ghost town—deserted save for a souvenir and convenience store. Tina checked Google maps and noted a small cluster of homes on the north side of Auraria, on the Dahlonega city limit. "Could this be where his brother lives?" She decided to drive out there to learn what she could.

There was indeed a small white sign along Route 9E south, stating, AURARIA. After less than two miles she saw a dilapidated building and then the store. She parked in one of the three spaces in front and walked into the building.

"Hi," she said. "Is anyone here?"

After a few moments a well-groomed man in his fifties, wearing a flannel shirt, overalls, and a blue blazer walked up to her with a smile. "Yes, ma'am, there is indeed someone here. That would be me. How may I be of service to you?"

Tina held out her hand, which the gentleman shook politely. "I'm Tina Spear."

"A pleasure, Miss Spear."

"I'm looking for the brother of a young man I worked with in Florida. The man's name is Jacob Plyer and I believe he lives in Auraria."

"No one lives in Auraria, Miss Spear. Not for the last sixty years, anyway."

"This is so odd. And confusing," Tina said. "The young man I worked with, Jacob Plyer's brother Ricky, died recently and—"

"Sorry to hear that, ma'am. Truly," he said, scratching his head.

"Yes. Thank you. In any case, the death notice said both he and his brother lived here in Auraria. Are there no homes here? No people living here?"

"I may know who you're looking for, ma'am. Is Jacob Plyer former military? There is a man comes by here probably twice, three times a month. Usually buys a soda or some milk. But I suspect he's just lookin' for cell service. Never fails to make a phone call or two while he's here. Last two times, came in with a young man looked a lot like him."

He paused, and Tina leaned toward him with expectation.

"I heard about the young man's death, too. Bright kid, far as I could tell."

Tina lifted herself onto her tiptoes without noticing. Her eyes widened. "So, you knew Ricky, I mean at least you saw him a few times. How did he seem to you?"

"Like I said, ma'am, he seemed like a smart kid. Bright red hair, right? Was probably a better influence on his brother than the reverse. Young man was always talking to the older guy when they came in here. The soldier would listen, shake or nod his head. He walked with a cane. Funny pair. Kinda' like the younger one was the older brother."

Tina's heart beat faster. "Do you know where Jacob Plyer lives, by any chance?"

"I might. Go up Auraria Road here, back toward Dahlonega. About a mile and a half on the left side of the road there're two mailboxes at the head of a dirt driveway. It goes up into the mountainside about a quarter of a mile. My guess is his house is the one on the right."

"I can't thank you enough. I'll head there right now." Tina grabbed his right hand and shook it with both of hers. Then she ran out the door to her car.

Though unsure what to expect, Tina did not imagine the well-kept yard and a fresh cottage-style home when she turned in to the gravel driveway and made her way up the hill. The driveway led to a stone berm that parted wide enough for a flagstone sidewalk to begin. Where the driveway stopped and the hill morphed into a cliff, Tina parked next to the army-green Ford pickup truck. She locked the car and walked up the sidewalk and onto the front porch. On either side of the stairs, azaleas flourished though their blooms had vanished in the onslaught of summer. The only sounds came from the trills of mockingbirds.

Everywhere Tina looked she saw the antithesis of Ruthann's dirty bungalow. She rang the doorbell.

A barefoot man dressed in faded clothes, holding a baby, opened the door. The baby squirmed and fussed. Before greeting his visitor, he focused on the child. "Hush now, Emma. Gimme a second here, honey. Shh." To Tina he said, "Can I help you, ma'am?"

It took Tina a few seconds before she could respond. The man before her looked so much like Ricky. "My name is Tina Spear. I'm trying to find Jacob Plyer. I was close to his brother, Ricky, who I understand died recently."

"You was close to Ricky? Say your name again, ma'am."

"Tina Spear. And yes, I was close to Ricky. I was his mentor for a year, after he was released from juvenile detention. He worked for me from time to time. I considered him a friend. Are you his brother Jacob?"

"I am."

The next few seconds were silent.

Eventually, Tina said, "I'm hoping to attend whatever service there will be for Ricky, Mr. Plyer. If you can tell me when the service will be, I'll be heading back into town to book a room for however many days I need to stay."

"No need, ma'am. We had a service for him yesterday afternoon."

Tina took this in slowly. "That's ... that's not possible. That's ... I can't believe this. Ricky died only three days ago. I came here to ... to say goodbye." Tina shook her head and looked away.

Jacob Plyer stepped out onto the porch, limping severely on his left leg, and closed the door behind him. The child continued to fuss, but he paid her no attention. Tina noticed Jacob's resemblance to his brother, his stocky chest, big arms, round head popping with reddish hair. Jacob's hair was longer than Ricky's and he had a rust-colored beard. He was likely six inches taller than she remembered Ricky. Tina took a step back.

"Ma'am, Mrs. Spear..."

"Or Tina. That's easier."

"Well, now, Mrs. Spear, this was just awful what happened here, truly awful. Side o' Ricky's head was blown off. I've still got bits of bone and blood on my wall and carpet. Even in Iraq, I never—"

"Good God! Please! Ricky shot himself here? Was he living here? Oh my God! How terrible it must have been. How terrible it still ...." Tina started to cry.

"Yes, ma'am. It's been terrible. Just awful. I mean ... Ricky was a tough kid, had a bad time, for sure, but I didn't expect this. I ... I didn't expect when he came here to live, he'd still be so ... so ...." Jacob swallowed hard and turned his head toward the baby.

"So what, Jacob?"

"So angry. So mad at ... everything."

"Mr. Plyer, I have to tell you, the person you just described is not the Ricky I saw last month. Can we go inside and talk, please? I'd like to know about Ricky's last weeks here."

Jacob steadied himself and lowered the tone of his voice. "Now's not a good time. We're not ready for company yet."

"You and this beautiful baby's mother. Of course." Tina reached out to touch the child, who recoiled from the strange woman. Jacob did as well. She pulled her hand back quickly.

"Emma's mom and me. Yes, ma'am."

"Did your mother come up for the funeral, Jacob?"

"My mother? My fuckin' mother's rottin' in prison in 'Lanta. She's, she's ... aw, fuck!"

"I'm so sorry. I meant Ruthann. Your grandmother. She adopted Ricky, so I think of her solely as Ricky's mom, and because you're his brother, I—"

"Ruthann's not a whole lot better. Didn't come up. Called and wanted to know if there was any money outta

Ricky's death. Bitch was thinking just 'cause she got five hundred dollars a month for adopting Ricky, she was goin' get some death insurance or somethin'. My grandmother … I swear. She's hardly any better than that bitch daughter of hers!"

Tina shuddered and stepped backward to the edge of the porch stairs.

"I'd like to come by tomorrow, Mr. Plyer, and talk to you some more about Ricky, if you think it would be okay."

"I think so. I'll check with my wife. Later in the afternoon, like today, would be best."

"Do you have a phone number I can use to let you know I'm on my way? I can leave a message."

"Cell service don't work so good out here, ma'am. Our regular phone ain't listed."

His eyes, glassy and distant, told Tina all she needed to know—for now.

"Best you come around four."

"Four tomorrow afternoon. Thank you. I'll see you then. Tell me, please, where is Ricky buried?"

"He ain't buried, ma'am. He was cremated yesterday, and we scattered his ashes along the creek, other side of the paddock there." Jacob gestured with his head toward the fence where Tina had parked, and to the forest beyond. "Ricky hung out in those woods lots a' times. Went swimming in the creek. Seemed only right his remains get scattered there." Jacob lowered his head and shook it. "My little Ricky … deserved better, damn it!" Jacob drew a breath, closed his eyes, and threw his head back. Tears streamed down his face.

Tina's stomach clenched into a stone. She turned to go down the steps. "I'll be by at four tomorrow, Jacob. I very much appreciate this."

Jacob nodded, after which he turned into the house and closed the door. *Clank* went a latching deadbolt.

As she descended, the stairs seemed twice as high and twice as far apart as when Tina mounted them. Every step back to her car was heavy and difficult, as though some enormous weight had moved her center of gravity above her head. She stumbled three times before she threw open her car door and dropped into the driver's seat.

Covering her face with both hands and shaking her head, she yelled into them, "This isn't right. This isn't fucking right!"

* * *

The Days Inn on Route 9E was as convenient as any other hotel, and a bit cheaper, with the added advantage of available upper-floor rooms. After checking in, Tina returned to the library for more research.

She learned that Georgia law requires the coroner to fully investigate any would-be suicide as a possible murder, until it is "nearly" conclusively proven to be suicide. "Nearly," in this case, meaning substantially more likely a suicide than a murder. This process can take up to 72 hours. Ricky hadn't even been dead 72 hours and was already cremated. A pit returned in Tina's stomach. Her hand on the mouse began to shake.

The Lumpkin County coroner's office address and phone number were on the webpage of county departments. She entered the phone number into her cell phone, closed the computer, and walked to the library entrance hall with purpose. Leaning next to the entrance doors, Tina pushed "Call" on her cell phone. She navigated the voice-mail system, to a clerk whose monotone "Lumpkin County Coroner's Office" answer made her wince. Was she expecting something cheerier from the morgue?

"Thanks for taking my call. I'm trying to find out about a young man who committed suicide a few days ago. May I please have an appointment to see the coroner? It will only take a few minutes."

"Friday at nine thirty is the next available."

"No, thank you," Tina said. "I've driven eight hours, only to be told I missed the service and ... and ... I need ... this is so hard to understand. So, please can I get in this afternoon? It'll be only a few minutes. I promise."

"I can't guarantee the coroner will be available, but I suggest you try later this afternoon, before closing, just before five. I'll let him know. Be sure to bring your driver's license."

"Thank you so much. I can't tell you how much this means." Tina winced at her effusive gratitude. It was ten after four now. She decided to head straight to the coroner's office.

The county coroner laboratory and morgue were in a building connected to the police headquarters by an enclosed walkway. It took Tina all of ten minutes to get to the morgue entrance from the library. Standing in front of a service window she wrapped her arms across her body and held her shoulders, listening for signs of life. Through the sliding glass window she saw an empty office chair in front of two blank computer screens. Next to one of them was a half-empty giant slushie.

"Hel-*lo*, is anyone here?" She tapped on the glass and waited for a few moments, then tapped again.

After a minute, a thin young man with a bird's nest of brown hair, wearing a lab coat, fell into the empty chair. He swiveled around and pushed toward the window. Before uttering a word, he looked at Tina and arched his eyebrows. "You're not Detective Tillyard!" he said.

"Your powers of observation are intact, young man," she said. Though she considered she may have offended him, Tina persevered. "I just need a few minutes with the coroner. I was told he might still be here."

"He's here, all right. We've been waiting for Detective Tillyard for twenty minutes now."

"If I can see him now, I won't be but—"

A man with milk-chocolate skin, in a sport coat, jeans, and sneakers burst through the entrance and rushed to the window, brushing Tina aside.

"Sorry I'm late, Roland. Can you let me in now?"

Ignored as though invisible, Tina stood her ground and exclaimed, "Ahem! Excuse me. Was I not standing here when you ran ahead of me?" He was lean, his shoulders perfectly square, like his jaw, but his eyes were soft, revealing, Tina thought, a heart larger than he might have wished. Her anger dissipated.

"Oh. My apologies, ma'am." He looked at Tina cautiously and slowly extended a hand. "Sergeant Devon Tillyard. I'm late to see the coroner."

Tina shook his hand, allowing it to stay moments after Tillyard loosened his grip. "Thank you, Sergeant. Is it Detective or Sergeant? The man at the counter called you Detective."

"It's both ma'am."

"Oh. Thank you, I'm here, Detective, to learn about a young man who committed suicide a few days ago."

Tillyard looked directly into Tina's eyes and lifted his chin. "Really?" he said.

She returned his gaze as if it were an indulgence. Tillyard was clearly athletic, yet he carried himself with a nonchalance that made his looks seem unimportant to him. Tina was buoyed.

"Ricky, or Richard, I should say, Plyer. I was his mentor and counselor for over a year and his friend for three years. I was told he committed suicide, and I drove eight hours straight as soon as I got the news. I was stunned to learn that he was released from the morgue and cremated not 24 hours later. That's not right!" A heaving sob erupted from her before she could control it. She quickly righted herself, wiped away her sniffle, and continued. "His brother Jacob told me this not two hours ago. This is absurd, Detective! How does a young man shoot himself and, in forty-eight hours, is turned into ashes while under the county's control? How?"

Tillyard stood like a column for a few moments, making direct eye contact with Tina. She held his stare with all the power and honesty her heart could summon.

The ridge of the detective's shoulders sloped as he exhaled. "What's your name, ma'am?" He smiled.

"I'm Tina Spear. I live in St. Augustine, Florida—as did Ricky, until five weeks ago, apparently."

"Would you speak with me outside, please, Ms. Spear?"

Tina scowled. "I'm not going to just go away, Detective. I'm looking for some answers. I deserve answers. And you know who else deserves answers? A smart boy who turned his life around, who's now dead. That's who."

With a loud exhale, Tillyard said, "Fine. This place will do." He looked at Tina without any expression and said, "I'm here, Ms. Spear, because I'm investigating Richard Plyer's death. Please don't get carried away—"

"Do not condescend to me! I buried a child of my own some years ago. I've fought for at-risk children my whole adult life, both for and against the systems we're told are supposed to support them. This isn't close to carried away, you ..." Tina felt the sweat soaking her clothes. She unclenched her fists at her side and pulled herself back.

"Now, please. How much can you tell me about Ricky's death."

"As I said, I'm here to see the coroner with my own questions. If you'll wait for me here or outside, you can come back to my office and we can talk."

The detective returned to the service window, and the assistant buzzed him through the double doors at the corridor's end. Tina opened the exit door and, on the threshold, drew in a series of deep breaths. "Finally," she uttered out loud. "Someone who might actually help!"

4

Anger Mismanagement

PAST

A week after Tina's first lunch with Ricky, she called Ruthann to plan a second. Tina wanted a conversation with him, not just a meal and a drop-off. Ruthann did not answer the five calls made over three hours' time. When the pattern seemed destined to repeat itself the next day, Tina decided to go pick up Ricky.

Driving to the sad bungalow in The Pines she clenched the wheel of her Audi until the pain reached her elbows. As she set the handbrake, she shook her head and muttered, "Am I doing the right thing here?"

She knocked on the outer screen door with some force and announced herself, repeating the gesture on the inner door. She heard noises, like furniture moving and a door slamming. A dog bark erupted and, as quickly, disappeared. As her hand went to twist the doorknob, Cole Hart flung the door open and wiped hair out of his eyes.

"Can I help you?" he asked.

A startled Tina settled her nerves and peered around him to look for Ricky. He was on the couch, Game Boy in hand. "Hello again, Mr. Hart. I'm here to see Ricky and, hopefully, collect him for lunch."

Cole held the door and stood on the threshold, on guard. "Ruthann didn't say nuthin' to me 'bout you comin' over today. Now's not a good time."

Tina was suddenly smacked with the odor of marijuana. She coughed and turned her face away from the ferret of a man in front of her. She shouted, "Ricky. Let's get some lunch together, okay?"

When Ricky didn't respond, Tina slipped under Cole's arm and into the kitchen.

"Hey, lady, look! This here's our home. You can't just—"

"I don't care if you're smoking marijuana. I don't. It's practically legal anyway. I'm just here to take Ricky to lunch." She walked through the kitchen, stood in front of Ricky, and held out her hand. "Hungry?"

Cole had followed at her shoulder, his breath heavy and stale. He went around her to stand between her and the rest of the house. "Come on, kid. Get up and take a lunch trip with the lady, heh?"

"You don't fucking tell me what to do, you got that?" Ricky looked at Cole without raising his head.

"Suit yourself, dumbass. I got shit to do." He stormed into the back of the house. The sounds of a slamming door and a hard lock echoed into the kitchen.

"Shithead," Ricky said.

After clearing her throat, Tina said, "I tried calling your grandmother a number of times, Ricky. I had no choice but to come over unannounced. Please come to lunch with me."

He looked up at Tina, put the Game Boy on the sofa, and stood up. "Okay. You're the boss."

She walked next to him as they left the house. "I'm not the boss. I'm your friend."

"Like rent-a-friend? I don't need another friend."

"Apparently you do. I know that man back there ... isn't a good friend to you. And Ricky, with your probation rules, you can't be around drugs, let alone use them."

"I don't fucking use drugs anymore. I quit that shit!" He stopped at the Audi's passenger door.

"Very good." Tina nodded. "Let's go someplace where we can sit down and eat a proper meal. And without a crowd. I assume this is okay with you."

"Just want a burger."

"I have a few places in mind. Come on. Please."

The Press was a small restaurant just outside of St. Augustine's center, hiding in a strip mall. In the car, Tina asked Ricky about school, as she had for her own adolescent sons, recalling their reluctance to speak at length to any adult. She gently probed his one-word answers for any opening, a portal, however small, to Ricky's vulnerability and trust.

Inside The Press they chose a table for two in a corner near the door. After the unsweetened tea and Coke arrived, Tina watched Ricky take a thirsty slurp.

"You'd better slow down before you get a brain freeze."

Ricky shook his head, continuing to suck on the straw.

"You don't get enough cola at home, I'm guessing."

He stopped. "Ruthann likes Dr Pepper and Cole drinks beer."

"Your stepdad didn't seem very friendly, Ricky."

"Cole's an asshole."

"How long was he married to your mom?"

"I don't know. Two years, maybe. Three. Who cares?"

"It's not a good idea for you to be around someone who smokes marijuana during the day and doesn't seem to have a job."

"No shit." Ricky looked out the window.

"Ricky, what I mean is I'd like to spend more time with you. Some evenings, maybe. A morning or afternoon on a weekend when we could do something together."

"Why? I mean, do they make you do this or is this just some … some … I dunno … some trick? Who are you, anyway, lady?"

Tina sat up straight and leaned across the table. "I'm the woman who asked to do this, that's who. I'm here to get to know you and help you any way I can." She leaned back and nodded. "But how about this. May I tell you a little bit about me? Do you think if you know more about who I am and why I do this, it will help you believe I'm for real?"

Ricky twisted in the chair and looked around for his burger delivery. He stopped fidgeting and shrugged.

"My husband Walter and I have … two boys. The youngest has just started college and the oldest is working for a state senator in Tallahassee. He wants to go to law school. We … uh … had a middle son, who would have been twenty years old this year. But he was killed in a car crash three years ago." Tina heard her voice start to shake. The passing of three years was not enough to drain the reservoir of her pain. She inhaled. "It's been … difficult for me, Ricky. And for my husband. These last few years."

"Was he driving?"

"Um … yes, Max was driving. He'd had his license for about six months."

Ricky shook his head. "That sucks."

"Yup. It surely does suck. Anyway, these days I run a small business here in town and try to give people a great place to work and earn a living. That's me, in a nutshell. It's who I am."

Ricky looked around again, avoiding eye contact with Tina.

"It's okay. I'm just another suffering parent. There are lots of us. So. Who are you?"

The food came, and Ricky's eyes lit up. He grabbed for the plate before the waiter set it down.

"Holy cow! This burger's huge!" He attacked his meal.

When both had finished their food, Tina pointed out to Ricky some sauce smear was on his right cheek. He went to wipe it with his hand.

"No, sir. That's what a napkin is for." She reached across the table and handed him his untouched napkin. He took it and, with an exaggerated flourish, wiped his lower face.

"So, Ricky," Tina said, "you know something about me. I want to hear something about you. What you like and want. Let's start there."

"I like burgers."

"Do you watch television? What shows do you like?"

"I dunno. Don't watch much. Ruthann and douchebag pretty much watch whatever they want."

"What movies do you like?"

"I saw *Transformers* in juvy. What a cool movie."

"In juvy. How did you end up going into a juvenile center in the first place, hmm?"

Ricky's smile transformed into a thin stripe. He looked away.

"Hey. I read the record. Your file from Seminole Forks. I know what it says. I want to know what *you* say. Please, Ricky."

"It's all fucked up."

"Okay. First, you don't need to drop the F-bomb every time something makes you angry. Second, I want to hear how you felt. What happened to make you want to fight the way you did?"

"I fuckin' didn't want to fight. I had to!"

"Okay. I'm sorry about all you had to endure. Why did you have to fight?"

"Mom was makin' me work for her. Just bad. She was mean and she hit me a lot."

"You mean your natural mother."

"Yeah, the one in fucking jail up in Georgia!"

"I'm so sorry. Please go on."

"No. This sucks. No use!" He stood up but was otherwise motionless. His face turned red.

Tina rose. "Ricky, dear. There's no problem. We don't have to talk about this."

"I ain't your dear. I ain't nobody's dear!"

With a nod and a sigh Tina said, "I understand. Do you want to wait here or outside, while I pay the check?"

Ricky swiveled his head as though, without warning, he couldn't recognize his surroundings. He sat down with a thud. After Tina paid the bill, they stood up together in slow motion, neither looking at the other.

They drove away in silence. Tina headed, not for Ricky's house, but for Vilano Beach. When she turned off San Marco, toward the ocean, Ricky looked up.

"Where ya goin'?"

"For a walk on the beach. I'd like you to walk with me. Are you okay for a walk on the beach?"

Ricky looked at Tina. "Got nothin' else to do."

There were few cars in the beach parking lot this early afternoon. Tina and Ricky walked in single file across the old boardwalk. The sea breeze swept their hair and cooled their bodies even as the August heat and humidity draped them. At the bottom of the weathered pine stairs spilling onto the beach, Tina removed her shoes and encouraged Ricky to do likewise. She led him through the soft beach sand to the ocean's edge, where the sand was compact and the walk less of a struggle. But Ricky struggled anyway.

"You okay?"

The sound of waves drowned her voice, forcing her to walk back to where Ricky was shuffling and wobbling, away from the edge of the water.

"I was hoping a nice walk on the beach would be relaxing. But you don't seem too relaxed. What's up?"

Ricky shook his head. Perhaps he can't swim, Tina thought. Maybe he knows someone who drowned in the ocean. Tina never asked. She led him up to an area where the sand was dry, but still solid underfoot.

"The sea can be pretty relaxing, you know, if you use it the right way."

"Huh?"

"I mean, a beach walk can be a good way to unwind, get away from a messed-up world. Even though you have to return to the same world, I find the beach is a way to feed my spirit. You know, nourishment for the soul."

"It's dumb."

"And why is it dumb? Tell me, please."

"This is like recess, you know. Fifteen minutes before you have to go back inside. Just s'posed to make the shit easier to swallow."

"Sometimes it's the best we can do until things change."

"Or you change 'em yourself."

"Is that how you got in trouble, Ricky? Trying to change your situation all by yourself?"

"You could say."

"I did say. You tell me."

"Sick o' takin' orders from Charity, my mom. And Ruthann. Didn't much care for the slick army dude from Georgia. Sick of them usin' me. Sick of being called dumb in school jus' 'cause I hated being there."

"Charity. Yes. A strange name for your mom, isn't it?"

Ricky nodded.

"How did she use you?"

He shook his head.

"You know, Ricky. I shared something deep and bad about my life to show you that I've been in a bad way.

Different from you, but someone you can talk to. I won't tell anyone anything you tell me. Not even my husband."

He looked at Tina with uncertainty. "I dunno. It's so fucked up."

"Messed up. I'm sure it was. Were you physically abused?"

"Nah. Cole hit me a few times, but I got big enough to hit him back. My mom would hit me when I was little, but … you know …. Ruthann didn't want to hurt me, so that I could keep carrying for them."

"Carrying for them?"

"Can we go back? This is weird."

"Of course. Let me get you home."

The walk to the car, though silent except for the lapping waves, felt like progress to Tina. There was much she still had to learn if she was going to help this young man.

5

Good Cop, Bad Cop

During their walk to police headquarters, Tina, though brimming with questions, made small talk about the town and asked about the detective's background. Devon Tillyard had entered the Georgia police academy at twenty-two, right out of the University of Georgia. He made sergeant in his home county of DeKalb at the age of twenty-seven, but was denied his application for lieutenant a year later. At thirty-one he applied to become a detective in Lumpkin County at his same rank and was accepted.

"Why do you think you were denied the opportunity in Dekalb?"

Tillyard looked at her with a raised eyebrow. "Why do you think?"

"You mean because you were a brown man in law enforcement? I don't think I can say much about something I know so little."

"There are plenty of African Americans in law enforcement, Ms. Spear. But this Black man was a college grad and wanted to move fast. In a lot of institutions I can name, the people in power want you to pay your dues. And the more I wanted to move up, the better the job I did, the more dues I had to pay. So, I moved out." He looked at Tina with half a smile.

Tina fell silent as she imagined Devon Tillyard's life, so different from her own. She wanted to know more. "Was it difficult leaving the county where you grew up, where your family lived?"

"My old man was a police detective all the time I knew him. Never wanted to be anything else. He turned down at least two opportunities to become a lieutenant. He was all about doing good, doing the 'right thing' in the community. He believed everyone knew what the right thing was, but he also understood people were either too desperate or too scared to act on their own. He forgot 'too dumb.' That's what got him killed. Trying to do the right thing for people too dumb to get it."

Tina got it.

They walked a bit closer and occasionally Tillyard's arm would bump Tina's shoulder. He apologized each time.

Tina just smiled and said, "No worries."

Within minutes of meeting Tina, Tillyard had opened up about something very personal. She liked him and hoped he was someone she could trust.

In the headquarters building, Tillyard led Tina to one of three desks in an open space. He pulled a chair out for her, and she sat down.

When he took his seat, Tillyard leaned toward her. "Tell me, please. What was your relationship with Richard Plyer?"

Tina expected and welcomed this question. She led the detective through the last three years of her counseling, mentoring, hiring, and befriending Ricky. She paused briefly and allowed Tillyard's silence to lead her next thoughts. "I watched Ricky grow from a sullen, angry kid to a happy, thoughtful young man in those three years, Detective. No thanks to his screwed-up family. He graduated in the top thirty percent of students at his high school four months ago. God knows, his grandmother wouldn't—"

"You mean Ruthann. His grandmother and adoptive mother?"

"I do. I actually had to pay her to come to her son's graduation. Long story for another time. She's a vile woman."

"And what is it you want to know, Ms. Spear?"

"At first, I wanted to attend Ricky's service and see if I could find out why, against all logic and things I know about Ricky, he would take his own life. But now, Detective ... perhaps you can tell me. Is it normal to cremate a suicide victim less than forty-eight hours after the reported death?"

"No, ma'am, it is not."

"Then can you tell me why this happened? Why on earth was his body not held, at least until the reports got released? This is crazy. It makes no sense!"

"All I can tell you is I'm investigating this."

"Well, I did some research, and it's actually against the law to inter or cremate a possible suicide victim before the coroner's office has ruled on the cause of death and released the evidence. It's a process which normally takes three days. *Three days!*"

"I'm aware of this. It's the justification for my current case."

"May I see the death certificate, at least? I mean, there must be a death certificate, and, oh, I don't know, a formal release from the coroner's office."

"Yes, ma'am. They are part of my review at this stage."

"May I see them, please?"

"No, ma'am, I can't let you see them. You're not next of kin and—"

"I don't have to be next of kin to see public documents. Isn't that so?"

"And these are not public documents. Not yet anyway. As part of an ongoing investigation, they are not considered in the public domain. I'm sure you've watched enough TV crime dramas to know this."

"And what, if I may ask, are you investigating, Detective?"

"The propriety of the cremation and reasons for it. I can't say any more."

Tina stood and reached into her purse for her business card. "I intend to find out what happened to my friend Ricky. I'd like to think we can …"

Tina sensed him at first, a shadow or a hint of breathing, a rise in the temperature of the air around her. She turned around quickly. A man had appeared behind her as if from a dimensional portal. A man like an oak tree. He was more than a foot taller than Tina. She heard Detective Tillyard's chair push back hard.

"Ms. Spear, this is Sheriff Caldwell. Sheriff, this is Ms. Spear from St. Augustine, Florida."

"Hello, Sheriff Caldwell."

Tina gulped. She could not remember when she had been in the presence of a man this large. His badge was level with Tina's nose and his stomach protruded slightly over his belt, making contact with her chest. She backed up, stumbling when she bumped into her chair. Sheriff Caldwell extended an arm and caught Tina's shoulder, preventing her fall. A hand the size of a cantaloupe held her steady.

"Whoa, there. Be careful, Miss," said the sheriff, with a slight laugh. He swiveled the chair around for Tina to resume her seat. When she did, she pushed back in her chair, closer to Detective Tillyard.

Caldwell walked to the side of Tillyard's desk. "What brings you all the way from Florida to our Appalachian paradise, Miss Spear?"

She brushed her pants and looked at the chief straight on. Or rather, up.

"I'm trying to find out why a young man so full of life and promise would kill himself. And why his body would be so quickly released from the morgue and cremated against your own protocol. I didn't even get a chance to pay my respects!"

Caldwell arched his eyebrows enough to reach the line of salt-and-pepper hair, cropped like a soldier's.

"And you are related to this boy, how?"

She couldn't help an exhale of exasperation. "I was his tutor, mentor, and friend for the last three years. I knew Ricky better than his own mother or his ex-stepfather did. And I cared for him more than any other person in his life. *That* is how I'm related to Ricky."

Caldwell nodded. "Richard Plyer, yes. We don't get many suicides here, ma'am. It's pretty good living all around. Detective Tillyard has the usual investigation of such tragic circumstances, and I'm sure he'll be in touch, won't you, Detective?"

"That's the plan, Boss"

"Thank you," the chief continued. "And thank you for your interest and visit today. We would appreciate, however, if you would allow us to continue our work. This way, we can get you the information you need sooner rather than later." He gestured the way to the exit.

"I'm not through with the detective. I'm hoping we can have a few more—"

"Not today. It's already late and I'm paying the detective overtime. Please take one of his cards"—Tillyard handed one to Tina from a holder on the desk—"and he'll be in touch with you tomorrow. I presume you're staying in town tonight. It's a long way back to St. Augustine, particularly at night."

"I am. I'll be around for breakfast. May I bring you some donuts?" she said as she cocked her head.

"Treats won't be necessary, ma'am.

* * *

The summer morning light streaked through the slight opening between the curtains in Tina's hotel room shortly after six. She was already awake, even though she had tossed and turned until at least two. She wasn't rested, but she was energized. She replayed the prior day's events over and over in her mind. The police had an investigation *after* the cremation. This confirmed the rapid disposal of Ricky's body was highly irregular. And if that were the case, there had to be a reason. Incompetence? A mix-up of some kind? But this was no big-city morgue dealing with a surfeit of murders and bodies. Was it at the request of the family— Jacob or maybe even Ruthann? But why? Why not let the normal process of death events play out; let their grief seep into the soil and the air; show respect for the life cut so short. Tina's eyes watered.

A thought struck her. She may not have been able to attend a service for Ricky, but Jacob had told her approximately where his ashes had been strewn. Before any more confronting of local officials and relatives, Tina would do this morning what she had wanted to do from the moment she had arrived in Dahlonega—say goodbye to Ricky.

She put on a pair of jeans, running shoes, and T-shirt. After a cup of black coffee and microwaved oatmeal, she was on the road to Jacob Plyer's home before eight. Tina drove past the Plyer driveway a few times in each direction to get her bearings. On the north side of Route 9E, not far from Jacob Plyer's home, she passed a clearing, a mere indentation in the woods. She pulled the car off the road as far as she could, her passenger door kissing the leaves of low branches. She put her phone and small zipper case from her purse into her back pocket.

A worn path wove through the woods. Wasn't it likely it went down to that stream Jacob had said was a favorite play area for Ricky? She wondered when Ricky had played here: pre or post juvy. Perhaps both. She walked slowly, listening to the birds and insects, marveling at the great canopy of ash, pine, and oak trees. When the trail bent toward the Plyer property, turning down an embankment, she heard rushing water. Buoyed by her reckoning, she quickened her pace and soon came upon a clearing and a rushing stream. The path hugged the stream through the woods. She walked slowly, thinking of her lost protégé and how he might have found some peace, even fun, in these woods. The stream eventually opened into a pool as wide as her house, where the water's rush slowed to a smooth ripple. In front of her was a thick rope knotted several times, hanging from a large, bent oak tree. This could be the place.

After walking to the edge of the pool, she saw some large roots over a bare patch of earth, inviting her to sit. With her elbows on her knees, Tina closed her eyes and let her mind play a hundred images of the boy-turned-man over the last three years. She walked to the rope, grabbed it after a few attempts, and hung her full weight from it, her feet on the lowest knot. Ricky's rope swing. Her momentum carried her over the water a bit. She hugged the rope as if it were Ricky himself. "I can't believe you're gone," she prayed out loud. Perhaps there was a real, if shallow, peace to be found here. She got off the rope swing and sat again. All was still for minutes.

The sound of shutting car doors interrupted her meditation. She opened her eyes but saw only the dense forest in front of her. A tiny yellow bird perching above her warbled a song like a tin whistle. The silence returned.

Tina rose to her feet and searched up the creek for a crossing of any kind. Where the land flattened out beyond the pool, large boulders- poked out from the water and a tree branch hung low for support. She slipped twice on the glistening boulders. But the creek wasn't deep, and she reached the other side wet only to mid-calf. She grunted her exasperation and persevered. She took out her phone to see if her compass app might be helpful. It wasn't. Her own sense of direction would serve her better. She slid her phone back into her jeans and continued. It wasn't long before she saw a meadow through the trees rising over a hill to a house. It was Jacob Plyer's house. In front of the house was a county sheriff 4x4 cruiser. It had the look of many of the vehicles she had seen yesterday at the police department. Tina stood on the edge of the meadow. Sweat streamed down her back. She leaned against a tree and would not take her eyes away from the front porch door.

When the door opened, she expected to see someone looking like Devon Tillyard emerge. Instead, two men—one thin, wearing a trooper hat, and the other, a mastodon of a man who ducked beneath the head jamb of the threshold—walked onto the porch. It could only be Sheriff Caldwell. He descended the stairs and before he opened the passenger side of the cruiser, he turned back toward the porch and pointed with his right hand. Was he saying something to a person out of view? The hulk of a man got into the cruiser, and Tina heard a car door slam.

Had this visit been part of the investigation Detective Tillyard was conducting? It had to be. Tina decided it was time to head over to the police department. She managed her way back across the stream with more ease than her first crossing. Stopping to take a deep breath by the large pool, she said, "I will miss you, Ricky. I know there's more to your passing than I may ever understand." She placed her palm on the rough bark of the oak tree with the rope swing and sighed.

In her car, Tina was all business. It seemed logical that after the police visit to Jacob Plyer's home there would be an update. First, however, she needed to find a donut shop. Armed with a box of Krispy Kremes, Tina took the stairs to the police building two at a time and stood in front of the service window. She was second in line. Tapping her foot and surveying her surroundings like an osprey, Tina approached the window when her turn arrived.

"I'm here to see Detective Tillyard. My name is Tina Spear."

"Yes, Ms. Spear. Detective Tillyard is busy now. Can you return later, please?"

"If you would be kind enough to tell him I'm waiting on him, I'd very much appreciate it. And here." She presented the box of donuts. "I've brought a little something for the force to enjoy this morning."

With a curled lip the desk officer looked directly at Tina. "Bribing a police officer is a crime, Ms. Spear."

"But presenting the whole police force with treats is more of a peace offering, isn't it?"

This made the officer laugh and she nodded gratefully. "I'll tell Detective Tillyard you're here. Please wait over there," she said, pointing to the line of chairs.

Over thirty long minutes passed before Tillyard opened the door at the far end of the corridor and invited Tina in. She hoped his smile meant he was genuinely glad to see her. But that didn't seem realistic.

She sat upright, full of inquisitive energy. "Well?" she asked.

"Well what?" rejoined the detective. "Tell me why you're here today, Ms. Spear?"

"Oh? You don't know? I want an update, of course," she said with more indignation than she felt.

"There's nothing new to report since yesterday afternoon. And if there were, as I said yesterday, we don't disclose details of ongoing investigations."

"I presume if Ricky was cremated, the coroner's report concluded Ricky died by suicide. Is this in the report?"

"Still part of the investigation. I'm sorry. The report will be made public soon."

"In that case, perhaps you can tell me what your sheriff was doing earlier this morning at the home of Jacob Plyer."

Tillyard sat back in his chair as if he had been pushed. He looked at Tina with a face at once angry and confused. He started to say something then reconsidered. "If, in fact, the sheriff paid a visit to the Plyer home, it was on an issue unrelated to the investigation of Richard's suicide and release from the morgue."

Tina sat back herself. "Oh?" She looked away. When she straightened her gaze at Tillyard, she continued. "Don't you think it highly coincidental that in the middle of this very unusual rapid disposal of a suicide victim, the sheriff paid an early-morning visit to the victim's brother? To the house where the suicide took place? This just … this doesn't smell right, Detective. If this wasn't part of your investigation, at least as far as you know, what do you think it was?"

"Ma'am, I have to ask, what makes you think Sheriff Caldwell visited Jacob Plyer this morning?"

"Because I saw him there, of course! I may have been far away, but it's no leap of faith thinking there isn't another officer the size of a refrigerator who would be a passenger in a police 4x4." Tina shared with him the details of her morning's remembrance of Ricky and showed the detective the lower legs of her blue jeans, still damp from her walk through the stream.

Tillyard looked confused. "I don't think whatever you saw at the Plyer residence was part of this particular investigation."

"As you already told me. With all due respect, that's horseshit. Forgive my blunt speech. But coincidences of this nature are not coincidences. You know I'm right. What this information should be doing is making you wonder what *is* going on. Am I right? If you don't know what your sheriff was doing talking to a person directly related to your investigation—and not someone, I suspect, he sits next to in church—maybe there's a loop here that you're not part of. Oh, I know I'm just an outsider. But don't tell me you don't believe me." Tina's intense look dared Tillyard to contradict her.

His gaze moved to take in the department beyond his office, and then returned to Tina. He muttered, "This wouldn't be the first loop I've been cut out of."

"Excuse me? What did you say?"

"Nothing. Talking to myself. Look, whatever you saw may have a bearing on this case, Ms. Spear, or it may not. That's for me, in the course of my investigation, to determine."

Tina stared at the detective and squinted. Did he need more information, more time? Did he need an external ally? "Where do you eat lunch, Detective?" she asked.

After shaking his head, Tillyard sat back in his chair and said slowly, "Normally, at my desk."

"But today?"

"I was thinking of getting out. Maybe heading to Miko's Diner on the road to Ellijay."

Tina rose and extended her hand. "Thanks for your help today, Detective." It was close enough to lunchtime for her to think about heading to a restaurant. A Greek diner sounded perfect.

6

Becoming Familiar

PAST

Returning from their stroll on the beach, Ricky walked into his house without any word. Tina followed, announcing herself as she stepped into the kitchen. The thought of surprising the obnoxious Mr. Hart again made her nauseous.

Ruthann stood at the entrance to the living room, cigarette in hand, squinting. "Might a' let me know you was plannin' to take the boy out today."

"I did, actually. I called you eight times over three days and left you two messages. Maybe it would help us both if you were able to pay more attention to your phone."

"I pay plenty attention to my phone." She took a deep drag and let the smoke escape through her flared nostrils.

"Ricky and I spoke about me coming around next weekend after school starts. I'll plan to be by around 10:00 a.m. to pick him up."

"Don't bother to announce yerself. Come on in, gather the boy, and get on out." Ruthann turned around and walked away.

"Thank you, Ruthann. Just as I've been doing." To Ricky she said, "I'll see you next Saturday, Ricky. At ten. Thank you." She let the screen door flap back hard on the frame as she returned to her car.

When Tina told Walter that evening that she wanted to spend Saturday with Ricky, her husband relaxed into a frown. His head sagged to his chest.

"I suppose it was just a matter of time before you found another child to take care of."

"Do not do this, Walter. I thought you supported my volunteer work. How could the time I spend with a troubled young person in need make you angry or jealous or ... I don't know what."

"You know the answer. We need more time to work through this ... struggle, Max's death. You and me together, remember? Even Dr. Arnau was—"

"I'm a little tired of you referencing Dr. Arnau like she was a priest. We've received some insight from her and, yes, we have a lot of issues each of us needs to address. But, Jesus, Walter. Working with Ricky is a big part of *my* therapy. What are you doing to work on yourself? Curtailing your pornography when I go to bed?"

Walter closed his eyes and shook his head.

"I'm sorry," Tina whispered. "That was not worthy of either of us." There was silence for a moment. Tina had more, though. "I need to develop more strength, more resilience, I think, before I can meet you like you're asking. Do you think you're strong enough, so individually recovered you think it's time to—"

"It's past time, Tina. Way past. Three years we've been grieving for Max. I don't want to grieve alone anymore." He sighed and looked at Tina. When she said nothing, he continued. "I need to grieve with you. I need to remember our son with you and let the tears flow *with you. We* lost *our* son. I'm not interested in achieving some place of strength by myself. Good God!"

Tina pushed back from the table. "I'm working on me, still. All right? I can't be there like you want right now." She stood, and Walter simply looked up.

"I've committed to this disturbed boy. When he's on his own—psychologically I mean—I'll be in a much better place. I will."

"I want us to keep our next appointment with Dr. Arnau."

"I'll be there." She cleared a few dishes and headed into the kitchen. Walter blocked her.

"This is beyond Max. This is our marriage. Our lives. You and me and this life we've tried to carve in this beautiful slice of paradise. I'm not willing to give all this up!"

"It's not my fault we're healing differently!"

"No. No, it's not. Nor is it mine. I've told you I'm with you for the long haul. I meant it then. I mean it now. I want you back. Does it mean anything to you when I tell you I want you one hundred percent in my life?"

"Of course it does! But it doesn't make what I'm going through easier or faster or any of the things you want."

Walter rose and picked up more dinner dishes. "I'll clean up," he said, walking into the kitchen. He placed the dishes in the sink and turned to look at Tina, standing next to her chair.

She was immobile, a totem of their grief. The sudden sound of running water from the kitchen faucet nudged her into motion. Without a word, she adjourned to their home office to attack the neglected administration of her business.

The next Saturday Tina gathered Ricky as she'd promised. Ruthann and Cole were both home but sequestered in their burrows. A smile came to Tina's face when Ricky lurched off the couch to greet her. He walked up to her side and stopped.

"Think of this as a casual day to hang out. Okay?" Tina said.

"Okay."

"When was the last time you took a stroll down St. George Street?"

"Where's St. George Street?"

This should not have surprised her. "St. George Street is the preserved main street of old St. Augustine and a very interesting place, Ricky. You'll see."

As they left, Tina yelled into the dark house, "Ricky will be back around three." And they were off.

Tina parked in the only parking garage in the town and led Ricky to the Old City Gate of the ancient city. "These stone pillars are older than the fort over there. Back to 1590, four hundred and twenty-five years ago. Looking through here, you can see all the way down St. George Street. See?"

Ricky peered down the long alley. "No cars, but lots of people. Like, too many people."

"It's only for pedestrians. Let's explore. You might find something interesting."

"Uh …"

Noticing his hesitation, she prodded him slightly. "It'll be fun. I promise."

Ricky took a step closer to Tina, arms folded in front of him.

St. George Street thronged with tourists and locals in the late morning. Ricky walked a few feet from Tina, who delighted in pointing out the various shops, the preserved buildings such as the Oldest Wooden School House in the US, and other small museums. In the window of one of the shops Ricky stopped to look at a mannequin of a pirate, complete with eye shade and braided beard.

"This is a pirate town. Always has been. Did you ever learn such a thing about where you live, Ricky?"

"They sure dressed weird."

Tina laughed. "I think this figure is what Disney thinks a pirate looked like. Not what they really looked like. But it might be interesting to learn more. There's a pirate museum about a block away. Would you like to go visit?"

"Sure," he said.

Tina opted for a guided tour and prompted Ricky to ask questions. He learned that the great powers of Europe employed pirates to raid their enemies. Some became heroes, such as Sir Walter Raleigh, while others became infamous and hunted, like Blackbeard.

"They didn't teach us anything 'bout pirates in school," he complained.

"Think about this, Ricky. Pirates were outlaws, robbing, pillaging, killing. I'll bet you weren't taught anything about Jesse James, Bonnie and Clyde, or Al Capone, either. Am I right?"

Ricky's silence confirmed her assumption.

"Which is interesting, since criminal activity is responsible for a great deal of why and how society has changed. Think about it. Most of our laws are designed to stop criminals."

"People don't need to be taught about criminals. Just makes 'em wanna be criminals."

"Why on earth would you believe such a thing?"

"I dunno. I guess 'cause, you know, people make good livings being criminals."

"And how do you know this?"

"Just sayin'. I know kids running' drugs, stealin' stuff. They got their own money."

"Did you meet these kids in Seminole Forks?"

"Some. Most when I was carryin' for Charity."

"And most of them were caught, Ricky, and had to pay for their crimes. Including you!"

"Not everyone gets caught, you know. Mostly jus' the dumb ones. I never got caught. But my mom, she—"

"Do you mean Ruthann or your real mom?"

"Both, I guess. They're criminals, but they—"

"Your mother, Charity, is in jail in Georgia. She got caught."

"My brother told me she was set up. Someone she worked with ratted on her."

"When we were together last week, you said to me you used to 'carry' for your mother. Did other boys carry for her too?"

Ricky walked faster through the museum. He passed the guide but slowed when he entered the museum gift shop. Tina caught up to him. She stifled the urge to grab hold of him.

"Hey. I told you. You can trust me. Let's go outside and walk. Okay?"

Ricky sniffed. "I guess."

"I find that talking about things with somebody you trust helps a person deal with whatever is bothering them. It does. And Ricky, I told you. I won't tell another soul anything you say to me."

He stopped. "We maybe were kids, but we weren't dumb shits. You know?"

"Who's 'we,' Ricky?"

"Me an' Noble an' some others."

"You all carried drugs for your mom?"

A slight shrug.

"It was dangerous, and you knew it was wrong, didn't you?"

"Noble, he was the smart one. Only got beat up and stole from one time. Me, some of the others, we got knocked around some. I learned early I had to fight just to do what Charity told us to do. I hated it. I hated it!" Ricky's eyes started to water, but he wiped them quickly. "I wish I had a dad. He could've stopped her!"

"It's okay. Let's not talk about such things anymore. Let's get some ice cream. We can talk about how this beautiful old street talks to us. How does that sound?"

Ricky had no reaction.

Tina walked slowly down St. George Street, and Ricky followed a few steps behind. As she walked up to a window to order ice cream, Ricky volunteered that he liked plain vanilla. With two cones in hand, they continued their stroll. Tina thought Ricky had opened a door to something important.

"Did you ever know your father, Ricky?"

The boy stopped walking and squinted at her, ice cream melting over his hand. He looked down and shook his head. "I wished I had," he said in a whisper. "Don't know nuthin' about him."

Tina grabbed a napkin and wiped the sticky cream from Ricky's hand. He took the napkin from her and continued to clean himself. They looked at each other and Tina nodded.

"Let's see what else we can find along this old street."

They walked side by side in silence, eating their ice cream as fast as they could.

7

It's Only Lunch

Only four other people sat in the Dahlonega eatery that easily could hold ten times more. Tina asked for a cup of coffee as soon as she was seated. The menu was glossy, full of pictures of tantalizing food, likely related to the actual food the way a Corvette is related to a dune buggy. Still, a Greek salad in a Greek restaurant seemed a natural choice. As her salad arrived, through the diner window, she saw a Dodge pickup pull into the parking space next to her Audi. Good guess, Detective, she said to herself. As though the caffeine had just kicked in, Tina squirmed in her seat. She was looking forward to working with the energetic police detective. Here was a man whose objectives were at least close to her own.

Devon Tillyard strode into the diner, took off his sunglasses, and looked around until he spotted Tina. "May I join you, Ms. Spear?"

Tina gestured to the bench opposite her and stifled a grin. "Of course you may, Detective."

He slid in, took up a menu, and as quickly put it down. The waitress came over to him.

"I'll have the same thing she's having."

"Black coffee and a Greek salad? That's all?"

"Yes, ma'am. Thanks." To Tina he said, "The food here is pretty damn good. Authentic Greek."

"Is there an abundance of Greek restaurants in Decatur, Detective?" Tina asked, smiling.

"All over Fulton and Dekalb counties actually," Tillyard said, unbothered. "But my real experience with Greek food was Tarpon Springs, Florida."

"You don't say!"

"I do say. DeKalb police force had regular training exchange programs with Pinellas County. Worked with Clearwater and Tarpon Springs police forces and ate Greek food at least three times a week. More Greeks in Tarpon Springs than all of Astoria, New York."

"Now you're just playing with me."

"Well, at least as a percentage of the population. In any case, food here is real Greek. So tell me again, Ms. Spear, why you think you saw the sheriff at Jacob Plyer's residence earlier today."

"You have to admit, he's pretty easy to recognize, even from a distance. He must be six foot eight and weigh, oh I don't know, maybe ..."

"Three hundred and twenty-two pounds. Most of it solid. Yeah. He makes no secret of his size. Pretty proud of it, actually. Intimidates the hell out of everyone in the squad."

"Humor me, please. Let's say I did see him over at the Plyers's and he did make some parting gesture to someone in the Plyer household. I guess it could have been threatening or benign."

"This person may have been indicating something to a relative or friend who happened to be there visiting."

"It's all possible, at this point. But putting the gesture aside, what could he have been doing there, and why wouldn't he have at least told you he was heading to the household at the center of your investigation?"

"Any number of reasons. Sheriff Caldwell doesn't report to anyone except the county council. He sure as hell doesn't report to me."

Tillyard wasn't looking directly at her. "Let me tell you something, Detective. I've got excellent instincts about people and situations. I'm a successful businesswoman in a town where businesses start and fail like seeds on a sidewalk." She pointed at him. "You know this isn't right and you sense it's related to your investigation. Now you have something to investigate."

"I've got more than enough to investigate, ma'am."

Tina nodded. "Well? Your coroner seems to be a source of some wrongdoing."

"Ma'am, I can't—"

"Oh, stop with that, please! You need someone like me who can stumble around and shake a few things up, don't you?"

This made Tillyard laugh out loud. He caught himself and looked quickly around the diner. "Okay. I cannot have you stumble around this investigation. Let's pursue your theory for a moment. You think the visit you observed was related to the suicide and abnormally quick cremation. What—"

"Exactly! You agree, right? Ricky's cremation was so quick. It was wrong and—"

"Still to be determined. I'm trying to look at it from your perspective. *If* your theory holds, what's your follow-through? If they're related, there's a purpose for it, driven by something … wrong. But wrong doesn't equate to sinister, in most cases."

"I'll go back to your coroner. Did you get straight answers from him? Was the paperwork all in order?"

Tillyard shook his head and eventually let his chin drop as he nodded. "The coroner is not a very forthcoming person, in the best of circumstances. And rightly so—normally. I'm guessing the sheriff himself told him he had to speak with me. When I finally did see the man, he wouldn't produce any autopsy reports until this morning."

Tina leaned in. "Well?

"I told you. You're not getting any data from me until this investigation is cleared up."

"Surely you can tell me if the coroner ruled Ricky's death a suicide."

Tillyard stopped moving, his face expressionless. Tina squinted at him, trying to decipher if this was stonewalling or communication of another sort.

"There is something, isn't there? Ricky may not have killed himself." She put her hand over her mouth and uttered a muffled "Oh my God! Oh my God! He could have been murdered."

"Do *not* jump to any conclusions, please," Tillyard said, his voice steady. "I said nothing, not even the slightest twitch to make you think this. Now, please! My job is to learn the truth, Ms. Spear. I, by myself, am going to track the evidence wherever ..."

Tina wiped the tears from her eyes.

Tillyard's countenance softened. "The full coroner's report will be made public today. I've got no idea where this will ultimately lead, but I can't risk having a civilian I just met suddenly become my ersatz partner."

"I'm more family to Ricky Plyer than any other person in his life. I had a right—"

"Hold on a second. You are a concerned professional who was very close to the deceased."

"Yes."

"I will share with you everything I can. By which I mean everything my duty and your standing will allow by law."

He leaned back in his seat. "So long as you continue to share whatever you learn with me."

Tina tapped her knuckles together nervously and looked away. It wasn't what she wanted. However, considering her sense that Ricky's death may not have been suicide, she would do whatever it took to stay close to Tillyard's investigation.

When they had finished lunch, they walked to Tina's car.

Tillyard told her, "I don't know where this is going, Ms. Spear, but it could be a dirty and maybe even dangerous place. You said you're going to see the brother this afternoon. Be careful. He may tell you things he wouldn't tell an investigator. I want you to call me after your visit. You will have to stay clear of the investigation, particularly if there's even a hint the department is involved."

A blanket of cold covered Tina. She shuddered and wrapped her arms around her shoulders. This was not what she'd expected to discover in Dahlonega.

8

Into the Clouds

On their return trip from lunch and the stop along St. George Street, an idea came to Tina.

"Do you know what an air show is, Ricky?"

The boy shook his head as he tried to get comfortable in his seat belt.

"Well, there are displays of airplanes and jets. There are stunt planes and skydivers. Different things to eat. It's a great deal of fun. This weekend, my husband Walter and I want to take you there. How about it?"

Ricky shrugged. After a few moments he said, "Okay."

The idea had great appeal to Tina. A forty-five-minute car ride with her and Walter would give Ricky more exposure to Tina. She feared, however, her marriage may not be the best example of a healthy adult relationship for a boy who likely never saw one. She resolved to speak to Walter. If they could be strong together for this young stranger, perhaps such strength could be a brick to start a foundation for themselves.

Dropping Ricky at home, Tina followed her young charge through the rusting appliances and debris.

Ruthann was watching television, a ghost of smoke rising from her fingertips. She looked over when Ricky and Tina came in. "Boy eat much?"

"I'd say his appetite improves each time we go out, Ruthann. I want to take Ricky out this Saturday for the whole day. My husband and I are going to the JAX NAS Air Show and I've invited Ricky to be our guest."

"The what? Some airshow, you say? Don't think it matters much. If it keeps the boy out of trouble, sounds fine." She took a drag on her cigarette and continued to stare at her television.

Ruthann had no idea of the Herculean self-control Tina summoned at that moment. When her teeth ground, something like a growl vibrated in her throat and she stood on her tiptoes, glaring at the older woman. "We'll be by on Saturday to pick you up, Ricky. Can you be ready to leave by nine o'clock?"

Ricky looked at Tina, then Ruthann, then back at Tina. "Sure. I'll be ready."

"Great. We'll see you at nine. Goodbye, Ruthann."

Saturday was a chamber of commerce day, as Tina often said. September days could be tricky in Northeast Florida. It could still be very hot, and hurricanes were an increasing threat. Today, however, the air was clear but for a few high strokes of white clouds. The temperature was going up to 85 degrees.

"This is going to be a good day," Tina told Walter.

"I hope so," her husband said as they walked to his Volvo SUV.

"Don't expect a lot of conversation with him. He's still shell-shocked from … I guess, from his whole life. I want him to see something completely new. I want him to get some life into his life."

"Life is a good starting place," Walter said.

Tina directed Walter to the Plyer home. When he turned into the driveway and maneuvered past an old washing machine and limbs of downed trees as far as he could, he let out a big breath. "Whoa! Who lives like this?"

"You don't have to come in. I'll go get Ricky."

Before either of them could move from their seats, the screen door clapped shut and Ricky was hurrying out of the house, head down, pulling on an oversized, all-white baseball cap. He shuffled to the front passenger door. Tina jumped out and opened the rear door for him. He looked at her as he shrugged and got into the back seat.

On the road, Tina said "Our driver today, Ricky, is my husband Walter Spear. Walter, this is Ricky Plyer."

"Hi, Ricky," Walter said, eyeing the boy in the rearview mirror.

"Hi," Ricky said, head down at the Game Boy he pulled from his jeans pocket.

Walter glanced over at Tina with a smirk. He started a conversation with her about a project to add a deck to their patio. Tina switched the conversation to a shopping trip they needed for home essentials. Walter added a few things to the list. They talked about the last movie they watched together on Netflix. Tina turned to see if Ricky was paying attention to the normal family banter. He was gazing through the window at the blur of passing scenery.

Eventually, the subject turned to their three children. As they remembered Max the conversation became slower, softer. Before either of the adults knew it, a silence fell between them. Tina looked out her window, eyes unfocused. The rest of the world had become white noise. Tina and Walter had each retreated to private places in a basement of memories and unfulfilled plans, too deep to allow a voice for their sorrow. But today there was a witness, a boy who was about the same age as Max when he died. Walter looked at Tina and grabbed her hand. She looked at him with imploring eyes as she slowly pulled her hand back to her lap. Ricky continued playing on his Game Boy in the back seat.

Just before the turn off I-295 for the naval base, Tina twisted around in her seat. "You told me a little about your brother Jacob, Ricky. You said he was in the army. What's he like?"

Ricky shrugged. "Jacob's Jacob. He was there for me when I was a kid."

"So you love your brother, do you?"

"I guess. Yeah."

"Did he enlist? Where was he deployed?"

Ricky looked up to see Tina's soft eyes and smile over her arm as she leaned on the back of her seat.

He nodded imperceptibly. "I guess he joined up when I was 'bout five or six."

"Did you see him while he served? I mean, did he get back home much?"

"Uh-uh."

"Where was he stationed?"

"Somewhere in Georgia, I think."

Tina's patience never wavered. "And from there he went to …?"

Ricky shrugged.

"Was he ever deployed overseas?"

"Couple a' times overseas. Got wounded pretty bad."

"I'm sorry. It must have been difficult for you, seeing your brother go off to war."

"Yeah. Some."

"How old were you when he was sent to wherever it was—the Middle East?"

"I dunno. I was twelve, I think."

It was, Tina understood, one year before Ricky was sent to Seminole Forks. It fits, she thought.

Walter steered the SUV toward Jacksonville, along Route 17. Soon the signs for various entrances to the navy base appeared, and Walter pulled into the line of cars "Looks like we'll be with ten thousand of our closest friends."

Ricky looked up and leaned over the front seat to peer through the windshield. His eyes got wide. When he sat back down with a bounce, a scowl smeared his face. Tina looked at him, puzzled.

It took much less time to park than the long queue might have indicated. Tina and Walter opened their respective doors simultaneously and stretched their limbs out of the car. Tina opened the door for Ricky, who didn't move.

"Come on, Richard Plyer! Time to have some fun!" She reached in to hold Ricky's hand, but he pulled it away.

"It's okay. You're going to be fine. We're going to see some very cool airplanes and flying tricks." When this appeal failed to budge the boy, she tried another tactic. "And I'm starving. I'll bet you had less breakfast than I had. How about we find a burger or a pizza stand."

"First things first," Walter cut in. "I've got to pee. How about you, Ricky? I think we need to find the restrooms before we think of food and drink, yes?"

The two adults stood with anticipation to the side of the car.

"Sunglasses?" Ricky asked.

Tina looked at Walter.

"Extra pair in the glove box," he said. "It's an old Boy Scout thing. Never, ever be without sunglasses."

Tina retrieved a pair of extra-large tortoiseshell sunglasses which she handed to Ricky. "I'm s'posed to wear these?" he said with a grimace.

"Only if you want to keep the sun from burning your retinas to tiny wafers," Tina kidded him. Ricky looked at her as if she had started speaking Hungarian. "You look fine.

Let's go find the restrooms," she said as she again extended a hand.

Ricky took hold of it tentatively and climbed out of Walter's SUV. The young man let go as soon as he was out of the car.

With Ricky between them, Walter and Tina looked at the signage as they walked toward the main runway where the spectators were gathering. The sidewalks filled with people, some rushing to get seats or find food, others ambling slowly with small children in tow. Walter saw the restroom sign and pointed to it. The threesome made a swing to the right and as they did, Tina and Ricky separated in the crowd. When Ricky lost sight of her for an instant, his head swiveled back and forth for a few seconds. Walter was right behind him, but Ricky didn't seem to recognize him. Finally, the boy yelled "Miss Tina! Miss Tina!"

Tina wasn't more than six feet away when she heard Ricky say her name for the first time. She also recognized in his voice the fear of a child. She stopped and turned around. "I'm right here, Ricky. Here I am." For a moment the stream of people slowed, and Ricky saw Tina. He ran between two people just as Walter reached for him. Ricky pushed one person aside and stood next to Tina, shaking.

She put an arm around his shoulder. "What's the matter, sweetie? It's okay. Don't worry, we're together now."

Walter came over to her other side. Tina lowered her arm and took hold of Ricky's hand. He pulled it away, and Tina took it again and held it fast. He looked up at her. She saw a part of him that was still a little boy, disconnected from the insular fifteen-year-old.

"Are you okay, Ricky?" Walter asked.

"I'm … I'm … not so good in crowds," he said as he clenched Tina's hand.

"But I know you're a brave young man. Just keep hold of my hand and we'll get through this together. Promise."

For the next hour Ricky stayed at Tina's side as his head swiveled and his eyes went wide behind the oversized sunglasses. Walter walked behind them, his hands deep in his pockets. The trio bought pulled pork sandwiches and sweet tea at one of the food trucks, taking seats along the main runway where bleachers had been set up. Tina wiped Ricky's face after he failed to maneuver the gooey overstuffed sandwich to his mouth. When she tried to wipe his chin a second time, Ricky's feigned resistance annoyed Tina. She put her sandwich down and pulled his head toward her to clean his face.

"Don't!" he said, squirming. "Stop it!"

"While you are my guest, you will look like a civilized person. At all times. Am I clear?"

He took another big bite of his sandwich and nodded.

"We'll see." Tina sniffed.

After their meal, Tina wanted to show Ricky some of the sights before the show started. She asked her husband to accompany them, but he demurred.

"The stands are filling up, so I'll stay here and save the seats," Walter said. "You two go ahead and explore." Tina shot him a questioning look, to which he turned his back.

There were a number of military displays for the attendees to take in. They walked by stationary fighter jets with stairways leading up to the cockpits. "Let's take a look inside, Ricky. What must it be like to be a fighter pilot!"

Ricky shook his head several times. "Okay. Let's at least get a selfie in front of this impressive airplane, yes?" Ricky again shook his head.

"Nah, I don't look so good in pics," he told her.

"I'm an excellent photographer. I can make even you look great. I can!"

Ricky couldn't stifle his smile and looked up at his counselor. "All right, I guess."

Tina snapped the photo, and Ricky had to agree the two of them looked okay. "I still look goofy with these huge shades."

"Nonsense. You look ... cool. You look like a young Eminem!"

Ricky laughed. "Don't look nuthin' like him."

"Not true. I think you could be his younger brother."

Ricky shook his head and smiled. "Don't think so."

Continuing their stroll, they came upon the howitzers and .50 caliber machine guns mounted on platforms with stairs and visitor walkways. Ricky stared at these exhibits, backing away from them slightly. Each time Tina asked him to accompany her to a platform for a closer look, Ricky shook his head and walked over to the next one. Tina needed to know why.

"Up close these displays are very cool, Ricky. You can see all the details of the gun barrels, the explanation of the holes for ventilation, and its history in protecting America. It's all very interesting. Come on up with me, won't you?"

"I can't."

"Oh? Why can't you?"

"'Cause I'm a felon. I'm not s'posed to be near any kind of weapon."

Tina laughed a bit but stopped when she noticed how concerned Ricky's expression had become. "I'm sure this condition of your parole has nothing to do with museum displays, now, does it? Besides, there is no live ammunition and no possible way this machine gun can be used. Come on."

"I'm a felon, Miss Tina. I can't be near no weapon of any kind. Part of my release. Those there ...." He pointed to the two machine guns. "Them are big weapons. No. I can't go near 'em."

Tina stood still, thinking. "All righty! Let's take a look from where you are and see what there is to learn." As she descended the stairway to the tarmac and went over to him, she noted the tension leave Ricky's shoulders and neck. She repeated some of what she had read about the guns' recoil and the heat it developed firing successive rounds.

"This isn't for me," he told her.

"I understand. Let's walk around a bit more before the show starts, and you can point out to me what you think is interesting or strange, and we'll see if we can figure it out together. How does that sound?"

Ricky nodded. She held out her hand again and he took it without hesitation.

After twenty minutes, just before the official start of the airplane acrobatics, the two returned to the bleachers to find Walter talking to two teenage girls, who, with their parents, were in the seats next to those saved for Ricky and Tina.

In a strong voice Tina said, "We're back, honey!"

Walter turned around and, with a smile that stirred a slight flutter in Tina, beckoned his wife and her charge. "Hey, Tina. You guys have been gone a while. Did you have fun?" To the two girls he said, gesturing, "Ladies, this is my wife, Tina, and this is the young man I mentioned to you."

After the introductions, the adults formed a conversation group and the teenagers stood swaying as they faced each other, avoiding eye contact. The shorter of the two girls raised her hand to her shoulder and waved it in Ricky's direction.

"Hi," she said quietly.

Ricky bent his head toward her and looked at her intently, though with his oversized hat and sunglasses, his expression was hidden. The older sister was not interested.

"Hi," she said, over her shoulder, and then turned back to the event field.

Ricky continued to stare at the younger girl. So much so she took two steps back, grabbed on to her sister, and giggled nervously.

"Are you some white rapper wannabe?" she asked.

Ricky said nothing, nor did he move.

After a few seconds of this, she said, "Uh … do you talk? You know, it would be polite if you would say 'hi' or something. Don't be a creeper."

As Ricky craned his neck toward the girl, he smacked his lips twice as if trying to swallow sand.

"Okay. Suit yourself," the girl said, turning her back to Ricky as she stepped up one bleacher row, next to her sister.

A man's voice boomed over a series of loudspeakers, greeting the throng, and announcing the start of the air show. Tina looked around and saw Ricky standing by himself facing the backs of the two teenage girls.

"Ricky," she called, "come on over here. The show is about to start!"

When still the boy hadn't moved, Tina went down to the tarmac, took his hand, and led him back up into the bleachers. She noticed beads of sweat on his cheeks beneath his sunglasses. Taking a tissue from her purse, she started to lift the sunglasses from his face.

Like a jack-in-the-box, Ricky's elbow came up and hit Tina's arm into her face. He turned around, jumped down to the pavement, and ran.

Tina reached back and grabbed her husband's arm. "Walter, something's wrong with Ricky. I'm going after him."

Walter rose from his seat to come with her, but she stopped him. "It's okay. I'll find him."

Walter held his hands out in front of him. "Tina, let me help you *and* him."

"I've got this. We'll be right back." She turned and raced through the crowd where she had last seen Ricky.

* * *

The announcement for the start of the show had drawn all the people strolling or just arriving, directly to the bleachers. They came at Ricky like a phalanx: a wall of faceless humanity surrounded him instantly. He could no longer run or even walk in the same direction. More people bumped him left, right, backward. He flailed his arms trying with all his might to ward off the horde of zombies blocking his path, crushing his retreat, not letting him go—but pulling him back, back from where he had just escaped. Back to fear and humiliation.

He closed his eyes and screamed as loud as he could.

He was still screaming when he felt a set of arms around him. He felt the crowd move away from him. He felt a hand on the back of his head and a voice in his ear.

Tina's voice said, "You're safe, Ricky. I've got you. You're safe."

His body reflexively lashed out, desperate for retreat. Slowly, as her arms grew stronger around him, he let himself go in a way he never had. His knees gave out and he collapsed in gasping sobs. The arms around him grew tighter, but ever more welcome.

Her voice said again, "I've got you, Ricky. You're safe now."

And he knew, for the first time in his life, it was true.

9

Ah, Family!

At four in the afternoon Tina turned in to the long driveway leading up to Jacob Plyer's home. She pulled into the space in front of the split rail fence. When she turned off the engine, Tina gripped her steering wheel hard to steady herself. After some deep breaths and long exhales, she sat still. When she left St. Augustine to attend a memorial service for Ricky, never for a moment did Tina think she might be investigating his possible murder. She was both repulsed and exhilarated by the fact she could somehow be instrumental to understand why Ricky had died. But she had no training, no experience to guide her how to conduct an investigation or to extract information from people with motivations she did not yet understand. The looming conversation with Jacob Plyer was but the beginning of this journey. Tina could barely imagine where it would take her. She was a child about to climb onto a raft in a roiling river.

After Tina rang the doorbell for the second time, a woman opened the door. Her short brunette hair was combed boyishly to one side, but a few falling strands gave her the look of an ingenue.

She smiled politely. "You must be Mrs. Spear." She extended her hand. "I'm Carmen, Jacob's wife."

"Hello, Carmen. I'm pleased to meet you. Please call me Tina. Mrs. Spear was my husband's mom." Tina smiled back.

The house had an open floor plan, belying the old exterior. Everything inside was neat. Perhaps, Tina observed, neater than a house with an infant and a recent gun slaying might warrant. Carmen offered Tina a seat on a billowy couch with a quilt throw over the top.

"Jacob's cleaning up the baby and himself," Carmen stated. "He'll be here shortly."

"Did you know Ricky, Carmen?"

"Sure I did. He was living with us for the past month."

"Did you know him before? I mean, when did you first meet Ricky?"

"About a year ago, I think. Just before Jacob and I tied the knot. He came up to visit. I guess he'd visited a few times since Jacob was discharged."

Tina said, "I knew Ricky had been up here a few times before he graduated from high school. He loved his brother and was hoping Jacob would have attended his graduation."

"Oh, I'm sure Jacob wanted to. But he's had a hard time since coming back from Iraq. He tries to be a stoic and all, but sometimes his memories … they overwhelm him. And his physical injuries. They're permanent."

"I'm truly sorry to hear that. I know what it means to have memories overwhelm you." A call in the middle of the night from the Florida State Police was one such recurring memory of Tina's. She banished it again.

There was a hallway above the living room, with a balustrade of natural wood in front of three doors evenly spaced apart. A baby's cry emanated from one. The door opened, and both women looked up. Jacob Plyer was carrying daughter Emma, who let out a piercing scream. Jacob cradled his daughter, trying to calm her.

"Carmen! Could you please help me with our little girl here? Baby?"

Carmen rose like a guided missile and flew up the stairs. Jacob handed Emma to his wife and the couple had a short private conversation without looking at their guest below. They descended the stairs side by side, Jacob's limp much more pronounced than Tina recalled from yesterday.

Jacob eased himself into the chair his wife had just occupied.

"I'm supposed to use a cane to get around, but damn thing ain't convenient."

"I hope you're getting all the care you need for this."

Jacob glanced up at Carmen. "Yes, ma'am. I believe I am. I took couple a' pieces a' shrapnel in my thigh, another in my gut. Tore my leg up pretty bad. They saved most of my stomach. But it pretty much hurts whenever I eat. They patched me up pretty sweet, I have to say. I know guys with injuries like mine, had to have their legs amputated. Some's in wheelchairs for the rest of their lives. I'm one of the lucky ones." He reached up and clasped Carmen's waist. "Real lucky, I'd say. This one decided half a man was better than none!"

Carmen shifted the baby and then took her husband's arm and held it. "Jacob Plyer, you will always be a whole man and more."

"Carmen was my nurse for my last two operations and helped me through PT at Fort McPherson. *That* was grueling. Most painful thing I ever did."

"I'm so sorry to hear this, Jacob," Tina said. "And thank you for your service." She cleared her throat. "I'm here because … Ricky and I became very close, and his suicide just doesn't make any sense to me. None. These last three years he was coming into a life he had built all by himself. A good life, you know? A life full of potential. He worked so hard to turn his life around. I can't understand what could have happened to make him want to end it. Can you?"

Jacob put his hand over his mouth and turned away from Tina. He took a few seconds to move his hand from his mouth to his eyes. His fingers were unable to stop a faucet of tears. "Ricky!" he said in a broken voice, looking to the ceiling. "My God. Ricky."

Carmen placed her hand on her husband's shoulder. Tina was still.

"He talked about you, Mrs. Spear," Jacob said. "Called you 'Miss Tina.' He told me you were the only adult who treated him like a person."

Tina's stomach contracted and she lurched forward for an instant. She took a few seconds to steady herself.

"He liked goin' to your business—studio, was it?—and helping out. He learned how to saw in a straight line, for God's sake."

Tina smiled and sniffled. "I didn't teach him how to saw straight. I tried to teach him the importance of high standards and how he should not be satisfied until whatever he was pursuing was the way he wanted it to be."

"Life ain't never like you want it to be, now, is it? It doesn't make a difference how hard you try."

Tina thought Jacob was about to spit.

"Oh yes, it does, Mr. Plyer. And sometimes, trying is the most important part. Ricky knew he had failed early on, and when I saw him last, he had learned from those failures, all those fights and robberies. All those lies he was told and told himself. He was learning from every single one of those and he was changing for the better."

She paused, waiting for a reaction from Jacob. He had the look of a forlorn animal.

She continued. "Damn it! Ricky *was* succeeding at building himself a future, a life so much better than the one he had as a child. You told me yesterday Ricky had so much anger. That may have been true over three years ago. But anger didn't drive the Ricky I knew this last year. Not at all."

Jacob's whole body twitched in his chair. In a paroxysm of pain, he thrust his bad leg straight out and grabbed it with both hands. He cried out, "Ahhh … Carmen! Carmen, honey, I need my meds! Please, baby!"

Glancing over her shoulder at Tina, Carmen raced into the kitchen and placed Emma in a highchair. The child fussed and reached for her mother, who had already turned away to pull pill bottles from a cabinet. She returned with three of them and a glass of water. Placing the water on the coffee table, she measured out a dosage. She handed her husband six pills: three blue and three white, which he gulped down with the glass of water.

"Jesus Christ, this shit is gettin' old. Arr …! Damn it. Is this fuckin' pain ever gonna stop!"

Jacob took a series of quick breaths through his mouth as Carmen put a hassock under his bad leg. His breathing settled back to normal.

Tina waited for the silence to take over for a few minutes, restoring some ease before she resumed the conversation. "Jacob, I so much wanted to say goodbye to Ricky at the ceremony. I have to tell you I was very surprised, and hurt, actually, that Ricky's cremation was so quick. Why would the coroner release his body and then … what? You had him cremated? I can't make sense of this."

Jacob's face was blank, his body as motionless as though a posthypnotic suggestion had been triggered.

"That was a very obtuse thing to say, Mrs. Spear." Carmen said. "I don't think any of this is your concern, is it?" she said. "We are Ricky's family. Not you."

Tina was unprepared for this challenge but could not retreat. "No. I'm not a blood relative, but I cared for and mentored Ricky for the last three years when, clearly, none of his so-called family would."

Emma started to fuss. Carmen raised her voice. "I saw Ricky take one of Jacob's pistols and blow his brains out! You can see it plainly. His blood and bones scattered on the wall." Her arm swung out like a loose girder on a crane, pointing to the stairway.

Tina saw a dark blotch the size of a melon against the brown wall. She tried to swallow. "I can barely imagine the horror," she whispered, focusing her will to cleanse the image from her mind.

Carmen pressed on. "If your life had been filled with a traumatic childhood and the terrors of combat, your friends blown into fragments next to you, what would you want to do?"

"I … I don't know. I can't presume to say what I would do in hell to those who've lived there. It must have been so traumatic for you both. I'm so sorry."

"We just want to get the whole business behind us as quickly as we possibly can. Put this immense tragedy into the past, with all the other pain and horrible memories."

Jacob still had not moved, though his eyelids had begun to droop.

"I understand, Mrs. Plyer. I do." Tina nodded a few times. "What I don't understand is how even a crushing need can still circumvent the normal police events and procedures attending a suicide. Things like a thorough investigation with a report, a release of the body to and from the morgue, reaching a decision regarding the treatment of the remains. Those things take time—by law!"

Carmen spoke in a slow staccato. "RC is a close family friend, Mrs. Spear. And you—"

"RC?"

"Rutherford Caldwell. RC. The sheriff? He and Jacob ... they have ... known each other a long time and, well, he understood what happened and decided to help out."

"Is that what Sheriff Caldwell was doing here this morning? Helping out?"

Carmen's head snapped back slightly, her eyes widened and as quickly softened. Jacob visibly stiffened and looked up at his wife. The two said nothing for a few seconds. When Jacob started to say something, Carmen patted his shoulder and Jacob went silent.

"RC," said Carmen, "like I said, is very close to Jacob and he checks up on him regularly. That's why he was here."

Something in Carmen's calm, measured tone is off, Tina thought. "Have you seen the coroner's report?"

"I think it's time for you to leave, Mrs. Spear. Thank you for your concern."

Tina was not finished but realized she had pressed the couple too far. She rose from her chair. "I'm very sorry, Mrs. Plyer. I ... I have no excuse. Please forgive me. I ... loved Ricky like he was my own son. I lost a son in a violent car crash when he was about Ricky's age, six years ago. I just want to have my own closure. I know you can understand."

Carmen regarded Tina with stern and wary eyes.

Jacob, groggy from his pain medicine, nevertheless looked up at Tina. "Ah, yeah. Like I said. Life pretty much sucks. I know you and Ricky were close. Sit back down, won't you? Please."

Carmen's displeasure was visible as she stiffened and walked to the kitchen with the baby.

"I only want to fill in the gaps, Mr. Plyer. Ricky was hard to get to know, early on. When my mentorship was officially completed, the time between seeing each other got longer. Would you tell me, please, how long after you left for the service did your grandmother adopt Ricky?"

Jacob's jaw clenched. "Ricky was seven."

"What was going on with your mother, to the extent she couldn't take care of Ricky, when she managed to take care of you?"

"She never took care of me, for as long as I knew her. I took care of myself. She would disappear for weeks—hell, months at a time—and Ruthann would call the child welfare folks and they'd argue about putting me into foster care. She, Charity, was charged a bunch of times with neglect, along with possession and prostitution. Not countin' all the other shit I don't even know about. She was in and outta rehab and jail. I swear, my mother's only desire was to piss off every human being on earth just for fun. My daddy was around sometimes, but he never lived with us after they separated. He sure as damn was never gonna take me in. He was military. Gone most times."

It seemed to Tina that Jacob needed to tell his story. She didn't want to be asked to leave again, so she asked tentatively, "How is it you never got into serious trouble, like Ricky?"

"Got lucky, is all. My first recollection is we lived— Charity, me—outside Atlanta. My dad, he was stationed at Fort Gillem. Saw him not too regular. I got decent grades in school 'cause I like to read. History, mostly. Revolutionary War, Civil War, the World Wars and all. And I played football. The coaches wanted me to play in college, but I … I didn't see myself goin' to college."

"Were you the one who took care of Ricky?"

Jacob stopped for breath. "By the time Ricky was born, my dad had been outta the picture for a while and Charity was doing anything and everything she could to get by. Dealin' drugs, hookin' up with sugar daddies, stealin'. Lil' Ricky was always dirty. He was sick, hungry. We got help from a couple a' neighbors—military families. Charity would be gone all the time. One day she comes back home, married to some loser named Cole. What a dumb fuck. Did anything Charity told him to, none of it legal. I was just trying to stay in school.

"We came back to Ruthann's house in 2003, when Charity went to jail the second time. When I enlisted, Charity was in some prison outside Jacksonville, and Ruthann yelled at me every day. Told me I was abandoning my brother. It was the welfare folks told her she would get monthly money if she became Ricky's legal guardian. It was horrible. You don't know. I had to ... save myself." Jacob looked up at Tina, his half smile fading into a quiver. He fought for control.

Tina nodded.

"Ricky was still little, but, well, Ruthann will tell you. He took it hard when I left. I came back whenever I could. I mean, I did my basic and MP training all in Georgia, so I got back from time to time. You know I was there when I could be, right? Ricky must a' told you."

"He did, Jacob."

"Ruthann was bad enough. But that cunt mother of ours ... Jesus, I'm sorry, ma'am. It's just that, well, as soon as she got outta jail she started dealin' again. Sendin' drugs over half the Southeast. She didn't give a rat's ass for Ricky or me. She got put in jail in Atlanta in 2007, got out then back again in 2012. I hope she rots there for the rest of her short fuckin' life."

Carmen had put the baby down for a nap and returned to put both hands on her husband's shoulders.

Tina shook her head. "Most of what you've told me is beyond my comprehension, Jacob. Some of this I knew from Ricky's view, of course. Some from Ruthann's. But this fills in some blanks for me. Do you think coming to live here overwhelmed Ricky? I mean, the memories of those terrible days. Could those memories be the reason he took his life?"

Jacob's head drooped. "I don't know. I just don't fuckin' know."

"What about Ricky's dad?"

Jacob stiffened and his lips thinned to a single line. He shivered as if drenched in ice water. "No one ... no one knows who Ricky's dad is."

Carmen said, "Mrs. Spear, I must ask you to leave now. It's getting on in the evening, and I haven't even started supper."

"Yes. Of course. You've been very generous with your time. Thank you. I'll be heading back to Florida in the morning. Before I go, could I trouble you for a glass of water?"

"All right." Carmen got up from her chair with purpose and went into the kitchen.

Jacob remained still in his chair. Tina rose, appearing to follow Carmen to the kitchen. But at the stairway leading up to the bedrooms, she stopped. On the stairway wall, at the uppermost step, there was a large red stain with smaller stains scattered around it. The section had been dulled from scrubbing. Tina stopped, extended her hand toward the wall, drew it back, and extended it again. She took one step up. When she looked back, Carmen was scowling and holding up a glass of water. Tina felt a gust of cold air blow through her.

"Thank you," she said.

Carmen crossed her arms and watched as Tina gulped the water and handed her the empty glass. The silence and stillness of the house was unsettling.

"Thank you again for your time."

Jacob nodded as Carmen bowed her head and said, "You're welcome, Mrs. Spear." She escorted Tina to the front door.

Tina had taken two steps down the stairs to the ground, when a camouflage-green pickup truck pulled into the driveway and parked next to her Audi. The driver was dressed in military fatigues and covered in dust. His dog tags clanged as he walked up to Tina with an all-business face.

He extended his hand. "Captain Virgil Lapis, ma'am. Whom do I have the pleasure of addressing?"

Tina put one hand to her throat while offering her other to the captain. "I'm Tina Spear. I was a counselor to Jacob's brother Ricky."

Captain Lapis shook her hand firmly. His eyes were gunmetal gray.

"Pleased to meet you, Ms. Spear, though I am sorry for these circumstances."

Carmen joined them in a rush. "Captain Lapis was Jacob's last commander at Fort McPherson. He checks up on Jacob. Part of his rehabilitation program."

"It must be comforting to have so many folks of authority checking up on Jacob," Tina noted.

Carmen ignored her. To Virgil Lapis she said, "Thank you again for coming over, Captain."

The two turned and went up the last of the porch stairs, the captain looking back to Tina with a slight tip of his cap. "Ma'am," he said.

Tina stood frozen for a moment, not knowing why. She shrugged off whatever had momentarily held her and got into her car.

On her way back to the hotel, she called Devon Tillyard as soon as she had a strong enough signal. "Detective, have you been over to the Plyer home yourself?"

"For the service, and to ask some questions of Jacob right after the suicide. I'll be back for a full interview in a day or two."

"Did you get the sense at any time, talking to Jacob, if he was off? Like he was trying to remember but couldn't?"

Tillyard paused, his breathing a slow cadence into the phone. "There's a lot of pain in the Plyer house right now. My guess is Jacob's suffering not just from a busted body, but from PTSD."

"I understand all that, Detective. What's bothering me is, well, I've been close to Ricky for three years and Ricky talked about me to him. A lot, apparently. Yet I was treated like, I don't know, an intruder. Mostly by Jacob's wife."

"Easy, there. You're still a stranger to them."

"I told you I've got a good sense about people. Jacob told me a lot of history, but almost nothing of the last week. And I got nothing from his wife except this feeling she couldn't get me out of the house fast enough."

"How about I give you a call after I speak more with the family?"

"I'd appreciate a call. Can I ask you a favor?"

"Asking isn't always receiving. Go ahead."

"Would you please find out for me what jail facility Charity Plyer calls home these days? I would like to pay her a visit. Jacob seems to think she's about the worst person ever to walk the earth."

A sharp clacking of keys on a keyboard filled Tina's phone. Then she heard, "Give me a few seconds here …."

Tina's surprise at the speed with which Tillyard addressed her request gave way to impatience. "Are you still there?"

"You know, you could look this up yourself online. The internet has done more for the Freedom of Information Act than any politician. But I've got it all right here. Let me see.

… Charity Plyer has completed six years of an eight-year sentence at Pulaski State Prison in Hawkinsville, Georgia. She went in on January 22, 2012 and is eligible for parole at the end of August of this year. Less than thirty days from now. Is that right? Sure is. Strange coincidence, isn't it? Her son commits suicide barely one month before his biological mother has a chance to get out of prison."

Tina's body was overcome with thousands of needles pricking her flesh. She pulled into a Dollar Store parking lot and stepped on the brake so hard the tires screeched and the car rocked in place for few seconds. "My God! Is she actually getting paroled?"

"Up for parole doesn't mean parole."

Tina shook her head. "This looks strange. It's one more piece of a puzzle I simply cannot understand."

"Sometimes a coincidence is exactly that: a coincidence. Is this weird? Oh yes, it is. It definitely is. But does this have anything to do with my investigation? I don't see it."

"You say that now. But loosely related events are circling around something. Ricky's suicide, the immediate cremation of his body, the strange visit of your chief to Jacob Plyer, and now their mother's potential parole? What the hell!"

"I've been doing this for a few years, and here's what I can tell you. Most loose strings don't tie together. Mostly, they're just false leads to be eliminated. Don't be thinking you have some grand conspiracy or anything. That's big-city stuff."

"Thanks for your time. Please stay in touch after I get back to St. Augustine. I'd like to know what you learn from Jacob—at least whatever you'll learn that you can share with me."

"I've agreed to call you after my visit tomorrow. I'll share with you what I can, and the rest … we'll have to see."

Tina hung up, put the Audi in gear, and sped back onto the road to the hotel. After she closed the door to her room, she flung her purse onto the bed and sat next to it, cupping her head in her hands.

She talked to herself out loud. "What the hell is going on? These events have to be coinciding for a reason. I just can't get to it."

It gnawed at her like a starving insect: Did Ricky's real mother, a woman not in Ricky's life since he was born, have anything to do with this mess? At the very least, Tina had to learn for herself what Charity Plyer knew.

10

Real Life Sucks

Tina was hovering over a printout of a lobby design for a client with two of her staff when a call came in from Rhonda Kingswood. "I hate to bother you like this, Tina, but I need your help. Ricky has been sent to the principal's office and no one can get hold of Ruthann. The office called me to come in, but I'm in Ocala. Is there any way you can get over to the high school and sort out what is going on with Ricky?"

"Of course I will," she told Rhonda. "What do I need to know?"

"You know everything I know. Thank you for doing this. Would you please call me back when you have a handle on the situation?"

"I will." Tina hung up and let out a breath. She was about to venture into an unfamiliar situation.

Tina gave her ID at the school visitors' entrance and was pointed the way to the office of Principal Vargas.

The neon corridors clanged with closing locker doors and the rush of students, sending a shudder through Tina. It had been at least a couple years since she had been near a public high school. She remembered all three of her boys. Like Simon and James, Max had been smart enough to get good grades, but unlike his brothers, he had not been smart enough to make good choices. When she was led into the principal's office her eyes focused on the back of a boy with slumped shoulders. But for the red hair it could have been Max.

"Thank you for coming, Ms. Spear. I'm Principal Rosa Vargas. Please have a seat."

Ricky sat in the last of four chairs lined against the office wall. Tina took the one next to his. Ricky moved away, turning in the chair to face the wall. Tina put her hand on his arm.

"We've got this, Ricky. You and me. We'll be fine." She smiled with kindness and confidence.

Ricky glared at her with defiance. "No, we won't. This isn't good." He turned back to the wall.

"Richard has been in a fight outside of class," the principal said. "The other boy was taken to the infirmary. He was only bruised. What is worse, however, is when Mrs. Trent, his social studies teacher, tried to break the fight up, Richard screamed and threatened her."

"Ricky, please tell me in your own words what happened." Tina's voice was calm and steady.

Ricky shook his head. "Why, so I can get sent back to juvy?"

"No, the opposite. So you won't be sent back. Please tell me what happened."

"Simms had no right. He's just another bully. Likes to make everyone think he's tough by pickin' on kids. Pickin' on me. Every day."

"Go on, please," Tina said. "It's important."

He looked at Tina and held his eyes on hers. She saw confusion, anger, and, she hoped, need. She nodded and squeezed his arm. "You can do it, Ricky."

"I was just walkin' outta class, headin' to my locker. He pushed me from behind, trying to knock me down. But I didn't go down. I dropped my books and I ... I walked up to him. I said nuthin'. Wanted him to know I wasn't afraid. He pushed me again and ... I don't know ... I couldn't stand him doin' that. So I punched him square in the gut and when he bent over, I hit him top of his head with my elbow. End of story."

"What about the teacher, Mrs. Trent?" Principal Vargas asked. "You threatened her!"

"I didn't threaten her. I swear. She came outta nowhere when Simms was already on his knees. She clapped her hands in my ears and said what a horrible boy I was. She said *I* was the bully! I ain't no bully, no way. So I screamed at her, 'I'm no bully,' and she was too stupid to know who the real bully was, and she"—Ricky's voice cracked—"she didn't give a shit about me!" He wiped his eyes with his shirtsleeve.

"I see," Vargas said. "But that's not what Mrs. Trent says, or what two other students told her."

"They're lyin'. Everyone's lyin'. Don't you women ever stop lyin'?" Ricky jumped out of his seat, red-faced.

"You had better sit down right now, Richard," the principal said.

"Ms. Vargas, if Ricky says he was bullied, then he was only protecting himself. You should at least admit to the possibility that your teacher did not see what instigated this, and quite possibly reprimanded Ricky when at least both boys should have been cited. If Ricky says he was bullied, and he alone was accused, I assure you that is what happened."

"Excuse me, Mrs. Spear, but you're not in a position to know what happened. Though I'm not surprised you would take the side of the boy. At this point we need to determine a course of action."

"I'd like to speak to Ricky alone, Mrs. Vargas. May I use your outer office, please?"

Principal Vargas looked at Tina. "I've been a teacher and a principal for eighteen years now. I've seen it all. Boys and girls lie to avoid trouble and only make it worse for themselves."

"I'm not new to parenting, Ms. Vargas. I raised three boys. I can smell a lie every bit as well as you can. And Ricky is not lying."

The principal stared at Tina, narrowing her eyes, thinking for a moment. She said, "You'd like to talk to Richard alone? Please stay here in my office for the next few minutes while I check in with my secretary." She came around from her desk. "You've got five minutes. Not a second more." She closed the door soundly behind her.

"Are you okay, Ricky?"

He rubbed his hands in his lap.

"Please. Talk to me."

"No one ever done … ever did that before."

"Did what?"

"Stood up for me."

"No one? Not ever?"

Ricky shook his head. "No one. Not my mom, not my grandma, no one in juvy. Not one teacher."

It suddenly came to Tina. All the women in Ricky's life had dismissed or abandoned him. She opened her mouth, but no sound came out. Eventually she said, "Ricky, look at me, please."

He did as she asked.

"When I said I was your friend, I meant it. Do you understand?"

"I ain't never had a grown-up friend. Don't think there's such a thing."

"So, what happened, Ricky? Just now. You said it yourself. I stood up for you, right? You said you can't recall anyone ever standing up for you. Well, things have changed, haven't they?"

No response.

"Ricky?"

He pursed his lips and nodded. "What are you going to tell Principal Vargas when she comes back?"

Ricky's too-familiar shrug returned.

"Think about this. You didn't mean to do anything wrong. You didn't mean to hurt anyone or threaten anyone. And you're going to apologize."

"Why! Why do I need to apologize? I was the one got shoved! Twice!"

"I know, but there's something else I know. You're the good guy here, and as the good guy, you can make this right. The Simms boy may never try to make things right. You didn't just hurt his body, Ricky. You hurt his pride. But if you apologize, not for anything that you did you thought was right, but for what you did that was wrong, people will see you not as a juvy boy, but as a good guy. Can you tell me what you think you might have done wrong today?"

With his hand on his chin, Ricky made the best display he could of thinking this through. "I guess, maybe, when I hit Simms on the head. Maybe I should have not done that."

"Maybe. But maybe it would have been enough to let him push you and go right back up to him. You told him you weren't afraid of him, didn't you?"

"Yes, ma'am, I did. I'm not afraid of him."

"I know. But when you hit someone, it's usually because you *are* afraid of them, isn't it? Afraid they'll hurt you or someone you care about. Afraid they'll continue being mean."

Ricky squinted at Tina. She smiled. As he stared at his hands, he rocked his shoulders from side to side. Finally, he sighed. "I get it, Miss Tina."

"I know you do, Ricky. What are you going to do when Mrs. Vargas comes back in?"

"I'll tell her ... well ... that I'm sorry I yelled at Mrs. Trent. I'll tell her I didn't mean to."

"And?"

Ricky's shoulder heaved. "And I'm sorry Simms made me so mad I had to hit him."

"That's close."

"I didn't want to hit him, but he needed to be hit, is all!"

"Then try this: 'I didn't mean to get out of control. I'm sorry.' Next, you can ask Mrs. Vargas, 'How do you stop the bullying, Mrs. Principal? When you want the bullies to stop.'"

"Yeah! They gotta stop!" Ricky said, nodding quickly. "Okay."

"Hold on. Remember what your goal is here. You want to stay in school. I'm sure the principal will want you to meet with Mrs. Trent at some point."

"If she does, can you be here, Ms. Tina?"

"I won't promise anything yet. I don't want to ever have to break a promise to you. Let's see how this goes, okay?"

Ricky's eyes glistened in a way Tina had not seen before.

11

The Visit

PRESENT

Having learned the prison visitor procedures online and calling before she left the hotel, Tina had a good three hours before she needed to be in Hawkinsville, the small town for which the major industry was Pulaski State Prison. She wasn't looking forward to her visit in central Georgia, and yet she felt—believed, even—a direct conversation with Charity Plyer could provide some insight that so far had eluded Tina.

She almost missed her exit off the interstate. But her adrenaline injected enough awareness to swerve from the passing lane to the exit lane without calling for stunt driver skills from other travelers. Even from Tina's sensibilities of living in the oldest settled community in the US, Hawkinsville looked to her like a town caught in a distant past, resurfacing only once every fifty years.

While the two-story, flat-topped buildings with their sand-brick construction and high razor-wire fences fulfilled her expectations of a prison montage, the floral gardens and modern symmetry of the entrance surprised her. She found parking in the half-moon-shaped visitor lot. She got out of her car and stood motionless next to it, listening to her own breath and the slight wind that swept like a spirit through the leaves of the oak trees.

Inside, Tina showed her ID, signed in, and was respectfully searched. An alert beagle on a leash, held by a stern-faced officer, danced around Tina, wagging its tail, sniffing eagerly. Tina left her purse with the desk officer and was led through a series of four metal-mesh gates, each with a clanking magnetic lock and a breach horn. It made Tina cover her ears each time she passed over a threshold.

Another guard took her to a room with teller-like windows and chairs. He pointed to one, where Tina took a seat and waited. Two other windows had occupants, the closest to Tina was an African American man with his palm on the one-inch-thick plexiglass. He said nothing. Tina continued to sit upright, with her hands in her lap.

After five minutes, a buzzer sounded and a guard ushered in a woman. Tina could tell, even in an orange jumpsuit, that this woman was slim and fit. As she approached the seat opposite her, Tina noted that this was very much a pretty woman.

Charity Plyer sat down on the other side of the window and said, "You got any cigarettes?"

While not the greeting she'd expected, Tina easily replied, "I don't smoke."

"Of course you don't. Well, let's get it over with. What the hell are you here for?" Her voice had a singing quality to it.

"My name is Christina Sp—"

"I know who the fuck you are. I asked why you're here, Mrs. Christina Spear."

A focus and determination rose up in Tina. "You probably also know I was a counselor, a mentor, and a friend to your son, Ricky."

"That don't surprise me. Ricky always was such a fragile child. Couldn't do much for himself except scrap and moan. Never liked helping me out much. Just a lost soul looking for a friend." Charity Plyer's mouth had a curl at one end that seemed never to leave. Tina couldn't tell if it was a constant smirk or an unfortunate physical gift.

"You do know, Ms. Plyer, Ricky committed suicide less than a week ago."

"I was so informed."

"Wow! You were 'so informed'? Your son Ricky, the one you so missed out on, your youngest boy, was a wonderful, smart boy. Full of life and promise. He had friends who cared for him and respected him."

Charity turned in her seat so she could cross her legs. She bent toward the speaker in the plexiglass. "Apparently, not enough."

Tina fought to keep her temper. "I'm here to visit you because I loved your son and I'm trying to understand what could have risen in him to make him want to take his own life. I was hoping you could give me some insight into why he might."

"Boy didn't like himself much. Not everybody's worth lovin', you know."

This took Tina with so much surprise that she launched herself out of her chair, which scraped the concrete floor like fingernails on a chalkboard. She gripped the arms of the chair hard, pulling it into the air as she rose. It was only a few seconds of rage. As her composure returned, she began to understand Charity Plyer. Tina pulled the chair back up to the window and sat down. If she was to get anything out of this woman, she could not let the convict get to her.

Tina's teeth were still clenched when she said, "Ricky had turned his life around. He was on his way to having a real life, and now it's gone. Was there something in his past you would share with me, that would haunt him so much he would take his own life?"

"Who says?"

Tina looked at Charity as a war correspondent looks at carnage. "I'm trying to understand a horrible tragedy, Mrs. Plyer. I was hoping you cared enough for your dead son. I'm trying to understand why another boy I loved is gone. But it doesn't seem to me you share that love, do you? I was wrong to think you had anything for me." She stood to go.

"Who says?" Charity repeated.

"Who says what? Are you asking if Ricky had a real shot at a good life? Or maybe you've already given me more information than I can digest. I believed in him and nurtured him more in three years than you could in a thousand lifetimes! What are you talking about?"

"Who says Ricky took his own life?" Charity looked directly at Tina, expressionless.

Unable to move, Tina stood there, her mind in a whirl. What does this woman know? How could she know anything about the events five days earlier in Dahlonega? Is she just playing with me or is there something more?

"The coroner's report, the chief of police, your son Jacob, and his wife. That's who says. They all told me the story. I was at Jacob's house yesterday. Nothing else makes any sense. In fact, none of this makes sense. Maybe there is no understanding the senseless. I don't know. Has someone told you something different? Are you saying Ricky didn't kill himself?"

Charity smiled. "Oh, I don't know anything for sure. But my son Jacob—he's not a well man. His wife, she's a damn Mexican wolverine. Don't know if she liked Ricky much. I'm like you, Christina Spear. I don't think all the facts are in the daylight."

"You and I are nothing alike, and I'm quite done being part of your game."

"Suits me," the inmate said, and pushed her chair back.

Tina decided this wreck of a woman was getting off too easily. "Is it true you're up for parole in twenty-three days?" she asked.

Charity turned again toward the visitor window and bent down. "Sure as rain, I am."

"What are you intending to do if you get out? You might not, you know. I'll bet you'll be denied parole. I mean, you're a lifetime serial offender, aren't you?"

"Oh, I'll get out, all right. I've got people in Georgia. I got people in the law vouching for me. You just take care of yourself. I'll be fine."

Before she could even think it, Tina said, "Law like Sheriff Rutherford Caldwell?"

After a few seconds of complete silence and stillness, Charity let out a shrieking laugh.

She shook her head and motioned for the guard. The two of them disappeared into the belly of the prison.

The visitors' guard came up behind Tina. "That's all today, ma'am."

Back in the Georgia summer sun, Tina felt cold. The slow walk back to her car was punctuated with the trills of mockingbirds, the only birds active in the midday heat. It was hard to fathom Charity Plyer. How does a woman, especially a mother, become so nasty, so unrepentantly selfish? It looked to Tina as if Charity had been surprised by Tina's reference to Sheriff Caldwell. Was there something of substance that Tina's sixth sense had summoned? Or was she grasping at dust? As she pulled away from Pulaski State Prison, Tina turned over in her mind everything she knew about Ricky's life, his last days, and the people inhabiting them. The hasty cremation of Ricky's remains could not be reconciled with anything in Ricky's past, however wretched. At least not yet.

She said, "Siri, call Devon Tillyard." Her digital servant asked her to repeat. She said the name more slowly, and the connection between smartphone and car worked its magic. Of course, she got Tillyard's voice mail.

"Detective, this is Tina Spear. I just spoke to Charity Plyer, and I have to tell you, she's just one big infection. Do you know if she has any connection to Sheriff Caldwell? Total speculation, here. But she claims she's being vouched at her parole hearing by someone in 'the law.' I'm trying to connect the dots and these two seem worlds apart. Carmen Plyer told me the sheriff is a friend of the family. Did he speed up the whole process as a favor? Is such a thing even possible? From what I can tell, if her son Jacob testifies at her parole hearing, Charity will go directly to hell. And, please, if you learn anything you can share, I'll be very grateful. Thanks, Detective." She ended the call with a button push on her steering wheel.

Two and a half days in Georgia and she was so much more unsettled than when she had left St. Augustine.

12

Home Is Where the Boy Is

Tina called Ruthann several times, never connecting. She left Ruthann a detailed message about what had happened at Ricky's school.

The next day, when she arrived for her scheduled meeting with Ricky, she announced herself and walked in.

"Ricky, it's Miss Tina. Ruthann?" She stopped in the kitchen and repeated her call.

Ruthann walked out of her bedroom, a cigarette clenched tightly between her remaining teeth. She pulled it from her mouth as she sucked in a billow of smoke. When she stopped and glared at Tina, she yanked the door behind her closed with a slam.

She said, "Ricky don't live here no more."

Tina blinked three or four times in an attempt to banish the alternate reality in which she found herself. "That's not funny. This is Ricky's home. You're his legal guardian. Where else would he live?"

"Cole got hisself a place over in The Shores. Livin' with a buddy, doing see-ment work or sumptin'. Thought it'd do the boy good to be with his stepdaddy for a while."

"Are you out of your—!" Tina got control of herself. "You can't just ship Ricky off to who knows where, far away from his school, because … why? You don't want to spend the money to feed him?"

Ruthann's eyes narrowed. "That what you think, is it, Ms. Know-it-all? Boy's a burden for me? Well, what you just said flat out ain't so. I loved the boy, I did. But he's a handful. He needs a man who can give him discipline."

"You are so mistaken, Ruthann. Inattention or physical discipline from a man who barely has his own life in order is not what Ricky needs. He needs love and he doesn't need any more of the women in his life giving up on him. Abandoning him. And that's what you've done here. You've abandoned your grandson!"

"Don't you fuckin' lecture me, you privileged piece a' shit. You got no idea what it's like to scrape for a livin'. Ricky's gonna be just fine."

"You don't know the first thing about me, you ... are you even capable of love?" Tina had never spoken like this to anyone in her life. "Are you still going to collect a regular government check for taking care of him?"

"And you don't know me neither, you high-n'-mighty bitch! None a' your goddamned business what I do with my welfare money."

There was no sense continuing this. Tina decided to report Ruthann's behavior to Rhonda as soon as she left. "How do I get in touch with Ricky?"

"Call Cole."

"His address and phone number, please."

"Always happy to oblige, Mrs. Spear." Ruthann dropped her cigarette into a half-empty bottle of Budweiser on the kitchen counter. She picked a pen out of a drawer and tore a piece of paper from a magazine sitting on the table. Scribbling on it, she handed the scrap to Tina. "Good luck," she said, and returned to her bedroom.

Deciphering the script written over the magazine print wasn't easy, but Tina managed. She called Cole from her car. When the signal went to an answering machine, Tina bit down hard and muttered, "Of course." She left a message for Cole, to make sure Ricky called her as soon as he could.

On her way home Tina was overcome with relief when her phone rang from Cole's phone number and Ricky's voice was at the other end. "Ricky, thank you so much for calling me back. How are you?"

"Okay, I guess."

"Are you going to be fine, living with your ex-stepfather for a while?"

"Hard to say. I think so. He's not around much."

It was all Tina could do not to curse Ruthann out loud.

"How do you get to school now?"

"Cole says he'll drop me off close by and I walk the rest. It's okay."

"We were supposed to meet today. Do you remember?"

"Can't today. Can you pick me up at school tomorrow?"

"I will. What time?"

"I'm done at three. That okay?"

"I'll see you at three at the front entrance. Don't forget."

"Okay. Bye." Ricky hung up.

Tina drove back to her office. She needed to dive into her business so she would not have to think about the Ricky's sordid situation. She called Rhonda Kingswood to report Ruthann. After the fifth ring, her shoulders drooped and she left Rhonda a message.

* * *

Twenty-six years of marriage had made Walter Spear keenly aware of his wife's moods and how they affected the contours of her habits. It was painful for him to watch Tina try to hide a recent explosion with one of her staff by obsessing over the amount of foam in her afternoon cappuccino. This evening, as they prepared dinner together, Walter retrieved the pasta water pot from under the counter. As he banged the steel utensil few times against the fry pans and a steamer, Tina stopped washing the bell peppers and shook both her hands next to her ears.

"Jesus, Walter! Do you need to throw everything around just to get one pot?"

Walter, pot in hand, looked at Tina. "No more than usual. What? Did the noise hurt your ears?"

"Yes, it hurt my ears. I can't hear myself think when you turn every pan upside down just to fetch a strainer." She was shaking.

"Okay." Walter set the pot on the counter and placed his hands on Tina's shoulders.

"Not now." She tried to shrug him off.

"Yes, goddamn it! Now. You're tighter than a drumhead. Worse than I've seen you in months. How about you take a few breaths and tell me what's going on."

Tina turned off the kitchen faucet and turned to face Walter, bracing herself on the counter. "It's hard to talk about. Hard to put into words even. Ricky's situation is even more screwed up than I could have imagined."

Walter tried to take her hand, but she pulled it away. They walked to their dining table like prisoners in a meal line, where they sat facing each other. Walter winced as Tina's voice went from despondent whisper to near rage, telling him about Ricky's changed living situation. No one was taking care of him.

The furrows in Walter's brow filled with sweat. He swiped his forehead with both hands and back through his hair. "No child should have to endure anything like this," Walter said.

Tina's shoulders heaved. "Walter, if you could have been there Tuesday at the school … it was everything I could do not to burst."

"You were thinking of Max."

Tina nodded. Though her eyes filled, she straightened her back and refused to allow a single tear to escape. "I'll be all right."

"You're always all right. Or so you want the world to believe. Jesus. It's okay to say, 'fuck it.' We both know we'll never have Max back in our lives. And Ricky can't ever replace Max."

Tina stiffened. "What an awful thing to say! Of course he can't. We've been through this too many times now. Our two living sons have been total blessings. But they're both out of the house. Neither James nor Simon needs us anymore. And that makes me sad. It … it makes me empty. They've dealt with their brother's passing so much better than we have."

Walter let a few seconds of silence gather around Tina.

"I know I can't give Ricky even a tenth of what he needs. He's had no chance in any of his living environments."

"Sounds to me as if juvenile detention was better for him than what he's got now. It was stable for a time and the system at least watched out for him."

"I have no idea if what you say is true or not, but it doesn't matter. Don't you understand? Maybe someday I'll learn what those thirty months were like for Ricky. But now, right now in the present, he's in nothing but a chaotic cluster-fuck."

Walter wrung his hands and looked from side to side. "Let's take him to the movies tomorrow night."

"You can't fix this with an outing. Are you mad? Movies? What movie?"

"Any movie. Jesus Christ, Tina, I don't know. But it's maybe a bit possible the little things can add up to a big thing in his life. It doesn't make any difference what movie. Let Ricky pick any one he likes. Let him be a kid, enjoying a shoot-up or a comedy or anything. You despair because

Ricky is caught in a horrible environment. Don't let yourself be so powerless, for God's sake. A few hours of mindless escape could do us all some good." He turned away from Tina.

"It's not as if our excursion to the air show was a rousing success," she said to his back.

Walter looked down for a moment. "Okay. That trip didn't go like either of us hoped. But this is just a movie. Something different, right? No big deal."

It was better than doing nothing, Tina agreed.

Friday morning, before Ricky's ride to school normally left, Tina called Cole's phone. Cole answered.

"It's Tina Spear, Cole. I'd like to speak to Ricky, please."

Tina heard the phone handset drop and then a distant yell. "Ricky! The Spear woman is on the phone for you!"

After a time Tina heard a faint, sleepy "Hello?"

"Ricky, would you like to go to a movie with Walter and me tonight? We'd like to take you out. Pizza for dinner first and later a movie. What do you say?"

"Huh? Tonight?"

"Yes, tonight. I'll get you after school, like we agreed. Walter and I will come pick you up later, at say five thirty. We'll get pizza, and you can choose whatever movie you want to see."

"Uh … I've never been to a movie theater."

Tina was slow to respond. She managed to clear her throat and say, "It's about time you did, right? Tonight, 5:30 p.m. Be ready. Yes?"

"Sure."

She turned to Walter, who was getting dressed for the day. She didn't feel as happy as she wanted. "He's never been to a movie theater. Never in his fifteen years of life."

"It means we're the source of another new experience for him. Why the hell are you so glum?"

"I get overwhelmed with sadness for him. When this happens, I can't help but wonder how many other children have lives like his, or worse."

"I don't understand you. You've done so much for this boy in four months—more than his family did in fifteen years. And what? You're unhappy because you can't do this for every frickin' child in the US? Tina, please! Don't do this to yourself and don't do this to us. You're on the verge of another small victory. Do not borrow trouble."

Her husband had a point. Why is this sadness never-ending? How on earth could she let a thought about impoverished children suck away the brightness of her progress with Ricky? "I can't get over losing Max," she said.

Walter closed his eyes and turned his face to the ceiling. "Oh, how well I know this. Look, Tina. You have got to compartmentalize your grief. Remember what our counselor said? Focus on the good times, focus on what made Max special. You let the grief out when it's safe, so it won't overwhelm you. Listen to me, please. I can't keep doing this. I won't."

"I know. Maybe I thought Ricky was the solution to get past my grief."

"That's not working, is it? And a boy from juvenile detention shouldn't be a solution to anything! I'm not saying he doesn't have something to give you in return. We both know he does. But you have to separate him from Max. If you don't, if you can't, then maybe you and I will have to …"

13

Listening to the Leaves

PRESENT

There was only one reason any coroner, and particularly one as punctilious as Tyson Landers, would complete a suicide determination so quickly, so lacking in procedural detail and follow-through: orders. This wasn't lost on Devon Tillyard. Since his diner meeting with Tina, the detective had become ever more certain his boss had ordered a speedy autopsy and suicide ruling for one Richard Plyer. While the detective would still have to prove his belief, the real question was why. Why would the sheriff take such an interest in a near stranger's suicide, a teenager who had lived in Dahlonega all of five weeks? What seemed like a mere uncrossed *t* had morphed into something Tillyard could not explain. The hair on the back of his neck crackled.

At his desk Tillyard listened again to the message left by the undeterred Ms. Spear. A connection between the sheriff and Charity Plyer seemed farfetched at best. But as he had told her, all the loose ends have to be run to ground, even if they fizzle and die. It was time for Tillyard to interview Jacob Plyer in earnest.

Carmen Plyer answered the door. She recognized Tillyard before he identified himself. She asked him at the doorway why he was there.

"Your brother-in-law's suicide, Mrs. Plyer, has some irregularities I've been charged with cleaning up on the report. I'm sorry for this intrusion, but I've got to put this paperwork to bed so I can get on after, chasing real criminals. You know, the real police work you taxpayers pay me to do. I won't be long. Promise."

"Wait here, please. I'll be right back." Carmen disappeared into the house. She returned a minute later and held the door open wide. "Please come in, Detective."

There had been no opportunity at the funeral service three days ago to interview Jacob. The Sheriff and chief deputy had been along with Tillyard, but not in any official capacity, offering their condolences and speaking in whispers to Jacob, Carmen, and a few of the others paying respects, including a military captain from Atlanta, connected to Jacob.

Stepping over the threshold and into the Plyer home, Tillyard noticed their daughter playing in a crib to his right. Little Emma shrieked in glee as she bounced a toy and crawled after it. Tillyard smiled. "She's a lot more energetic today than when I saw her at the reception," he remarked.

"Mood in the house is different," Carmen stated.

"That's a hopeful sign," he said.

Jacob was standing in the kitchen, leaning heavily on his cane. He extended his right hand to Tillyard. "Welcome, Detective. Please have a seat."

They sat around the kitchen table, Tillyard with his back to the window, where the streaming sunlight backlit his head. His face disappeared. Jacob looked at Tillyard wide-eyed and fearful, until Carmen went over and drew the curtains together.

Jacob shook his arms and his head. "Whew!" he said. "The sunlight made a silhouette of your head, like a saint. You ain't no saint, are you, Detective?"

"My mom, who loves me dearly, would never call me a saint, Mr. Plyer."

They laughed a bit.

Tillyard said, "I've had a chance to review the coroner's report on your brother's death. I have a few questions so I can be sure the story told by the witnesses is consistent with the story told by the body."

Jacob glanced at Carmen, who encouraged him with a nod and a smile. He said, "Sounds fair."

"Thanks. You said your brother was at the top of the stairs while holding a gun to his head and threatening to kill himself. When he fired, what did you see?"

A swallow of air stuck in Jacob's throat. "It ... it all happened sorta fast. I mean ... oh, shit."

"Take your time."

"I guess Ricky was just done, you know? He was pointin' at his head, wavin' the damn gun around."

"Where were you, Mr. Plyer, the moment Ricky pulled the trigger?"

Jacob's eyes darted from side to side. "I-I had just come out of my room to see what Ricky was so upset about. And I was ... I was kinda freaked out when I saw how, like, crazy he was, you know? Eyes all wide an' screamin' and all. When I saw the gun, I wanted to go and grab it from him. I was so damn shook up and scared seein' him like that. I can't say how far I was when he pulled the trigger."

"Do you think he could have been holding the gun on his head or do you think he might have been holding it far away?"

"Like if he was scared to pull the trigger or sumthin'?"

"Do you think he was scared? Can you tell me anything that might have precipitated his ... what ... snapping?"

"Ah fuck, I don't know! I was tryin' to get closer to him and tryin' to speak softly, he waves the gun and BAM! It goes off. I honestly can't say if he meant to hurt himself or not. Oh, Jesus!" Jacob pulled in a deep breath and screamed.

Carmen got up, took three pill bottles from the cupboard, filled a glass with water, and returned.

After the echo died, Tillyard gave Jacob all the time he needed to complete his recollection. Carmen poured out the pills, pulled her husband's hand to hers, and put the pills in his palm. She closed his fingers so he wouldn't lose any.

"Do I have to now?" Jacob asked his wife.

"Take half now," she told him.

Jacob complied. He closed his eyes after a deep swallow then opened them. "What were we talkin' about, Detective?"

"You were telling me why you think Ricky may have snapped."

"Yeah. … Shit, I don't know if he was scared, but he sure was mad, and he was cryin'. We were … we were talkin' earlier, how fucked up our ma and grandma were and how they … they used us. Used Ricky, mostly. He was talkin' about how the Spear lady treated him a world better than his own kin. … Aw, fuck, I just wish he'd shot me. I wish he'd shot me," Jacob said, sobs overtaking him.

Carmen slipped into the chair beside him and held his hands.

"Mrs. Plyer, did you see what happened?"

"I'm sorry, Detective. I was down here in the kitchen with Emma. I came to the bottom of the stairs when I heard Ricky yelling and a second after there was a gunshot. I'm pretty sure I screamed. The baby started to cry. It was … really bad." Her body shook.

Tillyard's lips tightened into a sliver. "There's no way to know for certain. But for your information—and we'll release the report to you tomorrow—your brother's wound was consistent with a 9 mm, fired from one to two feet away. Not from a gun directly held to his head. It's very unusual."

"I can't dispute what's in the report, Detective. He was outta control. Fuck, he might have shot hisself by accident.

You know, threatening to kill hisself but not exactly aimin' to. I yelled at him to put the gun down, but it was like he didn't even hear me. When that gun went off I-I felt like I was back in the war. I-I'm so fuckin' ashamed I couldn't do anything. Not one fuckin' thing."

"The ballistics report also said the gun had been fired twice. Where did the other bullet hit?" Tillyard glanced at the ceiling above the stairs, over the balcony; he looked at the railing and beyond. He could barely make out what could have been a small patch of plaster about six feet back from the top of the stairs. He sat down.

Jacob's eyes darted to Carmen.

She remained calm and said, "It must have been the first shot I heard, when Ricky and Jacob started yelling at each other. Is that right, Jacob?" She swiveled her body to look at her husband.

"Ha-had to been, I guess. I can't remember straight. Jus' can't imagine Ricky being so ..."

Carmen's eyes narrowed. "Jacob. You know how sullen and dark Ricky had been these last few weeks. I think, Detective, Ricky was mad at the world around him. Especially his mother. She's been in prison for the better part of six years."

"She's up for parole in twenty-three days. Do you think the possibility of his mother's parole may have triggered something in Ricky?"

Carmen answered, "We heard she could be released as early as August. Neither of her sons viewed that as good news."

"Good news, hell," Jacob said. "Just God spittin' in our eyes."

After a few moments Tillyard said, "I'll be asking Sheriff Caldwell this later, but I need to ask you, as well. Can either of you tell me why the chief might have authorized a fast-track release and cremation of your brother's body? Such action is only ever taken, in my experience, where there is some exigent circumstance like an infectious disease."

"God's honest truth, Detective," Carmen said, "RC was truly aware how …" She turned to her husband. "Jacob, I have to tell him."

Jacob shook his head.

"Yes, I do. It will help the detective understand."

Jacob let his chin drop to his chest.

Carmen turned back to the detective. "Among other ailments," she said, "my husband has been diagnosed with PTSD. He served two tours of duty in Iraq and in both tours was subjected to multiple IED attacks and firefights that killed his friends and, as you know, took a fair part of his leg and more. I called the police that night and asked for RC, since he and Jacob go back a number of years." Carmen stopped talking.

Tillyard leaned forward. "Please keep going, Mrs. Plyer. This is important."

She nodded. "As I said, Jacob suffers from PTSD, which RC knows only too well. When he saw my husband's condition that night—Jacob had taken his pain meds earlier in the evening—RC knew the only way to help him get back to some sort of normal would be to get Ricky's death behind us just as soon as humanly possible. RC was helping Jacob, Detective. Helping to keep him sane. It could have been Jacob picking up that gun and doing something no one could come back from."

Tillyard was still. "What was Jacob's condition when the chief arrived?"

Jacob's clasped hands shook. He raised them over his head and pounded them on the table three times in rapid succession. A startled Tillyard pushed his chair back and rose from it. As instantly as Jacob had exploded, he stopped, becoming a statue, save for shallow breaths and glazed eyes, somehow no longer of this world. He swiveled his head to look at Tillyard and opened his mouth. No words came out. Only a low, mournful groan.

Carmen jumped up. "I am so, so sorry, Detective. Jacob? Jacob, baby ..." She hugged her husband's head to her stomach and rocked him.

Slowly, his breathing lengthened. He closed his eyes.

As Carmen looked at the detective, her eyes narrowed. "I think you should go now."

Tillyard took two steps backward. "I may have a few more questions another time, but I have everything I need for now, Mrs. Plyer. Jacob, I hope you feel better soon. I'm very sorry for these events and I'm sorry you had to relive them. I'll make sure a copy of the coroner's report is delivered to you tomorrow."

He looked at Carmen holding her husband and looking down at him. Her face was no longer the image of compassion he had seen a moment ago. She seemed deeply unhappy. Not in any way sad. More disappointed, as if she had failed at something or as if someone had let her down. This is strange, he thought.

"No need to see me out, Mrs. Plyer. Thank you again. You all take good care now."

The front door seemed much farther away than he recalled, so he quickened his pace. With a look over his shoulder as he stepped across the threshold, Tillyard saw Carmen Plyer looking at him, her jaw muscles twitching. It appeared to him as the expression of a protector steeling herself to fight for the life of her family.

Tillyard sat in his car, engine running, while he analyzed what he had heard. Jacob Plyer wasn't sure about where Ricky was holding the gun. Okay. At least he had an answer for why, perhaps, the fatal shot was fired at least a foot away from Ricky's head. It was the most critical element of the coroner's report. In most circumstances it meant an accidental or intentional shooting by another person. It was rare for a true suicide. Was Jacob's answer a bit too compliant with the facts? Tillyard was willing to bet Jacob was addicted to those pain pills his wife fed him, which could help explain why Carmen seemed to take control of the conversation when she didn't want her husband to speak. Tillyard couldn't link this feeling to anything tangible. And why had there been an initial shot that went somewhere into the house? He needed forensics back to recover the bullet and get a trajectory.

His unsettled instincts couldn't be ignored. He needed to know more about Carmen Plyer. But more important than the good wife, was the sheriff. He's going to have to come clean. The coroner's report virtually put him on notice: this was no slam-dunk suicide. What had the chief been thinking?

14

The Appointment

Arriving home after a full day on the road, Tina was exhausted. She opened the garage door and saw Walter's parked SUV. With the engine idling, Tina sat with her hands on the wheel. The possibility of another tense dinner with Walter made her stomach turn. She didn't necessarily feel like being alone, however. Putting the Audi into reverse she backed out of her driveway and headed for her office.

She left Walter a message that she would be at work for a few hours. Then she entered the Spearhead Design studio. To her great satisfaction, Dale was leaning over the main layout table, where he and her chief fabricator were having a discussion. Dale stopped abruptly when he saw Tina and broke into a frown, which soon became a big smile.

"Glad you could drop by, boss! Any chance you've got some time to weigh in on the details for Clarkson's new office?"

Tina nodded. "I do," she said, and walked with a slight bounce in her step over to the table. Energy directed at a business task was more welcome than the two men could understand.

"Georgia go okay?" Dale asked.

"Not so much. But that's a story for another time. What have you got for me?"

The trio spent an animated hour before breaking. The two men left for the night, and Tina adjourned to her office. She read emails, reviewed contracts and design ideas, addressing work she could have easily put off until the next day. At nine o'clock her cell phone chimed.

"Hi, Tina."

"Hi, Walter."

"I made you salmon and salad. It's ready whenever you get home."

"Thank you."

"I also moved up our appointment with Dr. Arnau for tomorrow, one p.m. Please tell me you'll be there."

Tina stared at the ceiling and rocked slightly in her chair.

"All right. Yes, I'll be there."

"Thanks. See you when you get home."

"I'll be a few more minutes here. See you soon."

When she hung up the phone, her buoyancy drained in a flush. Rising from her chair she looked around at her office. It felt lifeless. The photos and paintings had lost their colors, the crystal awards on her bookshelf had become self-absorbed gnomes. She walked into the silent studio, taking in the empty workstations, the electric hum of the printer, the over-white lights exposing each detail beneath where no shadow was allowed. She was barely afloat. The feelings of the years after Max's death, before she met Ricky, had returned. But this time was different. There had been no questions surrounding Max's accident. Simply a teen who had lost control of his car, likely due to an irrelevant distraction. The only thing to do was grieve, blame herself, and her husband, and try to move on. But circumstances of Ricky's passing had questions, uncertainty, which had incomprehensibly become the cliff edge from which Tina was hanging. She gripped a paper on the nearest workstation and crumpled it. As she did, she let out a scream that rose up like compressed air from a breached tank. It reverberated off the high ceiling and walls before dissolving into silence. Cross-armed and sullen, she paced the perimeter of her office. After two complete tours, she realized she'd been holding her breath, which she corrected with a deep inhale. She closed shop and went home.

The next day, when Tina arrived at Dr. Arnau's office a few minutes late, Walter was already sitting in one of the two chairs in front the plain oak desk. As he rose, his arms twitched at his side. Did he want to give Tina a hug? Tina stopped at the doorway and Walter sat down.

"Welcome, Tina," said Dr. Arnau. "It's so good to see you." She extended a hand.

Tina accepted her hand over the top of the desk. "Thank you. I'm sorry to be a few minutes late."

"Have a seat, won't you?" The counselor indicated the chair in a superfluous gesture Tina found irritating.

"Tell me, Walter. You asked for this appointment to be moved up a week. What was your reason?"

"Well, first, I'm worried we've regressed. I mean, Tina has just been through another big trauma, and I'm not sure how we weather this when we're still struggling with losing Max."

"Tina, to what trauma is Walter referring?"

With tight-lipped restraint, Tina reduced the last three days to a chronology of events as if they were isolated from each other.

"We have discussed the possibility you may have transferred feelings for your middle son to your mentee. With these new circumstances, do you feel this is still true?"

"I … of course it is somewhat true. But we've dealt with this, haven't we?" She turned and looked at Walter. "Ricky was a boy in need. Working with Ricky helped me grieve and cope with my—our loss. And we've said before, sitting right here, I made that separation between Ricky and Max."

"What concerns me, Tina, truly concerns me," Walter said, leaning forward and looking into the desk, "is you've lost this boy too. And right away you've become obsessed with proving he didn't commit suicide. It doesn't feel like moving on to me. It … it feels like you're in another cycle of grief that shuts me out completely."

"Do you feel Walter has a point, Tina?"

With a sigh and a straightening of her spine, Tina said, "Walter's not wrong, Doctor. But I'm not wrong either. You can think what you want about my emotional state. I know something is terribly wrong about how Ricky died, and I may be the only one who cares enough to get to the bottom of it. If I've hung on to my loss of Max for too long, there is now a purpose. I need the unrelenting sense of injustice, the maddening remorse, to power me through this search for the truth. And I know here,"—she put her hand over her heart— "if I don't, the truth will be lost." Tina got up from her chair.

"Are you already leaving, Tina? You have twenty minutes left."

Before she could answer, Walter shot up from his chair. "I'm trying like hell to understand what you need, what you have to do. But I get no sense you care what I need. Do you? Just look at me and tell me you care about what I need, Tina. For the love of God. Look at me and tell me."

"I have to do what's right for me, Walter. You do what's right for you." She grabbed her purse and walked out of Dr. Arnau's office as if she was leaving a nail salon.

15

Looking Up

The movie Ricky wanted to see was *Transformers: The Last Knight*. It was the latest in a series of young adult sci-fi movies. Tina was a bit surprised.

"Are you sure this is the one you want to go see? Don't you have to see the others to know what's going on? There are some other action-adventure movies out, you know. I don't know any of their titles, but I'm sure Walter can tell you."

Walter nodded, his mouth full of pizza.

He began to speak, but Tina shushed him. "You can speak after you've swallowed, am I right?"

He tried to frown with his cheeks bulging of pizza, making Ricky and Tina laugh. When he swallowed with a loud gulp and took a big swig of water, he wiped his mouth with his sleeve, from elbow to cuff. "There. Let's see." He took out his phone and read off the theater's webpage. "There is *Guardians of the Galaxy Vol. 2*, and … wait for it … *War for the Planet of the Apes*."

"Yup. *Transformers* is the one. I saw one of the them when I was in juvy. We got to watch TV sometimes, you know. Pretty cool how they go from cars and trucks to killer robots."

Tina rolled her eyes. But a deal was a deal. The movie started in fifty minutes. "Ricky, when was the last time you heard from your brother in the army?" she asked.

Without taking his eyes off the slice of pizza in his hands, Ricky said, "He called over to Ruthann's last week." Back to pizza.

"So, how is he doing? He's been in the army for a while, hasn't he?"

"'Bout ten years, I guess. He's says he's goin' back to Iraq. After that, it's quits for him."

"Do you and your brother get along these days?"

Ricky started to speak with his mouth full when Tina held up her hand as she had to Walter.

"What? You asked me a question," came his muffled answer.

Tina let go an exasperated grunt. "Manners, Ricky. You can't be heard when you garble your words with a mouth full of food."

Ricky shrugged, looked at Walter, and swallowed.

"Much better. Now, tell me about your brother."

Ricky looked down. "Jacob's the only person I got close to a dad. He's got a place in Georgia, near where he trained. He wants me to go up there and stay as soon as he's back."

"How often have you seen him since he joined the service?"

"When I was little, he used to come home for a couple a' weeks a year. Couple a' times he came and took me up to Georgia"

"It must have been hard to get to know him, considering how long he was away each time."

"Yeah," he said, still looking down. Ricky brightened up and said, "Jacob, he's big and smart. He taught me how to throw a football. We used to go fishing together, go to the beach. Pretty much anything to get outta the house. Taught me how to fight."

Walter and Tina exchanged a glance.

Ricky stopped eating and looked into his lap. "Jacob's my brother *and* he's my friend. My best friend." He took a slow, furtive look at Tina.

"But not your only friend. Right?" Her hand inched across the table, but not far enough to take his hand.

Ricky looked Tina straight her eyes. "Not anymore. I got a friend who buys me pizza!"

Walter pushed his chair back from the table and crossed his legs, looking at his watch. "Movie's starting in less than ten minutes. Let's get some seats."

The film wasn't torture for Tina, it was mildly entertaining for Walter, and a runaway hit with Ricky. On their way to drop Ricky home, he asked if they could put the top down.

Tina obliged with pleasure. "A modern-day transformer, yes?" she said to Ricky as the top tucked itself into the trunk.

"That was so cool!" he said.

As they were driving back to Cole's, Ricky tried to stand up and get the wind in his hair, like a retriever. Walter politely encouraged him to sit back in his seat each time and to keep his seat belt fastened.

Tina couldn't pull the Audi into Cole's driveway. Two trucks and two cars crowded an open garage illuminated by a black light. Five men in lawn chairs huddled around a turned-up cable spool with more open bottles of beer on top of it than there were men. Lynyrd Skynyrd blared from a boombox at the rear of the garage. When one of the men realized there was a car parked in front of the house, he went over and tugged on the arm of another man, who walked to the garage wall and killed the lights. The second man walked between the vehicles in the driveway, over to the Audi.

"Evenin', there. Everythin' aw' right?" It was Cole.

Tina opened her door and stood behind it. Her eyes darted from side to side. "We're bringing Ricky back from the movies. I hope you and your friends are all well." Her voice brimmed with politeness.

"Sure. We're all good." He glanced back to the garage, where the men had all but disappeared into the dark.

There were sounds of shuffling bottles and crinkling, like the gathering of a plastic tarp. Tina thought she saw two of the men move something from the cable spool top and into a large container silhouetted on the ground, which they picked up and moved out of her sight.

Walter adjusted his seat for Ricky to get out from the back. Tina introduced Ricky's ex-stepfather to her husband, who walked four steps onto the grass and stuck out his hand. Cole looked at it for a split second, wiped his own hand on his jeans, and shook hands.

"Good to meet you, husband," Cole said.

"It's Walter," the husband returned.

Ricky didn't say a thing to anyone. He stuffed his hands in his pockets, walked past Cole, and strode in the grass to the front door, and disappeared. Tina's gaze had followed every step.

"The boy ain't much for manners, is he? Well, takes after his momma, that's for sure."

Tina didn't try to stop herself. "I don't think Ricky is very much like his mother. Either of them."

Cole lost his balance as he snapped his head toward Tina. He recovered quickly and laughed like he was trying to understand a joke but couldn't. "Uh, maybe. But since you ain't had the pleasure of meeting my ex, I'll go with my own observation, thank you."

"Just a hunch, Mr. Hart. I'm sure Ricky's tired and wants to get to sleep." A smile was plastered on Tina's face.

Looking confused, Cole stared at her in the streetlight glare. He turned around to walk back to his lawn chair confederacy.

"Thas' right. He got all tired from sittin' watchin' a movie. You take care now, Miss." His back to Tina, he waved as he continued to look at her over his shoulder.

In the car, Walter said, "That man has a handshake like grape jelly. I can't believe he does construction."

"What did you think of those men in the garage, sitting around?"

"Cole's drinking buddies? I'd say they scurried like mice as soon as you turned off the engine. And they didn't want to be seen, did they. The lights went off when you got out of the car."

"I don't know what they were doing. Whatever it was, they stopped. I'm pretty sure it isn't legal. That's no environment for Ricky."

"I agree. But please don't stir up a hornets' nest. Just check in with Ricky in the morning."

"I will," Tina said, staring over the beam of the headlights cutting the darkness as she drove.

16

Speed Trap

Devon Tillyard knew the sheriff had to be confronted for the questionable cremation of Ricky Plyer's body. But Caldwell had to know his detective would question him. It was all so odd. Why hadn't the sheriff come clean? Why had he let Tillyard investigate? These questions were actually easier to contemplate than the one continuing to gnaw at him: Was there something more deeply buried here that might explode?

As he planned his next moves, Tillyard decided to return Tina Spear's call from a few days before. He reached her cell phone while she was in her office.

"Ms. Spear, thanks for picking up. Is this a good time to speak for a few minutes?"

She hesitated. "My team is heads down on a project for a new client. It needs our full attention."

"If you can give me a time which suits you better, I'll—"

"You know what, Detective? There's no time like now. Let me get to my desk." Behind her closed door, Tina sat down hard and put both elbows on her desk. She switched the phone from her left hand to her right, to take notes.

"Okay. What's on your mind, Detective?"

"I'm returning your call from last week."

You cheeky SOB, she thought. "Are you, now? What did you think of my message?"

"You weren't exactly taken with Charity Plyer, and you had a feeling, based on no evidence, that she knew the sheriff. 'Bout right?"

"Good for you. And the sheriff is a friend of the Plyer family. So how about you tell me what you discovered during your talk with Jacob."

"Jacob Plyer is not a well man."

"I'd vouch for that. I think those painkillers contribute to his obvious depression."

"You and I share the same sense about his drugs. His wife said he and the sheriff go back a ways. Military, I'm guessing. Seems the sheriff was out to do him a solid by making quick work of a painful and ugly situation."

Tapping her pen on her desk, Tina turned this over in her mind. "She told me the same thing. But if this is nothing but a favor for a friend, why make it look so ... so ... suspicious, so fast he or someone appeared to be hiding something?"

Tillyard considered sharing the detail of the powder burns found on Ricky's hands but not on his skull, then decided not to. "Ms. Spear, I'm going to ask you for a favor. I'm going to take the sheriff on directly, but I have to have all my ducks aligned. I'll get nowhere if I don't have real evidence of what's going on. You seem to think there's some link with Charity Plyer. If it's true that Sheriff Caldwell and Jacob have some shared past, it's not too unbelievable to think maybe the same is true for Jacob's momma."

"She was also Ricky's mother, Detective."

"Right. So, I'm asking if you would go down this road for a bit."

"Say what? I don't understand."

"Check on the mother-sheriff connection. Ask the grandmother. Maybe you can give her a surprise visit and pose a few direct questions."

"Ruthann is one sharp-elbowed bitch, Detective. I see where Charity gets it. I can't say I relish more interaction with that harpy. But if you think she might have information to move this along, I'll see what I can do."

"I'll level with you, Ms. Spear, I don't know yet. But I … we have to flush something out."

"What do you know about an army captain named Virgil Lapis?"

Tillyard had to stop and think. "I believe I met him at Ricky's memorial service. Buttoned-up army officer from Fort McPherson. Why?"

"He came by the Plyer house as I was leaving. I don't have anything. Just a strange feeling he's out of place. And it makes me nervous, you know?"

Tillyard sucked in his breath. "He showed up again a day after the service, heh? Do you know why?"

"He's like the sheriff," Tina deadpanned, "just a concerned friend of the family."

"Okay. I'll look into Captain Lapis. I'm also going to look into Carmen Plyer. If I didn't know better, I'd say she was making sure Jacob was good and dosed up on his pain meds while I was there."

"Playing a hunch, Detective?"

"That's what I do. I pull on the loose threads until the sweater unravels."

"Or tightens into a knot. As soon as I've been in front of Ruthann, I'll give you a call."

"I'd appreciate it. Bye for now."

Tillyard looked around the sleepy police department in front of him. He turned in his chair to take in the glass offices of the sheriff and his second in command. The sheriff's had a museum-like cleanliness laid bare by the harsh fluorescent light. The other office had clutter on every surface Tillyard could make out. Cradling a phone while searching for a file or paper on top of his desk, the chief deputy was animated and engaged. The sheriff was not in his office. Everything seemed perfectly normal. Was there anything Tillyard might find to upset this unchallenged, slightly flabby department? There was no way to know. He was an outsider. The only way to the truth and its consequences, grave or benign, was to follow his instincts, which at this moment were telling him to be very careful.

17

Parks and Recreation

Ruthann Plyer was consistent in her communications: she never answered her phone or returned Tina's calls. If Tina heard from Ruthann, it was when Ruthann wanted something—a mercifully rare event. But Tina wanted Ruthann. She had to understand why, with no warning, Ricky was moved to his ex-stepdad's way station. After her last confrontation with the woman, she wasn't sure how Ruthann would react to more questions about her parenting. She decided to postpone the next encounter until she had a plan.

For most of Saturday Tina wrestled with how she might help Ricky, even while she tried to concentrate on new creative offerings from Spearhead Design. From her office she called Cole's house in the afternoon. As she started to leave a message, Ricky picked up the phone. He told Tina that Cole and his other roommate had gone "to work or somewhere to collect money." Cole, it seems, had been considerate enough to let Ricky know the boys were going to the Mardi Gras Bar straight thereafter.

This made Tina's heart ache. "You know, Ricky, I've been stuck in my office most of the day today. I sure could use a walk outside somewhere. Would you like to get out of the house and go for a walk with me?"

"Sure, I guess."

"How about I leave right now and pick you up. I'll be there in fifteen minutes. We'll go to Treaty Park."

"Okay."

Ricky was sitting on Cole's concrete stoop when Tina pulled up. When Ricky got up and walked to the car, Tina put the convertible top down. A smile brightened Ricky's face.

The parking lot at Treaty Park wasn't yet full. Families were picnicking, people were jogging and walking dogs. All the tennis courts had matches in progress. Tina and Ricky heard the bright crack of an aluminum bat from a softball game. She showed Ricky how to hold the lever that controlled the convertible top and asked him to use it. He hesitated at first and then let out a long "Coo-ool" as the roof clicked into place and the windows closed.

Along the main asphalt path circumnavigating the park, Tina and Ricky walked in silence for a few minutes. Tina asked Ricky if he knew the names of any of the birds they encountered along the way. He shook his head. She pointed out the few she knew well: cardinals, mockingbirds, red-winged blackbirds, all of which were distinctive for their appearance and their calls. They walked along the boardwalk by the lake, past the people fishing.

Tina stopped so they could put their elbows on the railing to look out over the water. An osprey suddenly dove into the lake, flapped around in the water, and emerged with a fish in its talons.

Ricky pointed at the raptor flying off. "That was awesome!"

Tina nodded. "Tell me how you're doing, Ricky. Are you having a better time at school?"

"It's okay. I don't get picked on like I used to."

"Do you have any friends?"

"Not like I had at juvy. The kids at this school are weird."

"It takes time" was all the wisdom Tina could muster. "What about living with Cole. How's it working out? Do you have your own room?"

"Nah. I sleep in the den most nights. It's got a couch and a TV. I can do my homework there."

With a sigh and a nod, Tina turned to Ricky. "Let's keep going."

Continuing their walk, they came to a sign: ROBERT-LARYN SKATE PARK. Ricky stopped and turned in the direction the sign indicated. They found themselves on the edge of 28,000 square feet of concrete with at least fifty people, most wearing helmets and gloves and careening over the hills, dips, and half-pipes, barely avoiding crashes and having the time of their lives. Ricky's mouth fell open. "I heard of these places, but I never seen one. This is awesome!"

"Do you have a skateboard?"

"Used to. They didn't let me take it to juvy. When I got home, it was gone."

Tina shook her head. "Well, is skateboarding something you want to start up again?"

"Hell yeah, it is."

"Where do they sell them?"

"I dunno. Walmart? Why?"

"I'm just thinking for now. Do you still have a helmet?"

"Never had a helmet."

"Oh. Okay. This gives me an idea. Let's keep walking."

Of course, Tina thought. A hobby like skateboarding was perfect. He could get out of the house, make friends, feel some freedom long absent in his world. She decided to research the sport a bit and eventually take Ricky shopping when she was prepared.

Ricky saw the big smile on Tina's face. He had to ask. "What's up? Why you lookin' so goofy?"

This made Tina laugh out loud. She shook her head. "You'll find out soon enough," she teased.

The following week, after their biweekly mentoring lunch, Tina pushed an envelope across the table to Ricky, with his name typed on it: MR. RICHARD PLYER. It wasn't quite official looking, but it didn't look personal either.

Ricky looked at Tina and gave his all-too-familiar shrug. "What's this?"

"It has your name on it. Open it and find out."

With more enthusiasm than Tina had yet seen from Ricky, he tore open the letter and pulled out its contents. He held a bright green gift certificate with his name on it for the amount of $250.00 at a local sporting goods store. Under "Special Instructions" it read: "To be used only for one assembled skateboard, helmet, and gloves." A ticket to the moon would not have been more exciting. He read it over and over, taking a second to glance up at Tina.

After reading it a last time, he put it face down on the table and exhaled. "Whoa. Whoa."

When he fell silent, Ricky beamed at Tina and started to squirm in his chair.

"Well?" Tina asked.

"Well, what?"

"Aren't you going to say anything?"

Ricky's face turned stern. His eyebrows bent down and he pursed his lips. Finally, he lit up with inspiration. "Can we go there now?"

"Ugh!" Tina cried. "What is the right thing to say when someone gives you a gift? You know what you're supposed to say."

With an open mouth, Ricky froze. Tina tilted her head and waited. No words came from either of them until Tina gave in.

"Ricky Plyer! Has no one ever taught you to say 'thank you' when you receive a gift? Or for that matter, when you receive anything nice from another person?"

He shook his head from side to side. When he stopped, his chin touched his chest and his shoulders heaved. It could have been a shrug, but it could have been something else. Tina reached across the table, over the upside-down gift certificate, and put her hand around Ricky's arm. They remained like that until Ricky looked up.

He opened his mouth to say something, but just stuttered.

"You're welcome, Ricky," Tina said. "Come on. Let's go to this store and get you outfitted."

Ricky was first out through the restaurant exit. When he got to the passenger door of Tina's car, he stopped and looked over the car roof, to his mentor. "Thank you, Miss Tina," he said.

Heading home after dropping Ricky off with his package of skateboard gear, Tina got a call. It was Rhonda Kingswood.

"Sorry I didn't get to return your call earlier in the week, Tina. What can I do for you?"

"Did you get a chance to listen to my message, Rhonda? Apparently, Ruthann Plyer has pushed Ricky out of her house to live with his ex-stepdad, who's renting a room from a work colleague or something. It seems pretty awful to me. Is there anything to be done about it?"

After a moment, Rhonda replied, "I'll go over and have a chat with Ruthann. You're welcome to be there."

"Our last conversation got a little heated, sorry to say. I mean, I showed up at my normal time to pick up Ricky, and poof, Ricky was gone. No phone call to me, nothing. I was livid!"

"I'm sure you were. Please keep this in mind. After all is said and done, she's Ricky's legal guardian and unless there is a very good reason to put a fifteen-year-old into foster care—keeping in mind he's served time as a delinquent—it's a difficult and, more often than not, unsuccessful avenue. I don't think there's much opportunity to change this situation."

When Tina didn't fill the silence, Rhonda continued. "At this point, you, Tina, are his best chance for developing his ability to build a stable life for himself."

Tina's grip on the steering wheel loosened and she felt light-headed.

"Tina? Are you still there?"

"Yes, Rhonda, I'm here. I'm just … I'm frightened. Cole Hart is certainly using drugs and, I'm pretty sure, from a few things Ricky's told me, he's dealing. It seems like such a … oh … I don't know. I want so much to get Ricky into a living arrangement that's even the tiniest bit supportive. Is that too much to ask?"

Rhonda took another long pause. "You are the environment he needs and responds to now. You give Ricky hope. You give him friendship and an adult in his life he can turn to."

"Please let me know when you plan to see Ruthann Plyer. Do you think she would speak or act any differently to you than she would if I were there?"

"Hard to say. If you want to be there, you should be. But I can't predict how she'll behave."

"Good God, it's like going after a wild animal. She gave some excuse Ricky needed male discipline, which is, of course, utter nonsense. There's not even presence from Mr. Hart, let alone discipline!"

"I'll give you a call as soon as I have some options for visiting."

"I appreciate it. Thank you. She's hiding something, Rhonda. I just have no idea what."

Opening the garage door from her car, Tina stopped with the motor running. Ruthann could not be her concern. Ricky was coming out of his shell, doing well enough in school. He, not his grandmother, should be the focus of her energy. All this chaos with Cole made Tina wonder who Ricky's biological father might be. Could he, or would he, have made a difference in his life? Tina shook her head. Of course not. What person, other than Tina, had ever treated Ricky as a normal human child?

18

One Answer Is Not a Solution

PRESENT

It struck Tina as odd she hadn't seen Ruthann for over two months, and only heard from her the one time: a show of rare politeness, to let Tina know her young mentee had killed himself. Ruthann may or may not hold any valuable information for Tina's quest, but she had to determine that for herself. Ruthann's current unavailability was normal. Besides, why would Ruthann want to grieve with someone who knew and cared for Ricky more than she?

It was a bright and hot beginning to the workday at six thirty in the morning. Tina stopped at her office to leave a bag of bagels and some instructions for the staff and continued directly to Ruthann's. She'd not been there since Ricky's high school graduation. For no reason she could understand, the drive to The Pines was less dreary than normal. The neighborhood seemed alive and thriving. In the everyday heat of the late Florida summer, life was proceeding with a superannuated normalcy.

Tina pulled into the driveway, noting it was as debris-free as she had ever seen it. She knocked on the outer screen door, shouting "Ruthann, it's Christina Spear!", and walked into the kitchen. She had never seen it so neat. No, it didn't measure up to Tina's standards, but it was a change for the better—welcome but incongruous.

"Ruthann, are you here? It's Tina Spear."

Silence. Tina heard a rumbling from one of the two bedrooms in the back. A faucet was turned on, then off.

After another minute, Ruthann presented herself like an offended dignitary. "Don't you have some nerve comin' to my home so early and unannounced!"

"Spare me your histrionics, Ruthann. You haven't returned a single one of my calls and you left me completely in the dark about the arrangements for Ricky's funeral. Which you did not attend." Tina looked at Ruthann and shook her head.

"You can just march yourself outta here this minute, woman. You got no cause to be here, and I sure as damn don't want you here!"

"You're mistaken. I have some very good reasons to be here. Starting with the fact you are the grandmother and legal guardian of a recently deceased boy I cared for deeply. Have you considered for even a second that you and I are both grieving? Have you thought there is now a hole in your life, and in mine, that won't be filled, ever?" Tina started to shake, but she steadied herself. "A wonderful young man who had worked hard, so very, very hard, to turn his life around, was taken from us. Look, I know you and I are so very unlike each other in every single way. But we have both lost someone precious and we're never getting him back. Do you get this, Ruthann?"

The older woman's eyes narrowed, her mouth softened, and she looked at the floor. "Ricky was on a new track, he was. He was happy to go live with his brother. Yup. Sorry the boy is gone. I surely am." She pulled out one of the chairs at the kitchen table and sat down.

Tina did likewise, never taking her eyes off Ruthann. "Can we agree, at least for the moment, this shared loss can … oh, I don't know … be acknowledged?"

"I suppose, for Ricky's sake it's the right thing. I don't want no hug or nuthin'. Ricky was ... gettin' better, ya know. He believed in somethin' better."

"He did, Ruthann. It makes me happy and so sad to hear you say it. I miss him. Do you miss him?"

Ruthann chuckled from the side of her mouth. "Hell, when the boy was here, he started cleanin' up after hisself, cleanin' up after everybody. Never thought I'd see such a thing. Even started in tellin' me or Cole what to do. Anyways, sure I miss him, I guess. I'm real sorry he's gone." Ruthann looked up, her lips twitching, her eyes casting about as if trying to follow a fly in the room.

"You know, Ruthann, there are some strange things about Ricky's death. Things which don't add up."

When her head bolted up and her arms and torso stiffened, Tina feared she may have pressed her advantage too soon.

"Like, what things?"

Tina shook her head. "You know what I'm talking about. A coroner doesn't even issue a suicide report within forty-eight hours, let alone release the body and have it disposed of. I missed the service even though I drove up the day after you phoned me."

With one hand on her chin, Ruthann nodded. "Seems odd, don't it? I heard they was movin' fast on account of Jacob's bein' depressed an' all."

"I suppose," Tina responded. "But there was an official release ordered by the sheriff's office more than a day before it should have been. Why would the sheriff order such a thing? A superfast autopsy, followed by cremation the same day? Doesn't it all seem more that a bit odd to you? Ruthann?"

The older woman's furrowed forehead, juxtaposed with her wide eyes, made her look irrational, wary.

She nodded a few times. "I never did consider it like what you're sayin'. But you know, Jacob probably couldn't handle all the stress and the ... the pain ... right? He wasn't in no shape to take care a' things."

"So the sheriff took care of them. Why would he do that, you think?"

Ruthann's shrug reminded Tina of Ricky during the first year. An involuntary shiver ripped through her. "Well? Do you think there's a reason I can't see? Why on earth would the sheriff do such a thing?"

"I don't know. How in hell would I know?"

"I thought you might, because of the relationship between Sheriff Caldwell and your daughter Charity."

The kitchen table shook as Ruthann's legs underneath bounced up and down. The salt and pepper shakers spilled over.

"You're fuckin' nuts. Don't be gettin' all bent just 'cuz you went to see Charity in prison. I don't know what she told you, but ... what you said, it ain't so."

Tina wasn't surprised by this outburst. The woman doth protest too much, she thought. A smirk grew on Tina's lips. She was on to something.

"Whatever is going on, Ruthann, it's got to do with Sheriff Caldwell. I'm asking you, for the love of Christ, to tell me what it is. You have to know. Carmen told me 'RC' was a good friend of the family. But I saw him at Jacob and Carmen's home when no one knew I was looking. It wasn't a routine visit from a friend. You have to know what's happening up there. So tell me!"

"You're talkin' crazy. Nuthin' I know's goin' on up there."

Tina doubted telling Ruthann anything she had learned from Detective Tillyard would get the older woman to budge from her position. "Isn't Sheriff Caldwell going to be vouching for Charity at her parole hearing? Your daughter told me as much."

"The hell, you say. Charity would never have told you—"

"What would Charity never have told me?"

Ruthann shot up out of her chair. "You leave right this second. You got no call to … to accuse me or my daughter or my grandson of nuthin'."

"I didn't accuse anybody of anything. I simply asked, 'What is Charity's relationship to the sheriff?' You won't answer me? Fine. I'll go. But I will find out. I won't stop. I'll get the records. I'll dig as deep as I need to." Tina stood and pushed her chair back into position. With an about-face, she shouldered her purse and walked toward the door.

Ruthann whispered, "RC is Jacob's pa."

Tina turned back sharply. "Say that again, please. The sheriff is Jacob's father?"

Ruthann nodded.

"Does it mean he was Ricky's father as well?"

"No, it don't. RC ain't Ricky's dad. He and Charity split long before Ricky was born. They weren't never married, so it didn't make no difference."

Tina needed to soak this in. She sat at the table again and motioned for Ruthann to sit down as well. She did so slowly, looking at Tina through slitted eyes, her mouth pursed like she'd just swallowed bleach. Tina could feel the hatred.

"Is the sheriff going to testify on Charity's behalf at her parole hearing?"

"I don't know. Maybe he will, maybe not. His choice."

"I was just shooting in the dark when I said that to Charity, but I saw it struck her. She was the one who said she had 'the law' testify at her hearing. Does it mean anything to the parole board if they have a prior romantic relationship?"

"Why you askin' me? I got no idea."

"Of course, it was a rhetorical question."

"Here's what I think. What's goin' on up in Dahlonega ain't at all what you think it is. Sounds like RC just trying to help out Jacob. What Carmen told you was straight up."

Tina didn't want to respond to this yet. She had to consider what all this meant. Why would the sheriff order such a quick and probably illegal disposal of Ricky's body? Even a father wouldn't go to all the trouble and risk just to spare his adult son the emotional pain of losing a brother, would he? Yet the aberrations of human behavior are rarely understood through logic.

"Jacob ain't been right since he left the army. You don't know. You got no idea."

Tina nodded and blew a long breath out through her nose. "Okay. I'll go. Thank you for the information, Ruthann."

"Don't thank me. I only did it 'cause you said you wouldn't let it die. Well, now you can let it die. Let it all be buried with our boy."

When Tina drove out of The Pines, she felt no resolution. The fact that Sheriff Caldwell was Jacob's father could mean there was nothing more to it than what Jacob and Carmen had said from the beginning, and what Ruthann wanted Tina to believe—the whole cover-up was nothing more than a father trying to spare his depressed son more pain. Nevertheless, the little voice escaping from the subconscious to warn the waking mind was clear in Tina's head: Something still is not right.

Back at her office, Tina threw her purse onto the sofa and sat down at her desk. Leaning back in her chair, she puzzled what to do next. Why has Caldwell's paternity of Jacob Plyer been a secret? That's silly, nonsensical, even. She picked up her office phone and dialed the Dahlonega Police Department. Tillyard couldn't take her call but would call her back later. Tina hung up, but let her hand stay on the receiver. She hit upon a long shot. She dialed Rhonda Kingswood. Maybe she could provide some essential insight into Ricky's enemies, friends, and juvy experience, anything which could have wreaked havoc in his last month. Or was she only grasping at a mist dissolving in the indifferent sunlight?

19

The World of Work

On a day when Tina was driving back to her office from a client in south St. Augustine, she saw Ricky skateboarding down the bike lane of Route 1 about a hundred yards ahead. She thought how dangerous it was for him to be going so fast, as if he were trying to match the speed of the cars whizzing past him. But, she noted with satisfaction, he was actually wearing his helmet. She slowed down and followed him when he turned onto Anderson Street. She pulled up alongside him, honked her horn, and waved. Ricky waved back. She stopped her car before the first intersection. Ricky came up quickly and bounced his skateboard up with a flourish. His momentum carried him farther than his judgment and he bumped into the back of Tina's Audi. Tina rushed to him but stopped short. Ricky pushed himself off the car and laughed a bit.

"I didn't do any damage, Miss Tina."

"I'm so sorry, Ricky," she said, breathless with worry. "I didn't mean for you to stop so abruptly. Are you all right?"

He nodded and took off his helmet. His hair had grown out and sprang from his head in rust-colored rivulets around his ears and forehead. Tina instinctively reached to touch it. Ricky ducked, but not fast enough. Tina managed to rub her hand quickly through his sweaty mat, pulling back the hair.

"Ricky Plyer, you've stopped getting haircuts. I'll bet you haven't been to the barber since we last saw each other." Ricky nodded. "Could be right there, Miss Tina."

"It's good to see you." She had to ask, "Are you still living with Cole?"

"Not at his old place. My grandma got a new house off a' Holmes Road. It's got three bedrooms. I think it's temporary but … it's okay." Ricky shrugged, adding, "Cole's moved back with my grandma."

Tina wanted so much to ask him more but realized there was a better use for this chance meeting.

"Ricky, do you have a summer job?"

"No, ma'am."

"Have you tried to get one?"

"Back in June, I applied to Mission Taco, but they already got someone."

"Is that all of it?"

"Yes, ma'am."

"Would you be willing to do some work for me, maybe three days a week, until school starts again?"

"Sure. I guess. What kinda work?"

"Work I don't have the strength or the time to do. Some of it would be at my office, working with the installers, and some would be at our house. Yard work, cleaning, nothing too difficult, and nothing you can't learn easily."

"Starting when?"

"That's the right question. How about tomorrow? Can you get your mother or Cole to drop you by my office, say by 10:00 a.m.?"

"Maybe. Where's your office, Miss Tina?"

"The fourth floor of the Treasury Building on Cathedral Place. It's the tallest commercial building in St. Augustine. So where are you off to now?"

"Goin' to see a friend."

"Oooo! A girlfriend?" Tina teased.

Ricky laughed sheepishly. "Nah, just a friend. Guy from juvy, gettin' back with his dad."

"Please be careful. I wouldn't want you to get into trouble of any kind. Right?"

"It's not like that, Miss Tina. Noble, he's, ah ... um, he's ..."

"Yes?"

"He's tryin' to stay outta trouble and asked me for some help. We're gonna go 'boardin'."

"Ricky, if I can be of any help to your friend Noble, please ask. I like his name."

"He don't." Ricky chuckled. "Says it makes people think he's all uppity."

"Uppity or not, if you think he needs more help than your friendship, or an adult friend, you let me know. Okay?"

"Yes, ma'am. I will."

"Good. Off you go. I'll see you tomorrow, and ..." He was riding away much faster than had Tina anticipated. She called out, "Ricky!"

He stopped but didn't come back.

"Call me if there's any problem with your ride tomorrow. You still have my number, right?"

Shadowed by an oak tree older than the Civil War, Ricky waved his acknowledgment and pushed himself on his skateboard along to his friend's.

Emotions inundated Tina. Ricky was about to start his junior year in high school, only two months after the end of her commitment to mentor him. Although she had signed on to mentor other adolescents who had "graduated" from Seminole Forks, none of them had responded to Tina in any way indicating the possibility of a mentor-mentee relationship. One girl had been overtly hostile and threatening. A young man, larger than a football lineman, ignored Tina completely, even though he interacted easily with all the other adults around him, including Rhonda Kingswood.

"You can't look at this as anything to do with you, Tina," Rhonda had counseled as they walked away from the home of yet another defiant adolescent. "These are kids, don't forget. Even though most of them are the products of broken homes, or abuse, or drugs, or poverty, some aren't. Some kids are chemically imbalanced. What they used to call bad seeds. Your heart goes out to every single child. I know. But it may be there is only one single child who can actually benefit from your heart."

Tina never did connect with another at-risk youngster as she wished. But the disappointment was tempered by her relationship with Ricky. It endured beyond the formal commitment. It struck her that Ricky was the same age now as Max was when he died. Tina bit her lip and pulled a tissue out of her purse to dab her eyes. In the direction Ricky had disappeared on his skateboard, the dense summer air shimmered like a mirage.

The next morning Tina wasn't surprised when, as she was going over construction details with her two installers, her cell phone rang.

"Miss Tina, my gramma can't get me a ride, and Cole's at work."

"Where shall I pick you up, Ricky?"

"Uh … how 'bout if I board over to the Route 207 light at Old Moultrie?"

"I'll see you there in fifteen minutes."

"Yes, ma'am."

Tina was rewarded to see Ricky, skateboard at his side, leaning against the streetlight pole at the intersection. She pulled into a business driveway. He slid his skateboard onto the floor of the back seat and got into the car.

Tina said nothing. Ricky said nothing.

At the Treasury Building parking lot, Ricky got out of the car first, and said, "I'm sorry I couldn't get a ride on my own, Miss Tina."

His words barely penetrated her subconscious. Ricky was looking over the top of her car and she could see his head. How had he grown twelve inches taller, and she not noticed? When her mind connected back to her ears, she shook her head as though finding consciousness after a snooze. "Not your fault. I'm glad you called, instead of letting the work opportunity fall through. That was very responsible."

Ricky nodded with a slight smile on his face, and Tina smiled back. When they were out of the elevator, Ricky stopped and looked at the active professionals in front of him. He stood for a moment, looking from side to side, as if watching a movie of something he could never experience.

"This where you work?" he asked Tina.

"This is my business, Ricky. Yes, it's where I work."

The high ceilings, multiple cubicles, clusters of people working over tables and in front of large LED screens must have appeared otherworldly to the young man. The buzz of the two large printers filled the office like the din of cicadas.

"Hi, everybody. I'd like you to meet Ricky Plyer."

All the work stopped. Everyone in the office came over to Ricky and introduced themselves, shaking his hand, and behaving as if they knew Ricky and were each happy to see him. When the reception line ended, work resumed. Ricky's face lit up and Tina's heart swelled.

"Let's go into my office for a few minutes to talk about your job. Afterward, I'm going to turn you over to Kyle, our installation manager."

Ricky continued to look around the workspace, swivel-headed, stumbling toward Tina's door. He bumped into Tina as she entered her office.

"Easy does it, Mr. Plyer. Have you never been to a business like this before?"

He stared at Tina with a goofy smile on his face. "This is yours? I mean, like, you own this business?"

She was at simultaneously complimented and vexed by Ricky's incredulity, but she gave him a smile and said, "Lock, stock, and barrel. I employ thirteen people full-time, plus myself. Have a seat."

"The elevator drops everyone into your office," he observed.

"Because our business takes up the entire floor. But you see, Ricky, this floor is much smaller than the floors beneath it. And it has fewer windows. Which explains why the rent is cheaper than most other downtown spaces."

Ricky looked at her like a cat looks at a television.

"Never mind. So, these will be your duties." She carefully explained to Ricky what the installers did and what her clients expected. She told him that Kyle managed the site installations and what that entailed.

"Do you think you got all of that?"

"Yeah, um … I think so. Maybe if you—"

"Don't worry. Kyle will give you all the direction you need. It's time to meet him."

From Tina's office, she and Ricky went through a door near the big LED screen marked "Production." Kyle Thornton turned in their direction as soon as they entered. He had a thick salt-and-pepper beard and similar hair that stood up in a pompadour. Tina reintroduced him to Ricky. He slapped Ricky's hand with a big wave of his arm and squeezed down.

Looking Ricky square in the eye, he said, "I hope you're ready to get to work. This is how we make money! It's all for show, until the interiors are built and installed. Am I right, Tina?"

"You are, Kyle. I'm sure you'll find Mr. Plyer able and willing to give you any extra muscle you need."

A young-looking man, taking meticulously stacked and bundled wood from a staging area onto a hand cart, stopped what he was doing and came up to Kyle's side.

"Ah, yes! And this is Roland Gleason, our aspiring master carpenter."

"Aspiring, my ass!" Roland asserted. "Kid, if it can be built with wood, I can build it."

This made Ricky break into a stuttered, awkward laugh. He took a step backward, toward Tina.

"So, you want to be a carpenter someday, Red?"

Ricky rubbed both his hands through his mop of hair and shrugged.

As Tina and Roland went back to their projects, Kyle guided the newbie. "Okay, Ricky. If Tina says you're working for us, then it's time to get started. Come over here, and I'll show you how things get done. We build the detail models of the design here in this shop. The full build is done at our warehouse on Route 1 and at the clients' sites. You with me?"

Walking over to a corner where the table saw stood next to a rack of other tools, Kyle attempted to put his arm around Ricky's shoulders. The boy moved away like he was ducking a big spiderweb.

As if to atone for his reflexive shudder, or perhaps to keep the stranger at bay, Ricky spoke up. "Is it just the two of you working with all this?" He pointed to the racks of wood, plexiglass plate, stainless steel frames, and bolts of cloth.

"It is," Kyle said. "And now it's the three of us."

"Ah … Miss Tina, she's the boss?"

"She sure is. She knows more about this business than anyone in St. Johns County. Maybe more than anyone in all of North Florida. She runs a tight ship, I can tell you."

Ricky shook his head. "How … how do you stand working for a woman boss?"

Kyle's halt was abrupt and stiff. He looked straight into Ricky's eyes. "Son, you have a whole lot to learn, don't you?"

He shrugged. I'm … just askin'. I mean, takin' orders all the time, and you have to do what she says and all."

"All right, stop right there. You don't have the first notion of what she does or how she works with me an' Roland, or how she makes decisions that make us all money."

Ricky lowered his head.

"I could tell you a dozen ways to Sunday how our boss keeps this business hustling and all of us working here, paid, and paid darn well. But I don't think you're ready yet to understand what I just said. You're gonna have to see for yourself, if you can keep your eyes and your head open long enough. Think you can do that?"

"Yes, sir."

"Now, don't go giving me this 'sir' crap. My name is Kyle and Kyle is what I expect you to call me. I won't mince words with you, but I won't call you names, neither. You gotta find your place here. Feel the rhythm. And here's the best advice I can give you. You ready?"

Ricky looked up and nodded.

"If Tina Spear is your friend, like she says, then act like you're her friend. 'Cause I'm here to tell you she will make you a better man if you listen to her and watch what she does. You understand?"

More silence from Ricky.

"Aw right. We have a truck to load with material for a new office up off Route 312. We'll head to the warehouse, and I'll show you the heavy lifting. Think you can help with that?"

"Yes, sir—I mean, yes, Kyle."

"Good. Let's get to it!"

Watching the interactions from her office, Tina felt some satisfaction that her young charge was going to be working with a positive male role model, maybe for the first time in his life. Kyle was a friendly good ol' boy at heart. She would check back later and assess the pulse of these new dynamics.

It was late afternoon when Kyle brought Ricky into Tina's office.

"How did it go, Kyle?" she asked.

"First off, I have to tell you, this carrottop has much to learn. *But.* He takes direction pretty well and seems to learn fast. That's a hopeful sign, I'd say."

Tina's smile broadened. "Ricky, what did you think of your first day of work, hmm?"

"It was okay."

"Just okay? Tell me what you learned out there."

With Tina's coaxing, Ricky told her in short sentences how he had loaded and unloaded the truck and he added other small details.

"You worked five and a half hours at $10.00 per hour, meaning you earned $55.00. Are you good with this?" Tina asked him.

Ricky's eyes got wide and his mouth formed an oval smile. "Wow! Fifty-five dollars?"

"Yes. So, I expect you are willing to do this three days a week, as we said, until school starts?"

"For sure!"

"Kyle, do you think you can keep him busy until he starts school in September?"

"No problem, boss. It ain't like we got a shortage a' work!"

With the deal cinched, Tina offered to drive Ricky home. When they got to the car, Ricky asked if she would drop him off at his friend Noble Dodd's home. Tina noticed he became sullen after she agreed.

"Ricky, what's wrong?

"Nothin's wrong."

"Come on, I know when something isn't right. I can see it in your face. You trust me, don't you?"

"Course."

"Then please tell me. Maybe I can help or maybe I can't, but I can listen."

Ricky continued to look at his hands folded in his lap and he let out a deep sigh. "Noble's gonna be back in trouble. It's bad."

"What kind of trouble, Ricky."

"I don't know if I should say. You can't tell anybody, Miss Tina."

Tina opened her mouth to say of course she wouldn't but stopped. If Noble was breaking the law, wouldn't she be obliged to report it? Particularly if Ricky might be implicated? She couldn't just watch and do nothing, could she.

"I've never lied to you, ever, have I? I don't want to tell anyone if you don't want me to. But if Noble is into something very bad, maybe you should be the one to say so."

"He's … he's dealin' drugs. Noble's dealin' and he's mulin' again."

"Muling?"

"He's carryin' drugs for other dealers. Big dealers from Atlanta."

"Oh, Ricky. That's so dangerous! He could go back to juvy, or worse! Why in God's name are you going to his house?"

"'Cause he needs me. I'm tryin' to talk him out of it. He won't end up in juvy again, Miss Tina. He'll go to jail."

"You have to stay away from Noble. You must. He could drag you down with him."

"No, Miss Tina. Won't happen."

Tina heard a conviction in Ricky's voice that was foreign yet uplifting.

"How do you know? Tell me, how can you know?"

"I just know. I only did drugs before juvy, though I seen lots. Watch it make people stupid, do stupid shit. I tell Noble every day. We go boardin' and we talk. He's ... he's not sure how to stop. He makes good money, and he tells me he's careful and all. But I know it ain't always so. I know he does drugs himself. He needs me. He was kinda' like my best friend in juvy. I'm not lettin' him down."

Tina's mind was racing between going directly to the authorities or saying nothing to anyone. "I won't tell anyone for now. But you need to promise me. Promise you won't get dragged into Noble's mess. Walk away when it looks too bad and Noble won't change."

"You never walked away from me."

"You, my young friend, are very different. You've continued to grow up every day."

"I'm not gonna give up on Noble."

"In that case, let's you and I talk about this from time to time. You should talk to him as his friend and as someone he trusts. But if he won't change himself, you can't make him. You may not be able to save him."

"I know, but I have ta try."

"I understand. Yes, you have to try. But please promise me you'll use everything you learned to keep yourself safe. I need to hear you say it. Promise me."

"I promise I won't get myself into any trouble with Noble," he said.

This put a tentative smile across Tina's lips.

Ricky pointed to the spot where he wanted to get out. Tina stopped the car. Ricky got out and pulled his skateboard from the back of her car. Before he closed the passenger door, he looked in at Tina. "You don't have to worry about me," he said as he shut the door.

She watched him skate toward Noble Dodd's home.

20

An Unbalanced Load

Instead of finding how to connect the dots, Tina was accumulating more dots. Her meeting with Rhonda Kingswood, their first contact since Ricky's death, was scheduled for midmorning. Rhonda agreed to meet Tina at City Bistro on Ponce de Leon Boulevard for coffee. Tina was looking forward to sitting down over a soy latte to assemble her ideas and questions with someone who knew Ricky, other than Ruthann.

Greeting Tina with a handshake and something close to a smile, Rhonda said, "Nice to see you again, Tina."

"Nice to see you as well," Tina said, and got right to her point. "I don't know what you've learned about Ricky Plyer's suicide, Rhonda, but there are a few things I've found that are irregular, bordering on the bizarre. Absurd, even."

Rhonda leaned into the table, holding her coffee in both hands. "When we were told of Ricky's death, we requested a report from the police. I apologize for not contacting you right away, but it had been over two years since you mentored Ricky. There was no way to know how your relationship with the boy had progressed—or not. It's always sad to learn of the premature death of any Seminole Fork alum. It's particularly hard for those we believed were making a successful transition to a normal life."

Tina nodded and said, "I saw Ricky less than two months before he supposedly killed himself. Two weeks before, he moved to live with his brother in Georgia. But here's what happened ..." Tina proceeded to give Rhonda a full description of the previous week's events, beginning with her phone call from Ruthann and ending with her last visit to Ruthann the day before.

"In less than twenty-four hours," Tina said, "the bloody coroner determined Ricky had committed suicide and within half a day released his body to be cremated. I still can't believe it! It's not right. And that vile mother of his, giving me no details and not even attending the service herself. I blame her as much as anyone for Ricky's death. She-she—"

Rhonda's eyes widened.

"She makes my skin crawl. Oh! Here's a little detail I had to pry out of Mrs. Plyer, the elder. The sheriff of the Lumpkin County police is Jacob's father. Do you believe that?"

Rhonda managed to place her coffee down gently and folded her hands into her lap. "I am at a loss. I believe everything you told me. Certainly, it is all possible. What do you think it means?"

"I think it means it's possible Ricky didn't commit suicide."

Rhonda said, "But if that were true, what really happened and why?"

"This is where I find myself now, and why I need your help. I need more perspective, more background, I guess, to help pull these pieces together."

"Such as ...?"

"What do you know about kids from Seminole Forks dealing drugs after they served their time?"

"You mean while they were on probation?" Rhonda's mouth tightened. "Drugs are what we deal with most often, before and after their sentences. Mostly using, but occasionally they've been dealing and a few times they've been transporting." Rhonda shook her head. "Lots of the kids have been used by interstate drug dealers as mules. It's awful."

"Noble Dodd was one of those, wasn't he? Noble and Ricky were apparently pretty friendly both in and after Seminole Forks."

"Yes. Yes, he was one smart kid. Diagnosed a sociopath, as I recall. It's been a while. We were very strict with him during his probation. And yes, I remember, Dodd was good to the point of being too good. You understand what I'm saying? Noble Dodd did all the work, was on time for all the check-ins. Was respectful to his mentor to the point where the mentor said there was nothing for him to do with Noble. He was the model of success after Seminole Forks."

"And what did you think?"

"Noble Dodd, I believe, continued to fool the lot of us. Besides, the model for success after Seminole Forks was Ricky."

Tears backed up in Tina's eyes. She had always felt in her heart Ricky was that model but had no acknowledgment until this moment. She reached around her chair for her purse and pulled out a tissue. "I'm fine," she said, drying her eyes. "It was ... special to hear you say that about Ricky. And that's my point. I refuse to believe he took his own life. Even if there were no suspicious ... anything around his death, I still wouldn't believe it."

"You and Ricky were the outcome the program had always envisioned. It's clear you remained in touch long after your mentorship was over. From what you're telling me, you became friends."

"We did, Rhonda. Thank you. But here's my dilemma. I can't seem to pull it all together. I can't reconcile Ricky committing suicide with anything I know, and I can't let go of the fact that what happened after his death is horribly unusual and for no reason I can fathom. But I don't have a working hypothesis of what truly happened. Only these disconnected anomalies, little events that make no sense. I'm grasping at straws here. Do you understand? Everywhere I turn, there are unanswered questions. Was his brother doing or dealing drugs? Was there some cover-up led by the sheriff? Did Ricky learn something or get into something so bad or hurtful it turned his life upside down?"

Throwing her head back and raising her hands in the air, Tina let out a grunt, causing a few bistro patrons to stop what they were doing and look at her. She realized she'd breached the bounds of coffee shop decorum.

"I'm sorry," she said to Rhonda. "I'm sorry, everyone," she repeated, looking around at the other tables.

Rhonda took hold of Tina's arm. "You're fine. And my instincts tell me you may be on to something. I have no idea what it could be. But look. Ricky's gone. How many dead ends are you going to chase before you grieve and move on?"

"His obituary was two lines, Rhonda. Two fucking lines. I'm sorry. He deserved so much more. He deserves the truth told about his life, how he had friends who relied on him, how he rose above his circumstances. And if he was murdered, I swear to God …"

"There is no reason to believe such a thing. None. And even if there was? It's for the police to investigate."

"The police are investigating. The detective on the case is well-meaning and a by-the-book cop. But he reports to that giant sheriff."

Rhonda leaned back. "I don't know if there's anything more I can do for you. I'm not saying you're wrong. I am saying you need to be careful. This business could consume you."

"You can tell me how I can contact Noble Dodd today. Can you do this for me?"

"Tell me why I should."

"He was the one friend of Ricky's who has been there from the beginning, and because he has been arrested before for drug dealing and transporting. I met him a year after I mentored Ricky. He knows who I am and he may even trust me. I need another way to look at Ricky, to find out what no one wants to tell me."

"I can do what you ask, but you must be very careful." Rhonda rose out of her chair and put her purse over her shoulder. "I see you've got a true believer's sense of injustice. I hope this serves you and doesn't get *you* killed. Noble Dodd was connected with some very bad people. People who would make Ruthann seem virtuous. You understand? Please do not, do *not* get hurt in this ... quest of yours."

Tina nodded without the slightest intention of veering from her course.

Fifteen minutes later, back in her office, she received a text with Noble Dodd's cell phone number and latest known home address. She took a minute to think what she wanted to say, how she would get him to meet her. She dialed the number.

On the first ring, someone answered. "Yeah?"

21

Past – More Than Lunch

PAST

After a silent dinner at home, Walter walked into the study with a copy of the *Wall Street Journal*. Tina remained at the table and called Ricky. Cole answered and, without any greeting, called out for Ricky to come to the phone.

"Hi, Ricky. I'm checking in to make sure you're still planning to come to work next week. I know it's only a week before you're back in school."

"Sure. I gotta ride lined up. It's all good."

"This makes me happy. There's another reason I wanted to speak to you. How's your friend, Noble?"

Ricky took a long pause. "He's, well, he's Noble."

"I'd like to meet him. Is he still doing and dealing drugs?"

"I shouldn't a' told you. It's fine."

"You trust me, Ricky. I know. If I tell you all I want to do is meet him and get to know him, without preaching or chastising, wouldn't it be all right?"

"I get you're worried an' all, but it's all good. It is."

"How about we meet casually at the skateboard park. And I buy the two of you lunch. How does that sound?"

"He knows you're my friend, Miss Tina. I told Noble about you."

"Even better. How about Sunday for lunch?"

"Okay, I'll ask him."

She thanked Ricky and hung up. Worry over how Ricky might be influenced by his longtime friend gnawed at her until it became a hole in her mind into which all other thoughts drained. She understood how overprotective this urge was. But she couldn't banish it. Taking the measure of Ricky's friend seemed the only way to exorcise the fear she'd conjured for his safety.

On Saturday, Ricky called her back.

"Noble will meet you, Miss Tina. I told him you just wanted to hang out and meet some of my friends."

"It's the truth. I'll pick you up at noon and we can go get Noble, yes?"

"How 'bout we meet you at the park."

"If that's what you want. It's a date. See you tomorrow."

When she hung up, Walter was standing in the doorway to their office.

"You can't let him go, can you?"

"Who are you talking about, Walter?"

"Both of them. Our son in the grave and the former delinquent making it on his own. You can't let either of them go."

"Oh, for God's sake, give it a rest. Ricky may be standing up on his own, but there are lots of opportunities for him to be dragged down again. I just want to meet this friend of his he's supposedly helping."

"Tina, it's been a year now since he's no longer officially your mentee. Do you think we might take this Sunday and do something together?"

"Come with me. Come to the park and meet these boys."

"I'm not interested in perpetuating this … what? This emotional lodestone you've tied yourself to. There's nothing there for me."

"You could come to support me. I'm trying to see if there is any danger to Ricky from this close friend of his. Maybe too close."

"You go. I'm sure there are projects around the house that need my attention." Walter turned around and walked away.

Tina rose from the office chair, holding her breath until she exhaled in a long release. Walter would have to find his own emotional lodestone.

Arriving at Treaty Park, Tina made her way to the skateboard arena. Ricky's mop of red hair was unmistakable, swirling through the throng of boarders. There was no way to identify Noble Dodd or even know if he was there. Leaning over the railing, Tina waved until she finally drew Ricky's attention. He completed two more half-pipe leaps. It all seemed impossibly dangerous to Tina, but Ricky completed each maneuver with a wobbling squat as low on his board as he could.

Ricky was sweating and breathing heavily when he snapped his board into his hands and leaned against the railing. "Hi," he said, breaking into a grin.

"Hi, yourself. You're pretty good on that contraption. Those jumps look awfully daring."

"I do okay. But there are some real good boarders here. Like, semipros."

"And Noble?"

Ricky pointed to a bench under an oak tree. Noble was seated, looking at his phone, his skateboard held upright between his legs. Ricky shouted at him and waved. His friend looked up, tapped on his phone, and ambled over to Ricky and Tina. He was a skinny young man, Tina noted, half a head taller than Ricky and probably thirty pounds lighter. His whole face seemed to droop. On his feet were a new pair of athletic shoes Tina recognized. They retailed for over one hundred and thirty dollars.

"This here's Noble, Miss Tina."

Tina thrust out her hand. Noble blinked at her a few times as he shifted his skateboard to shake Tina's hand. His fingers were long and delicate.

"Hey," he said.

"Hi, Noble. Thanks for coming to meet me. It means lot."

"Sure."

"I just wanted to know how you were getting along after Seminole Forks. Are you still in touch with your mentor, like I am with Ricky?"

Noble chuckled out of the side of his mouth. "The lawyer dude? He was okay. Kinda goofy and old school, ya know? I ain't seen him since over a year now."

"Where do you boys want to get lunch?"

Noble answered with no hesitation. "There's a barbecue place up on 207. Cyril's Ole Time BBQ. Can we do some ribs?"

Ricky nodded as his face raised in a smile. "Cyril's Ole Time, here we come!"

With their boards in Tina's trunk, Noble yelled out, "Shotgun!"

She turned and looked at Ricky, who shrugged. "He called it. He gets it."

The drive wasn't more than ten minutes from the park. It was enough for Tina to start her research. "Tell me about your parents, please, Noble. Are they together, and do you live with them?"

"Haven't seen much a' my daddy since I was eight. Momma raised me and my two sisters, but she gotta new man and, well, they hang out a lot."

"Do you like him?"

"Hey, lady, you like ask a lot a' questions, don't you?"

From the back of the car, Ricky laughed. "I told you. You can't put this on me."

"I know juvy is no easy lift and life after is sometimes even worse. I'm just checking in. Ricky speaks highly of you."

"Does he, now? Seeing as he's been beatin' my ass in boardin' and school, I don't see why." He turned and leaned his elbow over the back of his seat to look at Ricky.

"I just told her you're my friend, man."

"He did, Noble. And if Ricky says you're his friend, it means something."

"Tell his ol' lady that."

"You mean Ruthann doesn't like you?"

"Ask Ricky. She don't like anyone. And she cheats."

"Cheats? How does she cheat."

Noble crossed his arms and looked out the window.

Tina understood, telling herself to slow down.

Cyril's BBQ had large, well-kept picnic tables outdoors, where the trio settled in and ordered. The boys ate their ribs like cavemen, while Tina nibbled at her chicken sandwich and observed the friendship on the other side of the table. She saw Noble whisper something in Ricky's ear. It made him laugh for a few seconds—before he got angry.

"No way!" he exclaimed.

"Boys," Tina said, "I'm very happy you're enjoying your lunch. But please be polite enough not to whisper secrets to each other while we're all at the table. Okay?"

"Wasn't a secret, Miss Tina. Noble said you're like my mom in Atlanta, good-looking an' all, except ..."

Noble elbowed him. Ricky laughed and hit Noble on his shoulder.

Tina blushed. "How kind of you, I think."

"'Cept you ain't doin' time in prison," Noble said.

"Yes, that's been by design, I have to say." Tina laughed without humor. "Playing by the rules isn't always easy, we all know. And even I … have had my moments."

Ricky asked, "What kind of moments?"

"I think we all have done some things we wish we hadn't, right? I know when I was much younger, I didn't think the rules applied to me. But I managed to learn they did most definitely apply to me, before I got arrested or worse."

Noble leaned on the table with both elbows. "Do tell, now, Miss Tina. You more like Charity than you wanna let on?"

"I haven't met Charity. I won't presume to make any comparisons, Noble. I'll tell you, though, I try not to judge people until I've imagined myself in their shoes. But for some people, like Ricky's mom, it's impossible for me."

"She's one four-star bitch. I can tell you firsthand." Noble was stabbing at his plate, head down. "Got what she deserved."

"Fuck you, Noble!" Ricky jumped up from the table. "Shut the fuck up. She was an asshole, all right? But she didn't cheat you. You liked hanging around with that soldier jerk-off from Atlanta, all threats and commands. You and Ruthann …" Ricky trembled as he looked at Tina with anger and confusion rippling over his face.

Noble finished his ribs with diminished relish. Ricky eased back into his seat, wiping his mouth and hands with a wad of napkins.

Though startled, Tina was not surprised by Ricky's reaction. What did surprise her was how she saw the frayed edges of the adolescent friendship. Ricky and Noble were not like each other in the least, and maybe didn't even like each other. This observation nurtured her optimism for Ricky to remain apart from any bad choices Noble might make.

22

Cultivation of a Weed

PRESENT

Into the phone receiver Tina asked, with calm, "Am I speaking to Noble Dodd?"

"Who's this?"

"This is Tina Spear. I hope you remember me. I'm a longtime friend of Ricky Plyer. You and I met one time and I took you and Ricky to lunch."

"I remember you. You were Ricky's juvy counselor, right?"

"At the beginning, yes. But Ricky and I stayed friends, as you may recall."

"Is that right? What you want?"

"I'd like to meet with you, Noble. I want to talk about Ricky. He committed suicide last month."

Silence. Then softly, "Holy mother of shit. Not Ricky! That don't make no sense. Fuck!"

"This is why I'd like to talk to you. Can you meet me today, maybe this afternoon?"

"This afternoon, you say? How 'bout in an hour. I got shit to do this afternoon."

"I can be there in an hour. Where do you want to meet?"

"You come by my crib. Maybe bring some sandwiches. And fries. You know, the real deal, none a' dat Mickey D's shit. Like from a Mojo's barbecue or sumthin'. You cool?"

"Yes, I'm cool. Give me your address, and I'll see you in one hour."

When Tina hung up, she couldn't help wondering if the eighteen-year-old was living on his own or with his parents. She hadn't thought to ask Rhonda any more about his background. Now she'd find out for herself.

She asked Dale to come into her office and told him she'd again be going out in the middle of the workday.

"You can't do this today, Tina. Don't you remember? We're pitching the design for the new StarComm headquarters. This deal is huge!"

"Shit," Tina muttered. "Dale, I … I have to be gone a few hours. Can we push it back, maybe, to three?"

Dale brushed a hand through his longish blonde hair. "Tina, I don't know. I mean, do you think it's okay? We've been working on this for a month, nonstop. It's the largest project we have ever proposed. You can't just put this off for—" Dale stopped.

"Jesus. Okay. For what, Dale?"

"For some personal ghost chase. There. I said it. I'm sorry, but someone had to."

"What in the world are you talking about?"

He closed the office door. "Boss, you've been AWOL for weeks. We are all so sorry to hear of Ricky's passing, but your business is in a critical phase and it needs you. We need you!"

"Ricky still needs me, Dale. I don't think he committed suicide. I think he was murdered."

"Murdered! Christ, Tina. Isn't that a job for the police to handle?"

"The police may have been in on it." Tina had never thought this until now, disgorging her suspicion as if it had been Heimlich-ed from her subconscious.

Dale took a step away from Tina. Open-mouthed, he looked at her, his forehead tightening. Hands on his hips, he paced in a circle three times. On the third round he clasped his hands together. When he stopped, he looked at Tina with an anger he couldn't maintain. He looked away. "Maybe what you say is all true, and maybe it's just a theory of yours. I don't know. I—"

"That's right, you don't know." Tina glared at him.

"You're right. Here's what I do know. We're here for you and will be until ... well, until we can't. Right now, I'm worried. We're worried. You've never been like this, gone for days at a time, ignoring the great things we've got going on. And ignoring the ones going to shit."

"What are you saying, Dale? That we're in some kind of trouble?"

"Did you even know we lost three bids this past week? When have we ever lost three bids in a row? Boss, you have got to let this thing go, for the sake of your business. For our sake. We love it here and work our asses off for Spearhead Design. For you!"

"I hear you and I understand. I do. I will be back here soon, with all my heart and head. But I don't know when. I want it to be soon, very soon. But until I'm back, I need you, I need everyone, to do what you have always done—excel. You are such a great team. This is temporary, I promise."

"If you're going to be away like this for the next two days or two months, you'd better address the team and help us get a plan together. Please, boss."

"I will. I will. This afternoon. I'll be back by two, two-thirty at the latest. You know the StarComm proposal better than I do. Lead this for me. You can do it. And you have to do it."

His shoulders slumped, yet he held his head high. "We've got the pitch, boss. But we have to get on it right now. StarComm is due here in an hour and a half. See you later."

"You will, Dale. Thank you."

On her way to Noble Dodd's home in West St. Augustine, she stopped at Mojo Old City BBQ and picked up two pulled pork sandwiches and a basket of fries. In her car, the smell of slow-cooked pork, the richness of barbecue sauce, and the indulgent fried potatoes made her mouth water. The aromas in the air overcame her worry of prioritizing a personal imperative over the demands of her business, even if only for the moment.

She drove up West King Street, turned left onto Butler Avenue, and took it all the way to Gilbert, which dead-ended at the railroad tracks. How incongruous will this be, she fretted. Her new Audi parked in front of one of these houses? Strange. She never worried when she parked at Ruthann's, even though this neighborhood looked similar to where Ricky had lived. Noble's home, the last one on Gilbert, was less of a house and more of a tidy shack. When she locked her car, she pulled the driver-side door handle. Trust but verify, she thought.

Tall grass and weeds were everywhere, many topped with vibrant blooms. A din of buzzing drew her attention to a swarm of bees hovering at the plants by a stone berm marking the beginning of the railroad's right-of-way. Up three wooden stairs, she looked for a doorbell. Finding none, she knocked. A young man greeted her. Noble was well-groomed, with a head of hair from the sixties. His calm, inquisitive look morphed into a smile. He extended both arms to her.

"Mojo's smoked pork barbecue and fries! You done aw'right." He curled his fingers repeatedly into his palms, which Tina at first understood as, "Please come in", but which she soon realized was "Give up the grub!" She half laughed, handing him the overstretched plastic bag, the smell of barbecue oozing from Styrofoam containers.

Tina followed him inside, where the tidy shack transformed into a metro bachelor pad. Did Noble have a housekeeper or a live-in girlfriend? He turned into the kitchen and placed the bag on top of a spotless butcher-block table. He went to a cabinet and brought out two plates from a stack, pulled cutlery from a drawer, and grabbed a napkin holder with an unwrapped bag of dinner napkins. "Have a seat. You thirsty? I got Dasani, LaCroix, and sweet tea."

"A bottle of Dasani would be fine," she said, in a whisper. Tina had no idea of her preconceptions. Such notions held no substance for her until this moment. Observing Noble Dodd, dressed in a red polo shirt buttoned up to his neck, blue Tommy Hilfiger shorts, and leather sandals, Tina realized something. Noble Dodd was related to her notion of a nineteen-year-old living on his own, as Debussy was related to a garage band. Noble flitted about like a maître d', setting down a clean glass in front of Tina, pouring her water, grinning mischievously. Or was it malevolently? She was in shock and off balance. Noble had to notice.

Taking the seat opposite Tina, he ripped into the bag of take-out with abandon. "Miss Tina, I gotta tell you, that was some potent bad news you had. Hmmm. I never figured Ricky for anythin' like that. Nope. Not in a million years."

She pulled the remaining sandwich container out of the bag and put it on her plate without opening it. "It's the reason I'm here."

Nobel squinted at her as he bit into his sandwich. He swallowed hard and asked, "What you wanna know?"

"Why did you say you never figured Ricky for something like suicide?"

"Ha! When I saw Sliders, back in juvy, he was—"

"Sliders?"

"You know, flip-flops. It's what we called him 'cause he would jus' shuffle around in those sliders all day long. Like I was sayin', he was scared of his own shadow. All of us wonderin' how's a softy like this white boy—and I mean white-like-street-chalk boy—all carrot-topped an' shit—how this white boy could land here when he was so mushy. Ha. Well, one a' my boys picked on him so bad, you know, pushin' him, calling him marshmallow, we thought Ricky was gonna cry. Then *wham!*—Ricky smacks this guy maybe thirty pounds bigger than him, flattens him on his back. Ricky jumps on his belly, still wailin' on his ass like I ain't never seen. Blood spurtin' into the air. We all ran away, and Ricky got sent to the dungeon for three days. Nobody messed with Sliders no more after that."

"That wasn't the Ricky I knew, Noble."

"Turns out the caged Ricky, the Ricky he don't let out 'less he can't help himself is all bottled up. You know?"

"Ricky told me he was trying to get you to quit dealing drugs. Did you?"

Noble stopped chewing and put down his sandwich. "Ain't no concern a' yours, now, is it?"

"I know you were working for Ruthann. I've known for years. What I'm trying to understand, was Ricky into the life too, and I just didn't see it? Were there issues from his past, like this anger streak you mentioned, that ... could have overwhelmed him? Or were there things which could have gotten him murdered?"

Standing up slowly with his eyes glued to Tina, Noble walked backward to a cabinet, opened the drawer, and pulled out a black object. He came back to his seat and placed the object on the table. It was a handgun.

Tina shivered. "You don't need that thing, Noble. I'm no threat to you. I'm not."

Noble picked up the gun and held it in front of his face, looking at with curiosity, twirling it in his hand. He aimed it at the door and swiveled toward Tina. She gripped the side of her chair with both hands.

With a laugh, Noble put the gun back on the table.

"You gotta love a Glock. Works every time. Was Ricky into some shit that coulda' got him offed? Who knows? Coulda' been. 'Tween that drug-addicted brother a' his and them military freaks runnin' oxy and fent outta 'Lanta for his momma. That was … fucked up." Noble shook his head.

Tina's mind went to the army captain she'd met at Jacob's. "Like Captain Larus … Ladris?" She couldn't remember his name.

"The fuck you know about Lapis?" Noble shouted as his shoulders hunched and he grabbed his drink as if it were a life buoy.

"I met him last week when I was in Georgia. He came to Ricky's brother's house."

Noble began to pace the room. "Lady, you need to leave. You need to leave now."

"Noble, I swear. I'm just trying to know for certain what happened to Ricky!" She didn't move from her seat.

"I know you cared for Ricky, but you breathe a word we even met, and I swear …" Noble picked up the Glock and pointed it into the air.

"Can we please talk about Ricky? I'm begging you."

"That ain't how this works. I say you better leave, and you leave."

Tina felt both defiant and unsure. Her mind was racing as she tried to pull more pieces of the puzzle together. "I'll leave, Noble. I'm going. But please tell me, who else was busted with Charity, in Atlanta? How did she get so careless, anyway? You know what happened, don't you?"

The air in the room was getting humid from their sweat and quick breathing.

"Greedy bitch got what she deserved. You don't steal from the boss man and walk away." Noble stopped speaking and motioned with the Glock for Tina to keep moving through the doorway and out of the house.

As she left, she couldn't help but say, "Thank you, Noble. I promise I'll do right by Ricky."

"My advice: Don't be stickin' your pretty neck in places where it's goin' get chopped. Best either of us can do for Ricky is remember his floppy-haired ass and leave the rest alone."

Tina's nod had nothing to do with Noble's parting words. It was infused with resolve. Outside the front door she heard the steel clang of the deadbolt locking behind her.

23

Winning without Victory

One more time Tina went to Ruthann's unannounced. After three knocks on the screen door, she entered and called out, "Ruthann!" Tina waited at the door. Ruthann emerged from her bedroom in her usual huff.

"Hi, Ruthann. I wanted to talk to you about Ricky's graduation in three weeks."

"What about it? You coulda' called, you know. It ain't right you sneakin' up on me all the time."

"Oh, for goodness' sake, Ruthann, you think I want to drive over here? If you answered your phone or even returned a message, you wouldn't need to see me hardly ever!"

Ruthann crossed her arms. "You one piece a' work, lady."

With a sigh Tina said what she came to say. "I want to discuss only a couple of things. First, I know there are a limited number of seats going to the family and I was hoping there was a way you could share two of them with me and my husband."

"Fifty dollars should cover it."

"I'm … I'm sorry. Are you telling me you want me to pay fifty dollars for two family tickets to Ricky's graduation?"

"No, I'm telling you the tickets cost fifty dollars each."

After five seconds of silence, Tina said, "Ruthann, I know there are at least four tickets. How many are you going to use?"

"None. I ain't goin'."

"Oh, yes you are. You are going to Ricky's graduation for certain. You're the only family he's got in St. Augustine. You—"

"'Ceptin' Cole."

"Cole is not related to Ricky in any way. But if Cole *wants* to be there, I'm sure that would make Ricky happy."

"Why 'n hell would Cole want to get all dressed up, just to sweat in some auditorium with a couple hundred people breathin' heavy and listenin' to a bunch of silly speeches. No, ma'am. Cole don't wanna go to no graduation. Me neither."

"I'll tell you what. If you promise to go, I'll buy all four of the graduation tickets for fifty dollars each."

Silence.

"Seventy-five," came the reply.

"Done," yelled Tina in triumph. "I'll be back at five thirty today with three hundred dollars cash. And, Ruthann?"

"Yeah."

"Don't you dare think you will take my money and not keep your word. Not for a second. Do you understand me?"

"Come back with the cash. Gonna need to buy me a dress or sumthin'."

"Now, the second thing I wanted to …"

Ruthann turned around like a robot, walked back into her bedroom, and slammed the door. Tina looked straight ahead, letting a wave of revulsion, frustration, and anger rise up. She almost screamed but recognized for the first time it was something she did too often lately. The surge leveled in a simmering growl. "Ahhh! I'll be back in two hours with the money. You better have those tickets!"

As she let the screen door bang behind her, Tina muttered, "Ooo … that bitch!"

Back at her office, Tina breezed in, barely speaking to the staff, and took her seat behind the desk. There was a knock on the doorframe.

"Hi, Tina. Is everything all right?" It was her chief designer.

Tina put her hands to her head and smoothed her hair. She nodded and chuckled. "Thanks. I'm just dealing with a very aggravating person at the moment. It's a personal thing. I'll be fine. Here. Let me come out and join you. I've been meaning to talk to you about the design specs for …" At this moment her business and the work were more intensely satisfying than usual.

When, at the end of the workday, Tina showed up at Ruthann's screen door, the woman was standing on the other side, waiting.

"You got the cash?" she asked, showing no intention of moving to let Tina into the house.

Tina pulled a small envelope from her purse and showed it to Ruthann. "And the tickets," she demanded.

Ruthann pulled them from a back pocket of her jeans and thrust them through the partially opened door. Tina snatched them in a move so quick she surprised herself, as well as Ruthann.

"God damn you, woman!" Ruthann yelled.

After she verified these were indeed four tickets to the graduation ceremony, Tina passed the envelope with the money, which Ruthann grasped as forcefully as Tina had taken the tickets.

Tina removed one ticket and waved it in front of Ruthann. "You'll be needing this yourself," Tina said as she let it flutter to the porch floor.

Days later, Tina got in touch with Ricky. She wanted to help him with the rental of his cap and gown.

"No need, Ms. Tina. I've got it."

"You're sure, Ricky? I was hoping your grandmother would have helped out. I can, as well—"

"My grandma's got other things to spend her money on. Besides, this is for me. I have the money."

Ricky had continued to work for Tina when the school year resumed his senior year. In addition, she had vouched for him when he applied for work a few evenings a week at the Ace Hardware on San Marco Avenue. Transportation to and from work had been a bit of an issue, but Ricky sorted it out on his own.

Her chest heaved with pride. "Good for you. Your grandmother promised she'll be at the graduation. I was thinking of picking her up and driving her over myself."

"Whatever. She's peculiar, ya know? Anyway, we got rehearsals startin' next week. I may not be able to work at Spearhead, Ms. Tina. Is that okay?"

"Just be sure to take care of yourself, Ricky. And call me, if not next week, please call before graduation. I'll be there and I want to see you after the ceremony."

"Sure thing, Ms. Tina.

It took Tina all of the next ten days to get in touch with Ruthann by phone. She didn't want a ride to the graduation and, yes, she would keep her word to be there. Tina reminded her of their assigned seats. Ruthann had huffed that she didn't need a chaperone. Tina's nervousness grew.

The evening before graduation day, Walter prepared a simple dinner. It was well into the evening when Tina returned home. They exchanged perfunctory greetings. When they sat down to eat ten minutes later, no conversation spontaneously grew between them. There wasn't even the clatter of cutlery to cut the silence.

"Is this how it's going to be from now on?" Walter asked.

"You mean like it has been the last year?" Tina countered.

"You're right." Walter put down his fork and wiped his face with one hand. "So, tell me what's eating you, besides work and us?"

"Yeah. That's fair, I suppose. I'm thinking how much Ricky has grown, despite the awful woman who adopted him. I can't even tell you why I insisted she go to the graduation. Maybe it would be better if she doesn't show up."

"What does the boy want?"

"He's been nonchalant, putting on a brave face. Deep down, he probably wants his grandmother there. I think it's because he wants her to see the person he's become. Ricky has every right to be proud when he grabs hold of his diploma tomorrow. Despite living in four different houses over the last three years, with no parental guidance, between drug runners and lowlifes, Ricky's graduating in the top third of his class. I checked. It was all him, without a shred of help from Ruthann. Everything Ricky's accomplished will be wasted on her. She'll probably resent his success."

"Keep in mind he's not your son. He's your friend."

"Why do you do this over and over! Can't you please, please let go of the notion that my care for Ricky is not what keeps you and me apart?"

"Something's doing it and it's not me. All I meant was, you're overthinking and overreacting to everything going on in his life. For God's sake, Tina, you're the one who needs to let things go. Whatever it is making you obsess over every little aspect of this boy's life, drop it and have a moment of peace. Maybe think of the boys you … and I already raised, who are off on their own." He pushed back from the table. "Look, if you want, I'll go to work tomorrow instead of the graduation. You asked me to go with you, remember? Why? Don't worry, I'm not backing out. But I know the reason you want me there—to continue the fantasy for Ricky that it's possible to have a long, loving adult relationship." Walter dropped his napkin on top of his plate. "I won't let you down. That's my obsession, my craziness. *My* fantasy. Oh fuck, what a pair we are."

He cleared the table while Tina held her head, elbows shaking on the table.

* * *

Tina wanted to drive through The Pines to check if Ruthann would indeed make it to Ricky's graduation. When Walter reminded her of their conversation the night before, she agreed to drive directly to the ceremony at the St. Augustine Amphitheatre. They went through security and found their section. As they brushed past the first four parents of other students, Tina looked down the row of mostly empty seats. In one of them sat an older woman dressed in an old-fashioned flower-print skirt and a white blouse. On her feet were gray sandals with the slightest heel.

Tina stopped short, and Walter bumped into her. "Ruthann? Am I truly looking at Ruthann Plyer?"

Ruthann had the slightest touch of makeup around her eyes and maybe a hint of blush on her cheeks.

She turned her head to look at Tina. "Who else ya think it is? Jennifer Lopez?"

Tina closed her mouth and took her seat next to Ruthann. "You look … lovely today, Ruthann. Thank you."

Ruthann turned in her seat and leaned away from Tina. "What the fuck you thankin' me for? Coming to my son's graduation? You got some nerve." She turned back to face the stage.

Tina was speechless. The thought of strangling Ruthann passed quickly.

The processional took a full twenty minutes. The band played the same variation of Pachelbel's Canon in D three times. The relief felt by the attendees was palpable when the band changed to "Pomp and Circumstance" as the graduating seniors marched in. Though some distance away, Tina had no trouble spotting the shoots of red hair darting out from under the graduate's cap. When it was Ricky's turn to strut across the stage and grab hold of his honorarium, he did so with quickness and a big grin. Before he descended the stage at the far end, he turned to the audience and held his diploma as high as he could. Clapping erupted from a group of fellow seniors. Tina's heart soared. Ricky turned in her direction, his grandmother's direction, and blew a two-handed kiss. Tina shot up out of her seat and applauded as if she had heard Beethoven himself conduct Symphony No. 9. Tears came easily. Ruthann looked at her, shrugged, and stood and clapped—for all of two seconds. She sat down even as Tina remained lifted by the moment.

It took some time for all the guests to leave. Most were meeting the newly minted graduates along the back of the amphitheatre where concession stands, normally jammed with concertgoers, stood closed. The courtyard was overflowing within minutes. Ruthann followed Tina and Walter and waited with them in the crowd for Ricky.

When he finally sauntered up, Ricky had a young woman, also in cap and gown, by the hand. He went up to Tina, looked over at his grandmother, dropping the girl's hand.

He put his arms around Ruthann, who said, "Well, you done pretty good there, boy. Hope you make use a' yourself." She patted Ricky's back and then stood apart from him, looking around. "I'll be getting back now. Don't you get all partied out before you come home." She disappeared into the crowd.

Ricky looked again at Tina, who drank in the sight of him. From instinct or habit, she looked back at Walter, who appeared ready to roll his eyes at any moment. A spark of resentment flickered in Tina but was snuffed by the joy she felt for her protégé. He walked up to her with the closed-mouth grin she knew so well. She flung her arms around him. Ricky put his arms around Tina's waist, put his head on her shoulder, and closed his eyes.

He pulled himself away, taking hold of the hand of his friend. "This is Gail, Miss Tina."

"Hi, Mrs. Spear. Ricky's told me a lot about you. It's great to finally meet you." She held out her hand.

Before accepting it, Tina put her own hand over her heart, nodded slowly, and looked at Gail. Tina reached out and took Gail's hand with both of her own.

"It's such a pleasure to meet you, too."

Behind Tina and Walter, two boys walked up past them and grabbed hold of Ricky, punching him playfully. One was a tall, lanky boy who had received one of the graduation awards. The other was shorter and pudgy, wearing a different type of robe. He carried a clarinet.

"Hey!" Ricky yelled.

They laughed and then coughed as they realized the proximity of two unknown adults.

"Miss Tina, this here's Ralph," said Ricky.

The tall boy stuck out his hand, which Tina and Walter shook.

"He's the smart one. This here other one, this is Jessup. He's the musician. You couldn't tell, right?"

Jessup waved his clarinet in the air.

"Ralph's folks are havin' a graduation party now. Ralph here finished top of the class. What a nerd!"

Tina said, "I saw in the program that you received an award yesterday, Ricky. For most improved student year on year."

Ralph shoved Ricky with his hip. "Ma'am, there was only one direction he could go. Jus' nobody knew he wouldn't stop."

Ricky shoved Ralph back and turned red.

Walter moved in and introduced himself with a smile and a handshake, to each of the students. To Tina, it felt like in intrusion.

"Can we give you a ride somewhere?" Tina asked.

"Nah," Jessup piped up. "Folks are waitin' on us over at the parkin'. We're goin' to meet up at Ralph's."

"Ricky, can we give you and Gail a ride over to your friend's home?"

"That would be awesome. Thank you." He looked at Gail. "Ask your parents if you can come with us. Maybe they can pick us up at the end."

Gail nodded with excitement and disappeared to find her parents.

"Gail seems very nice. How did you two meet?"

"School."

"I would never have guessed. How long have you known her?"

"Not long. Well, I'd seen her junior year. Knew who she was, but I didn't have a class with her or nothin'."

"And …?"

"We started talkin' one day after class, and right after, started studying together. She's real smart."

"Apparently, you're pretty smart yourself. You never told me you were getting an award. Most improved student? I'm very proud of you."

Ricky blushed and looked at Tina. His gratitude did not bloom into words but flowed into his eyes; it swelled in his chest with a breath taken deep into his lungs. Tina and Ricky looked at each other for no more than seconds, yet everything silently felt or unspoken between them was completed.

Ralph's home was a three-story Victorian on at least an acre of land in the Lincolnville neighborhood. Purple, white, and crimson bougainvillea spiraled up and around the large front porch columns, which were festooned with congratulation banners for the graduates.

While watching Ricky and Gail walk through the gate to the festivities, Tina's tears of joy for Ricky's success comingled with those shed for what Tina never had—never could have—with Max.

She wondered when she would see Ricky next.

24

Shrinking Possibilities

Noble Dodd's assessment that Ricky would not have killed himself hadn't relieved any of Tina's confusion, though it had girded her resolve. She fumed to think Ruthann had gained custody of Ricky when his mom went to prison, just so she could use him—a child—to serve her drug business. But Tina had to consider how much truth there was. It was a revelation to understand that Noble might have had his own agenda by telling her such a thing. She had to be careful.

By the time she returned to her office, it was midafternoon. Her team had completed their initial presentation to the StarComm directors. The office was subdued. She asked Dale to follow her into her office.

"So? How'd it go?" she asked him.

"Well, I think the StarComm group liked what they saw, but they thought we were a bit too boutique for their needs."

"Meaning too small."

"Right. They needed a commitment from the owner on a plan to scale up to meet their needs."

"But you and I and Kyle, we discussed how we were going to build, and quickly. We were ready for that question."

"We were. But without a firm commitment from you, Tina, as the owner, I don't think they were convinced."

"Shit. I'll give Don Blanchard a call right now."

"I think it's the only thing that has a chance to pull this back our way." Dale said. "Tina, in six years, this is the first time I ...." He stopped and nodded at Tina.

"You what, Dale?"

"Nothing. Please let me know how the call with Mr. Blanchard goes."

"I will," Tina affirmed, punching the speed dial on her cell phone.

It took her three tries to reach Don Blanchard. When she did, she apologized profusely for her absence and asked him for five minutes. She didn't plead or beg. She drew straight lines from what the StarComm group wanted to how her firm would deliver. The StarComm COO was cool but did not disagree with her. He went on to express his disappointment with Tina's absence.

Though crestfallen, Tina persevered enough to get a second on-site audience with a smaller StarComm team to make a final pitch. When she clicked off her phone, she dropped her head to the desk, folded her arms around her ears, and closed her eyes. I've got to be careful, she thought. I can't let this business, these great people, down.

For the next ninety minutes she was the proverbial captain of the ship, pumping up her team, letting them know the hunt for the great whale was still on, and encouraging them to come up with new ideas for their creative work and for doubling their company resources in less than two months. The office hum returned.

Back in her office, she sat and relaxed a bit. She remembered she needed to get back to Detective Tillyard with everything she had discovered and get the details of his investigation—presuming her information merited a more forthcoming detective than she had thus far encountered. It was 5:35 p.m. She enjoyed the idea of speaking to him again.

Her call was transferred to his desk, and Tillyard picked up.

"This is Tina Spear, Detective. I hope you're well and have a few moments for me."

Tillyard leaned forward in his chair. "This is as good a time as any, Ms. Spear. What have you got for me?"

Tina thought, How typical. I've shared everything I have with him and he's given me nothing.

She said, "Okay. I'll go first. I'll put a caveat out here to begin with. Some of this, I believe, and some of this I'm not certain about. I don't know."

"Okay, Ms. Spear. Maybe between the two of us, we can figure out what's what."

She provided the details of her conversations with Ruthann Plyer, Rhonda Kingswood, and Noble Dodd, subduing her emotional responses.

When she stopped and drew a loud breath, Tillyard whispered into the phone, "Damn if most of what you told me doesn't make perfect sense. First, it should be easy to verify if Sheriff Caldwell is Jacob's father. That's a simple birth certificate check. That could explain most everything about the burial of the coroner's report and the quick cremation."

"Burial of the coroner's report? This is news, Detective."

"Yeah, I know. Happened the day after we talked last. Sheriff actually took me off the case."

Tina leaned onto her desk and held the phone closer to her face. The information saddened her far more than it should have.

"I kept a copy, though. If it gets out, it'll cost me. But look. I never told you, but there was a discrepancy in the report, or at least something that should have been investigated and wasn't. There was no GSR—no gunshot residue—on Ricky's skull, but there was on his hands. Both his hands."

Tina blinked three times in rapid succession. "What could such a thing mean?"

"The report concluded that he held the gun away from his head with both hands and pulled the trigger with his thumb. But that's a dumb way to commit suicide. I don't understand this one yet."

"This doesn't tell me anything, Detective. I'm sorry."

"Yeah. So listen. Last week I told you I was working on a hunch. I got twitchy from the way I saw Jacob Plyer and his wife interacting. She seemed more controlling of him than I recalled at the memorial."

"At least you got to go to the memorial."

"Right. Anyway, I did some background checking on Nurse Carmen. I needed to know her last name before she married Jacob. That took me to their marriage license. Would you like to guess what Mrs. Plyer's family name was before she got married?"

To Tina, this seemed wholly unlike the Detective Tillyard she knew. He had built up his reveal in a way that was downright playful. "Please do tell me, Detective."

"Navarro. Her name is Carmen Navarro."

Tina was silent. "Navarro? It might as well be Smith or Jones. Why is this of any significance?"

"Carlos Navarro is the head of one of the three largest Mexican drug cartels. Carmen Plyer is Carlos Navarro's niece."

Tina turned this over in her mind. A drug lord's niece was Jacob Plyer's wife and Ricky's sister-in-law. Okay. But if she was in the US military, she was a US citizen or close to being one. It could mean she has or had virtually no ties to her uncle.

"Detective, this is one more isolated puzzle piece in a damn sea of puzzle pieces. I don't see how this means anything."

"I told you before, even if there's nothing to them, you can't ever take coincidences or tangents at face value. So, I dug a bit more. I checked with some of the officers I know in narcotics in Atlanta. Turns out, Fort McPherson has come under investigation for losing a whole lot of synthetic opioids over the last five years. And for receiving shipments of those same drugs, far in excess of what should have been their normal allotment. Carmen Navarro Plyer is an army nurse stationed for a time at Fort McPherson, now working at Camp Merrill, near Dahlonega."

"Ah … okay. A disturbing coincidence. But still, this information is nothing more than a prejudice because of her family name."

"You're right. It's quite possibly the full extent of it. From what you've told me, Jacob's grandmother might just be a dealer and had pressed her grandson and others into drug running. Years ago, and maybe still today? I have to figure how to go to the sheriff with all this."

"Hold on, Detective. Could Sheriff Caldwell be involved? Do you think Jacob is involved in the drug business? I mean between his grandmother, his mother, and now, his wife …" Tina covered her mouth with her hand.

"I know what you're thinking, Ms. Spear. I'm considering this too. But we still don't have enough information."

"I'm coming back to Dahlonega, Detective. I have to spend some time with Jacob. He's in a bad way."

"Instead of coming all the way up here, why don't you confront Ruthann? She's the one who should be sweating."

"Because I don't give one shit about her, that's why. She can go to hell. I'm trying to learn what happened to a promising boy, that's all! And what happened to him, happened in your town. The rest of this screwed-up business is all your department. I don't care that they're running drugs. I don't care if Sheriff Caldwell is Jacob's father. I don't care if the lot of them overdose and rot in their houses." She stopped to catch her breath. "I just ... want the truth, Detective."

"Don't we all? Well, look at it this way. Ricky's death may have been directly related to drug dealing by his brother or his brother's wife, or both, or neither. From your perspective, it makes no difference whether or not the chief covered up the autopsy and closed the investigation to ease his son's pain or to cover up a crime. But it makes a huge difference to me. You do get this, right?"

"Yes, Detective."

"Good. I can't stop you from coming up here, I know. But I think if you take another run at the grandmother, you might find out something that will break this for us."

"Jesus. I ... I don't know. I need to think about it and talk it over with ... someone. I can't take this to my husband." Why on earth did I say that? she asked herself.

"Look. I don't want you to take any more risk or do anything you wouldn't normally do. And you sure aren't going to do anything the police should do. But you're right. Too much about this doesn't smell right. You did great getting Mrs. Plyer to tell you about the sheriff. Do you think you could get her to give up more? Think about it and get back to me."

The cubicles were all empty when Tina left her office for home. It was all so normal. But this typically long day had been fueled not by the energy of her business, but by the chaos of her compulsion. After her conversation with Tillyard it was impossible to concentrate on StarComm or any other project. How would she confront Ruthann Plyer?

How would she react? Could Tina trust any reaction? It was just too much. A framed photo on her desk stopped her. It recalled a day ten years in the past. Tina, Walter, and the three boys before any of them had reached their teens, were sitting on a dock on Robinson's Creek, the marsh reeds bent in the background, the sun hidden yet bright behind them. Such a time seemed more than a lifetime ago—another person's lifetime. Would it ever be possible to hold on to the little that remained of her family and repair her relationship with Walter? With this question echoing in her mind, Tina grabbed her purse and headed home.

Walter's Volvo was in the garage. Tina heaved a sigh propelled by a gut-wrenching ambivalence. She felt her energy escape into the air like the unwinding of a steel coil. Walter was at the table, eating dinner. Opposite him was a place set for Tina.

"If you're hungry, I've made enough for us both," her husband said, raising his eyes but not his head as Tina entered.

"I … I'm not very hungry." She stood still behind her chair.

"Tough day at the tip of the Spear?" he said as light-hearted as he could.

"Well, yes and more." She folded into the chair like a bird falling from the sky. The day's conversations overwhelmed her in a torrent. She covered her face with her hands.

Walter's eyes went wide, his mouth tensed. He asked her, "Is this something you're ready to discuss?"

"It's everything, goddamn it! Everything is falling into shit and I can't stop it."

"You never could, and it was never on you alone to stop any of 'it' in the first place. And yet, here we are—"

"I know. I know. I'm obsessed, conflicted, obstinate. I can't think straight. Ricky was not supposed to die. I don't— I can't let this be the end, this whimper into nothingness."

"You just can't let go, can you? Not even when your family is about to disintegrate. You hold onto Max's passing like a—"

"Stop it! This is not about Max, you …! Max was our son. Ricky was … something else."

"You say this all the time, and still you can't make me believe it. I know how you've been with Ricky for these last three years. At first, I thought this opportunity was the very thing to bring you back. But it was the opposite. You used Ricky. You attached all your sorrow, your guilt, your need for some different outcome for Max, to this boy. And the outcome is horribly, ironically, no different. I can't help you, Tina."

"I'm not asking for your help. I just need … Jesus Christ, I don't know what I need. Do you really think I'm unhinged because his suicide, or whatever it was, affects me like it has? Something is wrong. Something is very wrong, and I can't figure it out. All I want is for this whole shitty business to be over." She pounded the table. As tears dripped down her face, she pushed her cheeks up to dry them. "I can't let this nonsensical tragedy fade away without the full light of day! It has not one fucking thing to do with our dead son. Get that through your head, will you please? Nothing!"

"Ricky was killed by his brother's gun with Ricky's own hands on it." Walter's statement of fact did not faze Tina.

"And who else had their hands on the gun before? And why had Ricky picked up a gun in the first place? And why, why was I not there to say goodbye to him!" Tina's voice broke into a wail for a few seconds, until she regained her composure.

"I've never in my life seen you like this, Tina." He handed Tina a box of tissues. "There's only one thing to do. You pursue this until you can't. You take a leave of absence, and you do everything you have to for the next two weeks. Two weeks. With those two weeks, set your mind that you're going to return to Spearhead and put wherever you are at that point on hold. This whole business may be too much for you or for anyone. You can't let this take you down. Ricky would never have wanted for you to end up like him."

Tina recalled the warning from Noble Dodd's display of the Glock. "Is that what you think, Walter? That I'm heading for a breakdown or a gun barrel?"

"It doesn't matter what I think. It only matters what you do. We have no future, you and I, until and unless you get this behind you. Do what you have to." He walked into their home office.

She picked up her purse from the table and entered their bedroom. She sat on the bed, going over in her mind what she should do, what she could do. It was a few minutes before she heard the door to the garage close hard, followed by the harsh rumble of a Volvo motor.

PART 2

Charity, Jacob, and Ricky

25

Family Matters

The fun of living with RC around Atlanta in 1986, for twenty-year-old Charity Plyer, was short-lived. RC was good to her when he had time off from his construction job, but he could be a real downer when she wanted to stay out with whatever new friends she had made. The day she became pregnant with her first child, the universe became her enemy. She was on the pill, for God's sake! She had no intention of becoming a mother. RC needed to know this.

Coming home for dinner on a chilly fall evening, Charity hung her head and told RC in a whisper, "I'm gonna have a baby."

"Say again, Char. You're pregnant?"

Charity nodded.

"Oh my God! You're pregnant. That's freakin' fantastic! I'm going to be a daddy."

"Oh? You think this is just fine, do you, Mr. Hot Shot?" she said. "You're gonna be workin' all day. Gone a week at a time. Maybe get a damn foreman job like you been after. I'll be the one stuck with a cryin', sucklin' creature needin' my attention twentyfour-seven for the next umpteen years. That is not the life I'm goin' for here."

"Say what? You didn't go off the pill on purpose? What the hell? Never mind. This can work out great for us. I mean,

I can ask for a raise, even without a promotion. There's a lot of new work goin' on over at the military bases. No reason the boss can't make me a foreman, with all the new work." RC went silent as his thoughts started to fly. "We probably should go ahead and get married, right? That's it, Charity! We should do the deed and become a family!" RC picked up Charity and twirled her around like she was six years old.

"Put me down, you fuckin' whale!" she screamed.

He did as she asked, with the care of a jeweler.

"Get married? Now I know you've lost your mind. You recall when I said I'd come to 'Lanta to live with you? We put no strings on this arrangement. You do recall what I'm sayin', don't you?"

"Sure, I recall all of it, Char. But things have just changed big time. Look, I have to go to South Carolina on a project for a few days. I want you to think about this. Think about what this means for us. For the family we can have." He pulled Charity into a hug.

"I'll think about it, all right," she promised.

Two nights later, while RC was working in South Carolina for the week, Charity went out to a new bar in Decatur and ran into an old friend. A single, male, old friend. It made her feel alive knowing she was attractive to someone besides RC. Sexy, even. The warmer she felt at the bar, the further her thoughts ran to independence, romance, having anything she wanted without consequences. And what stronger statement of her independence, of her own agency, could she make than to have sex with whomever she wanted, whenever she wanted.

Three days after RC's return, Charity had difficulty dodging phone calls from her erstwhile lover of the prior week. When RC confronted her, she disgorged the truth in a stream of defiance.

RC's mouth dropped open and his eyes ignited even as they filled with tears. When Charity halted her defense, RC's vocabulary shrank to a howl and four-letter words. When he trembled, the air in the apartment vibrated like an impending storm. Struggling to gain emotional equilibrium, he said, "I wouldn't marry you for anything on this god-forsaken planet!" He pounded his fist on the countertop and then held himself rigid. "But you are carrying our child, goddamn you! My child. And you will bring our baby into this world, Charity. Fuck's sake." RC wiped his head and sat down. He couldn't look at her.

"I'll make sure you have enough for supporting the child. But I can't take this … this … pit of your … your spittin' on us and what we coulda' had!" He rose again. "I'm outta here. And don't you think for a single second of aborting our child. You hear me?"

"I can take care of myself and my baby just fine. But if you leave me now, RC, you forfeit any right you think you have to this child."

"Good God, listen to yourself! You got no skills, smart as you think you are. How you gonna make a living? You fucking … I-I—"

Charity stood, hands on hips, watching RC hit the sides of his head with both hands. After a minute of this, he stopped and whirled around to face her.

"Here's what's gonna happen. I'm done. I'm moving out, but I'll figure out a way to pay the rent and help with the baby. You need to apply for welfare tomorrow and figure out the rest of your life. You are so full of yourself, so God-damned self-indulgent …, it's got you all twisted. Not one other person in the world matters except you."

"You're damn right about that!" she yelled back.

There was nothing more for RC to do but save himself and try to save the baby. He moved into a rented room and the following week he enlisted in the army. RC looked back only to be sure Charity had a healthy child.

Charity applied for and received welfare and began to use her evenings to troll for a partner—someone she could control with her sexuality and her cunning, someone with an income, maybe even a business. This plan was much more difficult than she'd imagined. Men were very happy to buy her tequila shooters and share their coke and their beds with her. But either they didn't measure up on her checklist or they were too wary to get entangled.

Until he was formally inducted into the army, RC had two rents to pay. This proved financially untenable, but not so untenable as moving back into the apartment with Charity. Unless, of course, Charity moved back to her mom's in Florida.

"I can't afford both places," he told her over the phone one night. "You've got to go back to Florida. I'm stoppin' rent on the apartment."

"Hell, you say! I'm not goin' back to live in that backwater town. Nothin' there but the past and old farts."

"You don't have a choice. Besides, if you do, I can still send you some money. If you don't, you'll make things worse for you and the baby. You'll end up killin' yourself and our child. Be as smart as you think you are and tell Ruthann you're movin' home."

They argued for another five minutes until RC, exasperated, hung up.

Charity hated the fact that RC was forcing her into a decision. But the more she considered it, the more it made sense—at least until after the baby was born. She chuckled as she thought of Ruthann as a gramma. The next day she told her mother she was coming back to St. Augustine to have her child. Ruthann's rant and scolding washed off

Charity like rain over a rock. She would regroup in her mother's home and figure things out from there.

26

Time Served

When RC called to tell Charity, in her cell, that Ricky had apparently taken his own life, she was numb. But then, she'd been numb for a few years.

"Did he really, RC? Jesus H Christ. Fuck. How'd it go down? Tell me straight now."

"You know he was at Jacob's place here. Well, seems the two brothers got into it, calling each other names. Ricky got depressed and picked up one of Jacob's handguns. Just fuckin' tragic."

"Never knew Ricky to have it in him, RC. Damn. Seems, you know, off. Like there's something else goin' on. You levelin' with me? Jacob didn't off him, did he? Go crazy in some drug-addled rage?"

"No, Charity."

"No complicity of that lyin' cockroach Lapis, protecting his little empire?"

"If you want my testimony at your parole hearing, you just shut up about any association with Lapis. Jacob's in a world of pain and doesn't need your paranoid ranting. Hear me?"

What Charity heard was a snarl, not something she recognized as normal for "the whale." "Fine. Hearing's in three weeks. Can you get me out to come to Ricky's service?"

"I'm doing everything I can to make sure you can't. Service is tomorrow, after the death certificate and cremation. You're stayin' put until your parole. That was our deal."

"You cold, fucking, whale bastard. Seems awfully quick work there, Constable. What you got going on?"

"Keeping you away as long as possible." He hung up.

In the evening, Charity used her daily outgoing phone call to reach her mother. "You going to Dahlonega for Ricky's funeral?" she asked.

"I sure ain't. You know I got no car no more, and I sure as hell ain't takin' no bus. Something don't smell right up there, and I don't want no part of it. It's bad about Ricky. Really sorry the boy is gone."

"How's the trade, Ruthann?"

"We're doin' fine. Cole is a pain in the ass, but he gets stuff where it needs to go. Even recruited a girlfriend's daughter up in Jacksonville."

"You be careful with those new folks."

"Don't you worry, missy. Your old boyfriend's been busy *training* us. He's got these *procedures* now. We got more checks and balances than the government!"

"Is he? Still workin' with Carmen's cousins?"

"How the hell would I know? He don't share shit like that with me."

"All right. Sheesh! Anything else going on? You know I can't have nothing getting in the way of my parole hearing."

"So far, so good. Spear woman might be trying to get to the service for Ricky."

"What I hear, could be she has trouble gettin' there on time. Don't say nuthin', Ruthann. Just do your business. Got that?"

"Got it."

"I'll be in touch." Charity hung up.

Days later, when her cellmate was out in the yard playing softball, Charity stretched out on the top bunk. While revenge never left her thoughts, she knew it could not be the first project she undertook after her release. She would have to ease back into some kind of regular life, a life recognizable but not too threatening. Jacob's home was the perfect situation. Grandma Charity gets outta prison, helps with the new baby and cares for her wounded son, relieving his overworked wife. Charity chortled under her breath.

It was a shame about Ricky dying and all, but Ruthann had warned her. Ricky wasn't coming back into the business. He changed in a way Ruthann couldn't understand and that's all there was to it. Except it wasn't true. This counselor Spear, she created the problem. She had the backbone to come to see Charity in prison. She was disruptive. She was the one who turned her youngest son against her and who, if Ruthann could be believed, would not stop until she knew for sure what happened to Ricky. "She's a fucking loose cannon," Charity said out loud. "You, Mrs. Spear, are on the watch list. Better fucking stay in your lane, bitch."

Charity Begins at Home

PAST

"Hurry your ass along, missy. You're gonna be late for work!" Ruthann yelled at her daughter.

Charity continued primping in the bathroom. After all, her large tips depended as much on her obvious curves as they did on her waitressing skills. Satisfied, she grabbed her purse and walked past her mother, toward the door.

"Ain't you at least gonna kiss Jacob goodbye? He does call for you, ya know. When you're gone. Which is all the time!"

"The hell you talkin' about, Ruthann? I'm here all damn day lookin' after the boy."

"You mean after you got outta bed 'round noon, killed your hangover with a handful of aspirins and a full pot a' coffee? You think just 'cause I ain't here I don't know how you behave? You didn't get home till 4:00 a.m. again. I get off my shift and what do I find? Jacob needing changing, needing to be fed. You ain't fit to be a momma, child. You gotta do better by this boy!"

"Maybe you should adopt him and make it official you're his momma. You do recall RC was the one wanted this boy so bad. He shoulda' taken Jacob right after he was born, but no. Course, you can't be no single papa while servin' in the army. Fuck's sake, Ruthann, I'm doing my best here, all right? And whatever you think about what I'm doing at night, I'm workin' the whole time. I got some things goin' on maybe I'll fill you in on, so long's you keep lookin' after the boy."

"What sorta work?"

"Money makin' work is all you need to know for now. Be a good gramma, and I'll tell you all about it soon enough." Charity walked out with a strut, got into the old Pontiac she shared with her mother, and headed to the restaurant.

Ruthann heard the cries from baby Jacob. "Shit damn, that girl's too smart and too stubborn. I'm comin', baby boy, I'm comin'." She took Jacob out of his crib and bounced him gently while she talked to him. "Damn, I wish your daddy could take you for a while. Glad for the money he sends and all, but I just ain't got the energy you need, little one. You're wearin' me out! And so's your damn momma."

* * *

Big tippers at the restaurant could also be connections to other opportunities, Charity discovered. It was easy enough to flirt with the mostly male customers, but as often as not, she was asked for a quid pro quo of one sort or another. Not a night passed without an invitation to go out, to hang out, or to perform some favor. If the offeror was good-looking, wildly generous with his money, and had something fun in mind, Charity would agree to meet him and pursue the offer. By the time Cole Hart wandered into the restaurant one evening in 1990, Charity was fed up being a waitress and a part-time mother.

He and a friend came in late for a meal and a beer. Charity swished over to their table right away.

"You boys are comin' in a bit late for dinner. Lucky the cook's still on duty. If you're nice, I'll be sure he takes special care with your order." She stuck out her hips so her jeans creased invitingly just above her thigh. Cole was practically drooling.

"I'll have whatever you're cookin'," he told her with a stupid grin.

Charity laughed. "Now, I know you can do better than that. B'sides, I ain't cookin' tonight, darlin'. But I'll be sure to get you what you need. Have you looked over the menu?"

"No need. What say you order for me." He smiled at his buddy, who laughed and ordered a cheeseburger and a Michelob.

"Two Swiss burgers, two Michs, and a special order a' sweet potato fries," Charity said as she wrote on her order pad.

She swiveled to go toward the kitchen and looked over her shoulder. Cole had unconsciously turned his chair around and was watching Charity with the goofiest eyes she had ever seen.

She already had this looker hooked. Could be a good night, she thought.

28

As a Matter of Fact

In a pantomime evolved into ritual, Walter took a cup of black coffee in a to-go mug and left the house for work without a word. Dealing with the collateral damage of her work and homelife became a recursive frustration fueling Tina's darkness. Today she decided to head to Ruthann's before going to her office.

A black Mercedes SUV backed out of the Plyer driveway as Tina approached the house. She noted the out-of-state license plates—Georgia. The driver turned and looked at her when the car drove past. Tina likened his expression to an inquisitor staring at a heretic.

She cursed Ruthann under her breath. The woman didn't own a car, making it impossible to tell whether or not she was home. For the fifth time in as many days, Tina banged on the porch door, announced herself, and proceeded to the kitchen door, only to find it locked with a bolt installed since Ricky's death. She banged on the curtained glass of the door a few times and shouted Ruthann's name.

As soon as Tina turned to leave, the door unbolted and Ruthann appeared.

"Jesus Christ," Ruthann said. "Don't you never give up?"

"I don't know," said Tina, more honestly than she'd intended. "We'll have to see how this all plays out, won't we?"

Ruthann stepped onto the porch and closed the door. "Nuthin's playin' out here 'ceptin' your crazy need to see what ain't here. You're lookin' tired, Miss Tina. You should get some rest and let all this go. Be so much better for your health, I'm sure."

The hair on the back of Tina's neck spiked, but she didn't change her expression. "Oh, I'm tired, all right. I'm tired of your lies, tired of your foul mouth, tired of you covering for something you know was wrong that took your grandson's life. And you have the gall to look me in the eye and tell me you know something about my health? Well, here's what I know about yours. You and your drug-running cohorts are done. Using adolescent boys to carry illegal drugs, Ruthann, will get you a bunk next to your daughter for the rest of your days. And, oh, how I look forward to that. But, you know, it won't be me getting it done because—and please open your ears here—I don't give a shit what you do. I only want, and have only ever wanted, the truth about Ricky's death. I don't know if you know and won't say, or if you are more clueless than I am. I haven't been your enemy, you sorry woman. You want me gone? Easy! Be straight with me now. Right now, this instant, or … or I will do my best to fuck up your shitty life. Which is it going to be, Ruthann?"

Tina could see Ruthann's jaw muscles tighten like violin strings. Was Ruthann about to attack her? As if reading Tina's mind, Ruthann rushed back into the house and pushed the door hard behind her. Without thinking, Tina ran full force with her shoulder against the door, bursting it open and knocking the older woman to the floor.

Ruthann tried to right herself, when Tina kicked her with blind rage and a scream like a war cry. Ruthann thudded to the floor and tried to crawl away. Tina jumped on her back and flailed at her head, her shoulders, her neck, hitting Ruthann fast and hard. She punched the side of Ruthann's face. Breathless grunts erupted from the older woman. Ruthann got one arm free and uselessly waved it, trying to land a blow. Tina slapped the arm down hard. She raised her arms over her head and held her fists together, preparing to hit Ruthann as hard a blow as she could. With another scream, she shook all over and halted her assault.

Tina's exhausted breathing slowed. Looking at Ruthann splayed and motionless on the floor, Tina felt outside of her own body. How on earth was she capable of this? Backing up slowly she wiped her wet hair from her face and braced herself against the kitchen counter.

A low groan rose from the floor.

"You stupid, pathetic woman!" Tina cried. "My God, I can't believe this."

Ruthann rolled over, screamed in pain, and then lay still. "Fuck! You broke my fuckin' back. You broke my fuckin' back!"

In shock, Tina knelt by Ruthann's side. "Oh no! Ruthann, I never meant ... how could I have ...!" She pulled out her phone and dialed 911.

"Fuck's sake," Ruthann grunted, "don't call no cops!"

"I'm not leaving you like this and I'm not taking care of you, either. I can't believe this! I just—. Hello, yes, I'd like to report an assault and I need an ambulance." Tina completed the emergency call and then filled a glass with tap water. Tina tried to make Ruthann drink; she only swatted at the glass and at Tina, who rose from her squat and vomited all over Ruthann's kitchen floor.

The paramedics put Ruthann onto a stretcher as she cried and cursed. When Tina asked about Ruthann's condition, they said it would have to wait until she could be examined by a doctor, but she was stable for now. A police officer asked Tina to sit at the kitchen table and answer a few questions. Tina spared nothing in her recounting of events.

Tina asked if she could do some cleanup while the officer interviewed her.

"At this stage, ma'am, you've already done everything you're going to do here. I'm afraid I have to book you for breaking and entering and second-degree assault." He asked Tina to turn around. He recited her Miranda rights.

"Are the cuffs necessary, Officer? Please. I'll go with you without any fuss."

"I'll take them off when we're at the car, ma'am. Off we go."

As she walked through the wreckage of Ruthann's home, up the debris-strewn driveway, hands bound behind her, Tina's energy fell away. Without warning, a strange feeling came over her. She was content. Happy, even. Her shoulders straightened and her chin rose. She looked victorious rather than vanquished. As the squad car turned out of the driveway, Tina smiled.

The booking process felt detached and somehow not real. Tina's belongings were taken, and she was given a quick health inspection after the photo and fingerprinting. She was allowed the one call. Deciding who to call was painfully difficult. But she managed to dial Walter's number. She gave him the condensed version of events.

"Holy shit, I can't believe you! How could you let this happen? I-I—oh my God! Okay. Look, I'll come down there right away. Has bail been set?"

"Probably be done after you get here. And Walter?"

"Yes, Tina."

"I'm sorry to have to put you through this, but I am not sorry Ruthann is in the hospital and out of commission. She's a wretched piece of—"

"I swear I don't know who you are anymore. I'll be at the police station in twenty minutes."

Her bail was modest. Tina was a business and civic icon in St. Augustine, with not even a parking ticket to her name. The first judge decided to recuse herself from setting bail because of her personal friendship with Tina. Walter posted the bond and drove Tina to pick up her car.

After five minutes of silent driving, Walter said, "Do you even recognize yourself? Do you see or understand who you've become?"

Tina turned her head to look straight at him. "I do. I'm righting a horrible injustice."

"Like hell you are. You're just creating a vortex of suspicion, animosity, and now, violence. It's not getting better, Tina. It's escalating! Can't you see that?"

"Maybe escalation is precisely what has to happen to get to the truth."

"Jesus. There isn't any truth here."

"Of course there is. I'm getting closer. I know I am and I'm not alone."

"Alone? Damn it! I'm alone! And I'm done. Either you stop your obsessive sleuthing now and work with me on our marriage, or I'm moving out and we can see where your truth takes us."

Her look changed from defiance to resignation. "If that's what you want."

"Fuck you, Tina. That's not remotely what I want. It's what you've driven me to."

Tina looked out the window as they entered the Plyer driveway. She told Walter, "I'm going to go home, take a shower, and call my office. Thank you for coming to get me and posting my bail. I know you don't understand this, but I'm not wrong. And I'm under control. I've—"

"Bullshit. You beat a woman into the hospital. You're not under control in the least."

"Learned a lesson. An important lesson. But I know how to get the answers. Finally. Please hold on. Please. A bit longer, if you can."

"I'm working late tonight," he said, driving off and leaving her standing like a specter next to her car.

Tina was in a trance driving home. She needed to talk with someone with a shred of sympathy for what she had endured and would likely continue to endure. Someone who would let her talk, even for a few moments, so this wave of self-loathing and sadness could pass over without harm, without changing her course. She dug her phone out of her purse and yelled at her car to dial the first person who came to her mind. A voice answered after three rings.

"Detective Tillyard."

Tina was composed. "Hello, Detective. It's Tina Spear. I … I wanted to let you know I just beat up Ruthann Plyer and put her in the hospital."

Silence. The detective reoriented his mental compass. He slapped his forehead. "Did you truly, or are you pranking me? Neither of which, by the way, squares with what I know about you."

"Apparently, you are getting to know me, as I get to know myself. Finally," Tina said.

Tillyard was silent as Tina recounted her latest exchange with Ruthann.

29

After the Arrival

PAST

The year after Ricky was born, Charity became engaged to Cole Hart. Of all her male associates, he was the least resistant to her control of the drug business. Most of them balked at her use of her son Jacob and his high school friends as mules. The rest eventually realized they were never going to be more to her than commodities with a short shelf lives. With a combination of emotional dependency, good looks, and a slight deficit of gray matter, Cole Hart made the perfect subordinate in her enterprise. Better in some ways, even, than her mother. Besides, Charity needed Ruthann to help look after baby Ricky.

On a cheerful fall afternoon, Ruthann said to her daughter, "Let me get this straight, missy. You got yourself knocked up by God knows who and—"

"I know who." Charity was busy packing small bags with pills and didn't look up. "All that matters—"

"Know who or not, his daddy ain't here to take care o' him, is he? What? So I'm the one who needs to look after your kid? Again? You're livin' under my roof. I already took care o' you and Jacob. Now you gotta take care of this little baby."

Charity grunted and continued her work.

"You do recall that I did most of the work with Jacob? When you was hauled off to jail in—what was it, '93? Who looked after your boy all those days and who made sure we had a roof while you took off partyin' and drug dealin' and who knows what else? Your turn, Charity. Ricky is your child. Best you get straight and keep them welfare people off our backs. You hear?"

"Long as we're settin' the record, who's been bringing in the money to this family these past three years, heh? Me, that's who. You even quit waitressin' so you could help with the business."

"All true. And now you're gonna marry your favorite connection. Why? So we can collect more of what we bring in? You think maybe he'll take care of baby Ricky? I knew you was strange, deary, but I didn't know you was from Mars."

"You know, Ruthann, you worry too much and think too little." A smile crossed Charity's face. "You've seen how my number one son has taken such a shine to his baby brother. There's half your answer right there. Stop frettin' over who'll look after the baby and start focusin' on how we keep growing this business without bringing the law down on us. Stay on the numbers and the money. Jacob will do much o' the babysittin', right? 'Specially if we had him mule less— you know, more time with baby brother."

The porch door creaked open and slapped shut.

"That you, Jacob?" Charity called out.

"Yeah, Ma, it's me," Jacob said. He walked through the living room on his way to his bedroom, without a glance at either of the two women.

"I got some good news, son," Charity said, still smiling at her mother. "You're gonna have a stepdad pretty soon. I'm gettin' hitched to my good friend Cole. He's pretty fond of you, and I know you and he worked together a few times."

Jacob stopped. His head snapped in the direction of his mother. He opened his mouth to speak. Nothing came out except his energy, sucked into a void much greater than his anger. He shook his head. "I don't give a fuck what you do anymore."

The cry of a waking infant in the far bedroom took hold of his attention. Neither of the women stirred. Jacob's shoulders lifted and he hurried out of the living room to take care of his baby brother.

"Well, ain't you the one!" Charity yelled after him.

In the bedroom, Jacob looked at the baby in the old crib, crying in stuttering sobs. Jacob picked him up and the crying subsided.

"I'll bet you're hungry, Ricky. Right? Let's go see if those hags thought to make up a bottle for you this afternoon."

He carried Ricky to the kitchen, stopping to ask if either Charity or Ruthann had made up a bottle for Ricky.

"Should be one on the counter," Ruthann said.

Jacob shrugged. Why it wasn't in the refrigerator was obvious.

"It's too early for his evening feed," Charity said. "I'm trying to get him on a regular schedule so he don't fuss all the time."

"I didn't know babies kept to adult schedules," Jacob said.

"It's all about the training, Jacob."

He ignored his mother. He grabbed the bottle while still holding on to Ricky and sat down on a kitchen chair. Before he could tilt the food toward his little brother, Charity was off her seat and snatched the bottle from his hands.

"I told you I'm trying to get him on a regular feeding schedule."

"He ain't no dog, Ma. He's a hungry baby."

"Like you would know anything about takin care o' babies."

"They teach us plenty about babies in school," he lied.

"Oh, do they?" Charity turned and winked at her mother, who raised her eyebrows in surprise.

"Yeah, they do. He's gonna grow into a person soon, ain't you, Ricky?" Jacob reached for the bottle, but Charity pulled it away. "Gimme the damn bottle, Ma, for shit's sake. He's hungry!"

Charity leaned toward Jacob and slapped him hard across the face. It was more than enough to sting. His eyes burned with tears and anger as he hugged his baby brother, who started to cry.

"I see your pa's weakness in you, Jacob. You gotta do the hard things in life if you wanna get anywhere, if things are gonna be like you want 'em. You hear? Now, you let this bottle be for another hour before you feed Ricky. It'll be fine."

Jacob carefully got to his feet and carried Ricky off to their bedroom.

"Damn kids," Charity said as she reached for a cigarette. "Good thing you can put 'em to work."

* * *

The day Jacob got his driver's license, Charity was jubilant.

"This will make your courier job a whole lot easier now, won't it?" she told him.

"Huh? How does this make takin' your dope around any easier? Taxi's still best. I don't know how to get to most of them places you tell me. Besides, you take the car out most every night."

Charity smiled at Jacob and encouraged him to think more about what she had in mind.

"You gonna buy me a car o' my own?"

"You're close. It'll be my car, and you'll get to drive it. So long as you keep drivin' for a few more years. You get my meanin'?"

He did. The cost of a car at his disposal meant he was indentured to his mother's drug business. Jacob' shoulders drooped as he walked to his room.

27

30

A Surfeit of Badges

The phone rang in Tina's office. It was the St. Augustine Police Department. "Just to let you know, Mrs. Spear, Ruthann Plyer is being held over for observation at Flagler Hospital, but at the moment there seem to be no substantial injuries," Officer Chamliss said.

Tina let out a long breath she wasn't aware she had been holding. "Mrs. Plyer has so far declined to press charges, but in exchange for dropping the charges she wants you to pay for the medical costs associated with the 911 call and her subsequent care. Does this sound fair to you, Mrs. Spear?"

"It does, Officer. I hate to say it, but I may be getting off lightly in the long run."

"Very likely, ma'am. You beat that woman up pretty bad. In her own home."

She hung up and sucked in another breath.

That evening she preceded Walter home, fixed herself a light dinner with two hefty glasses of a reserve Rioja, put in an hour reviewing project charts, another hour on Facebook, and got ready for bed. She had fallen asleep with her iPad on her lap when her cell phone rang. She saw the time was eleven thirty-three. Walter was not in bed.

"Mrs. Christina Spear?" a voice said.

216 / Throwaway Boy

"Yes."

"Ma'am, this is Sergeant Wilmot of the St. Johns County Sherriff's Office. Your husband is Walter Spear, correct?"

"Y ... yes, it is."

"Mr. Spear was the subject of an attack at his place of work tonight, about an hour ago. He's been beaten up pretty badly. Paramedics have stabilized him and have taken him to Flagler Hospital."

"Oh my God! *No!*" Tina yelled into the phone as she put her free hand to her mouth. "I'm heading there right now, Sergeant!"

"Yes, ma'am. I will meet you there."

During the fifteen-minute drive to Flagler Hospital, all Tina could think was she had put Walter in danger. This attack had to be the consequence of her willful, reckless crusade. When she asked for Walter Spear at the emergency entrance desk, two law enforcement officers came up to her. The man introduced himself as Sergeant Jason Wilmot. The woman was Deputy Denise Paul. They asked if they could accompany her to see her husband.

"Yes, yes, of course. Oh my God, poor Walter. Officers, do you know what happened?"

As they walked into the emergency ward, Tina learned that security cameras in the office captured two men wearing ski masks when they broke into Walter's business. He had been alone. It seemed their sole intent was to harm her husband, since nothing was stolen and a note had been left on his desk. Walter had suffered a broken jaw, a broken arm, and a severe concussion. She rushed into room 8. Three women were tending to her husband: one administering an IV and two working on a splint for his left arm. One looked up and came over to Tina.

Without extending her latex-gloved hand, she said, "I'm Dr. Lansing. Are you Mrs. Spear?"

"Yes, I am," Tina said. "How is my husband? Will he be all right? May I go to him, please?"

"You can, but please don't touch him or move him until we're finished. I want to get another set of X-rays on his arm and his jaw. He's getting an IV with antibiotics and a mild sedative, more for pain management than sleep, at this point. Does he have any allergies to medicines?"

"None I'm aware of. He's going to recover fully, right, Dr. Lansing?"

"I'll know more after the X-rays, perhaps a CT scan to check for internal bleeding, particularly in the brain. He's responding well so far."

Tina moved quickly over to the side of Walter's bed. The top of his head was bandaged like a mummy. Red stains appeared sporadically, oozing through the gauze. He turned his head slowly toward her and raised his right hand.

Tina took it in both of hers. "Dear God in heaven, I can't believe this has happened. I'm so, so sorry!" She heaved a sob before dissolving into tears.

Walter slowly extracted his hand from hers and held up his index finger, waving is slowly back and forth in front of her.

She laughed and wiped the moisture from her face. "Oh, yes. I can blame myself if I want to!"

Walter's eyes closed.

Sergeant Wilmot cleared his throat. "Mrs. Spear, we do need to speak to you for a few minutes. This is an active aggravated assault investigation. We hope you can put us on the right track."

She nodded and left the room with the officers, where all three stood in the middle of the hallway.

Wilmot said, "It appears the sole purpose of the break-in was to hurt your husband, but not kill him. We've spoken over the phone to his business partner. He can't think of anyone or any reason why someone would to this. Can you?"

"I-I don't know, officer. You said there was a note of some kind had been left on his desk."

"Yes, ma'am. Before we get to the note, what can you tell us about potential enemies your husband may have? Maybe enemies of you both."

Tina's mind raced. Would divulging her actions of the last two weeks help her cause, help find those who hurt Walter? Or would their telling only make things worse? Desperately beyond her experience, she had but her moral compass to guide her. Walter was already collateral damage. Evasion wasn't only pointless, it was counterproductive.

"I'm the one who has enemies, Sergeant. Not Walter. Even my husband's business competitors think of him as an honorable workaholic."

"Who are *your* enemies, Mrs. Spear, and do you believe them to be capable of this kind of violence?"

"Can we please sit?" She motioned to the sitting area at the far end of the corridor.

Seated between the officers, Tina told them her story, focusing on the most recent revelations from Noble Dodd, but leaving out much of what she had learned from Dahlonega. When she completed the tale of her own violent encounter with Ruthann, replete with self-recriminating detail, she looked up from her lap and into the face of Sergeant Wilmot. Her eyes were swollen and dark. "I was just trying to find out why a wonderful young man took his own life. How could I have known it would lead to this ... this brutal, shitty business. Poor Walter!"

Wilmot nodded to his colleague, who pulled a cell phone from her side pocket. She extended an arm, holding the phone, to show Tina a picture taken at Walter's office when they arrived. It was a message on copy paper scribed with blood which must have been Walter's. It read "STOP T. SPEAR."

"It means, Sergeant, I'm the one responsible for my husband being beaten to a pulp." Tina hung her head.

"Organized criminals, Mrs. Spear, will very often target family members for their intimidation. I'm sorry to say it's very effective. From what you've just told us, we can start with the assumption that these perpetrators are part of an illegal drug distribution business. Are they working with Ruthann Plyer? It's hard to say. But you are apparently getting very close to bringing light and, possibly, heat onto this operation. Close enough that they felt the need to take this risk to stop you. It also tells us these people may be from outside of Florida."

"When I drove to Mrs. Plyer's home yesterday," Tina said, "I saw a black Mercedes SUV leaving. It had a Georgia license plate. I think there were two men inside, but I'm not sure."

Wilmot looked at Tina. "What time did you see these men leave the Plyer home, Mrs. Spear?"

"It had to be between eight and eight twenty in the morning."

"What's the name of the officer working your assault case?"

"Officer Chamliss."

"We'll notify Chamliss and check his report for the timeline we're talking about."

Dr. Lansing came up to the sitting trio. "There you are. Mrs. Spear, we need to keep your husband overnight and maybe for another day, depending on what the X-rays and CT scan tell us. He's also going to require dental surgery in the near future, after we repair his jaw."

Tina shut her eyes. "I understand, Doctor. May I see him now?"

Wilmot stood, as did his colleague, who said, "You should go be with your husband. If there is anything else we need from you, we have your cell."

"Thank you, Officers," she whispered as she turned quickly to follow Lansing back to room 8.

The next day, Walter was moved to a private room after his X-rays and the CT scan. The good news was that his arm likely would not require surgery. The not-so-good news involved the CT scan; while showing no internal organ injuries, it confirmed a severe concussion where his head had been sutured up like a football. There had been no brain bleed, but additional observation and hospital rest was necessary, and the jaw surgery had to be scheduled.

After spending the night, Tina left Walter in the hands of his medical team and went home shortly after 6:00 a.m. to shower.

At her office Tina called a quick meeting of the staff to let them know what had happened, and that Spearhead was going to redouble their efforts to win the big clients in the pipeline and complete all outstanding projects on time and on budget. The hum of work rose throughout the morning.

Just before noon, her cell phone rang. When Tina saw Detective Tillyard's name on the screen, a feeling like double tequila on an empty stomach overcame her. "Oh my God," she said, to answer the phone. "Is this Detective Tillyard? So soon after our last conversation?"

"Are you all right, Ms. Spear? You sound a little off this morning."

"Oh, Detective, if you only knew! If you stay on the line for a few minutes, maybe you will know." She put her phone on speaker, elbows on the desk, and her chin in her hands. "You called me, so you go first."

"Jacob Plyer is in the hospital with an oxycodone overdose. He's in a coma."

31

Another One Gone

PAST

Charity's marriage to Cole Hart lasted nineteen months. Cole, predictably, proved less pliant in marriage than the eleven years leading up to it. He believed the institution afforded him more privileges with his wife than she was willing to accommodate. Access to Charity's finances, for example, and a say-so not only in how she ran her business, but how she ran her life. They fought about everything. He took as much time as he could to move out.

Since Jacob started high school, he came home from class or football practice in the late afternoon. If either Charity or Cole was home, he put his backpack on his bed and took Ricky out in his stroller. If only Ruthann was home, he'd check with his grandmother on Ricky's status and play with him for a few minutes before dinner.

Cole and Charity were rarely home after five o'clock. Jacob didn't know if it was because happy hour had started somewhere or if the waning daylight made it safer for the two of them to venture outdoors. Jacob called them vampires.

For a while, care for Ricky was a free-for-all.

"Ma, where you goin'? Ricky's crying. He needs changin' or food or somethin'."

"Now, you listen closely, Jacob. I've been takin' care of Ricky the whole time you been at school and working my business at the same time. We all gotta pitch in here. This means you, Mister. I'm still workin' most evenings, so you do as you're told here and watch out for the baby."

"Me? Why's it gotta be me? Gramma's gotta help too, right?"

"Your gramma is working with me and hasn't got much time to look after the baby at night. You settle in on your homework and look after the boy. Shouldn't be too hard. You share the room with him and all."

Ruthann was no help. "I had one child too many as it was," she told Jacob.

Charity gave her a cold stare.

"I ain't of a mind to be a mother all over again," Ruthann said. "But don't you worry, we'll manage all right."

"See there? Your gramma's staying right here if you need help," Charity said. Whenever she said this, which was often, she gave herself permission to leave the house.

Jacob was as grateful as he could be for his time alone and with Ricky. But a baby wasn't real company, not a friend to hang out with or a fellow lineman on the football team. The baby needed watching and changing, feeding, and bathing. No way could he keep this up. And yet he did. Even after Cole moved out of the house, Charity was still out most nights, and Jacob could not allow Ricky to struggle in fouled diapers or wail incessantly when hunger or isolation overwhelmed him.

Ricky took his first steps when he and Jacob were alone in their room. Ricky was fourteen months old.

Jacob, proud as any dad, announced to the household, "Ricky's walking'!"

He took the infant out of the bedroom and into the living room, perched Ricky on his legs, and rolled a ball for him as if he was a pet. Ricky gleefully went after it and plopped down as he reached the toy. Charity and Ruthann glanced up from their seats at the table in the kitchen.

"Come on, now. Get up and come back over here," Jacob told him.

Ricky waddled around on all fours and made it up onto two feet. He started his return to Jacob, only to fall on his face and begin to cry.

"Figures," said Charity. "Boy should be up and on his own by now, gettin' into mischief. Maybe it's a blessing he's a slow learner."

"Hell, you say!" Jacob's anger rose. "He's only a little over a year old. He's no slow learner!"

"If you say so," Ruthann said. "Your mamma was walkin' before she was a year old."

Jacob picked up Ricky, checking him for signs of injury as the baby continued to cry.

"He'll be fine," Charity said. "Just put him back in his crib." She rose from her seat and rattled her car keys as she opened the refrigerator. "Ruthann, you wanna get some milk and bread and maybe some peanut butter or somethin'. Could probably use some sandwich meat."

"Jesus, girl! You got the fuckin' car! I gotta take a taxi. You pick up the damn food, why don't ya!"

Another argument. The rhythm of life. By the time Ricky was four, there wasn't a civil conversation to be heard in the Plyer household. Charity and Ruthann hardly got along better than Jacob and his mother. The daily grind of school, looking after Ricky, and the twice weekly errands on which Charity sent Jacob felt like cannon volleys chipping away at his fortress. The regular and frequent cries of want from Ricky forced the threesome out of their isolation and into paroxysms of accusation, defiance, and dread.

The year after Jacob graduated from high school, Charity was arrested for possession with intent to sell, and prostitution. Ricky was five years old. Charity lied, saying she had consensual sex with the man, who was apparently a drug dealer on a police task force watch list. She was not collecting money for sex. She was collecting a debt the man owed her. It took a well-placed lawyer three months to negotiate her sentence down from five years to three. Charity never admitted a shred of wrongdoing.

It was immaterial to Jacob whether his mother was guilty of the crimes. She was going away to prison. Away. He would no longer be forced to suffer the coercion, the berating, or the indifference from her. And he could leave.

The day after his mother was sentenced and remanded, Jacob enlisted in the army. When he returned home from filling out the forms, Jacob found Ricky alone, playing in the dirt outside the porch. Jacob shook his head and looked down. Ricky squirmed and screamed when his brother picked him up.

"Ricky, you stop this. You're a damn mess. Gotta get you cleaned up." Jacob walked into the house and called, "Ruthann! Can you help me here? Ricky's a dirt pile mess!" His voice reverberated through the empty house. He called again as he searched for his grandmother, with Ricky still fidgeting in his arms. "Jesus H. Christ. I can't fuckin' believe Ruthann would up and leave you by your lonesome. Where'd your gramma go?" He put Ricky down.

"I dunno," the boy mumbled. "I wanna go back outside."

The elder brother scratched his head. "Not now. We gotta get you cleaned up. It's time for supper."

Ricky turned and ran for the porch, Jacob fast on him. He caught Ricky as he got to the door and picked him up again.

This time Ricky started hitting Jacob, screaming at him, "Let me go! Fuck you! Let me down."

Jacob put Ricky down and smacked him openhanded on the side of his head. The boy shrieked and erupted into tears, but he kept squirming. Jacob hit him again.

"Damn you, Ricky. You stop. Ya hear me? You gotta wash up, and we have to find Gramma. I don't want no more lip."

Ricky tried to pull away, but when Jacob raised his hand again Ricky stopped and sat on the floor, sobbing. Jacob let go of Ricky and put both hands to his head, walking around in a circle.

"Shit, shit! Ricky, I'm sorry. Damn it!" He bent down to pick up his brother.

Ricky fought Jacob again, but with less vigor.

"Come on, boy. Look at me. Let's get you cleaned up and get something to eat. Aw' right?"

Ricky looked away.

Jacob shook his head. "I can't take this, Ricky. I just can't."

After he washed and dressed his little brother, who fought him every second, he took Ricky into the kitchen to forage for supper.

* * *

One week before his call-up for duty, Jacob went with Ruthann to visit Charity, who was a year into her sentence. They met her around a small table in a secure common area at the Lowell Penitentiary in Ocala. Four guards were stationed along the perimeter. No one else was in the room.

"Neither a' you two looks worse for wear. Ruthann, you bring cigarettes?"

"Course, I did. They's with the guard. You'll get half of them, I expect."

Charity sniffed. "Not even. Jacob, what you up to? First time you visit your momma in hoosegow. Where's your brother?"

"Left him in the car. He didn't want to come in."

"Says you," Charity told him.

Jacob looked away and shook his head. Turning back to his mother, he said, "I came to tell you to your face, I'm leavin'. I've joined the army and I've been called to duty next week."

Charity looked at Jacob without expression for a few seconds, and then burst into a cackle. "What, you gonna follow your walk-away daddy? Ha. You ungrateful shit for a son. You abandon me because, why? I put a roof over your head, money in your pocket. Just when I need you to carry on with your gramma, you up and leave."

"Why do you care? You can't control me no more, Ma. I'm done with runnin'—doin' your business and taking care of Ricky like he's a damn orphan. Two of you ain't half a' one mamma to that boy." He looked at Ruthann.

"Somebody had to keep the business runnin'," Ruthann said. "We coulda' been ripped off a dozen times, but we stayed on track. We did 'cause of me."

"And me, Ruthann," Charity said.

"Oh, you some brain, aw right, getting yourself locked up 'cause you got careless—again."

"Jesus Christ, you two!" Jacob shouted in a whisper. "Stop it. I'm leavin', and Gramma's gonna officially adopt Ricky, right?"

"It's near as done, Charity," Ruthann replied. "Welfare will pay decent, so I can keep him outta foster care, but it won't be easy."

Charity sniffed. "Don't much matter. But at least you can keep him till he starts earnin' his keep. You know, takin' over the runs from this turncoat son here." Charity leveled her eyes at Jacob.

"Ain't you somethin'," he said. "Gotta boy growin' into a man, and all you can think about is how he's gonna serve you." Jacob pushed his chair away from the table. "I said what I came here to say. Goodbye, Ma." Jacob walked over to the exit. The guard buzzed him through to the next security area and he was out.

Ruthann bent forward to speak quietly to her daughter. "This place is the shits, girl. You gotta stay outta trouble and get home soon as you can."

"I got only one more year if I play this right," Charity said.

"From what I see, this here's a real sad life. When you get out, you gotta do better."

"I gotta do smarter, Ruthann. And I'm startin' in here, learnin' what I can from these wacked bitches. You stay the course, and I'll be home soon as I can."

"Place makes me sick to my stomach." She stood and stepped back.

Charity didn't move.

"I'll be on my way now."

When Ruthann left the prison, Jacob was in front of Charity's old Pontiac, kneeling in front of Ricky, with both hands on the boy's shoulders. Ricky shook his head as he punched Jacob's hands. Jacob got up when he saw Ruthann walking toward them. Ricky turned and pounded his fists on the car and then pulled at the door until it opened. He climbed in and slammed the door.

"Boy's learnin' fast, life ain't no picnic," she said as she opened the passenger door.

"Stop, Gramma. Okay. Ricky'll understand someday." In the driver's seat, Jacob turned around to look at his brother. His face was streaked with tears and his mouth was bunched up like an airless balloon. "You'll be fine with your gramma, Ricky. She'll take good care of you."

"Fuck you both," the seven-year-old said with conviction.

32

A Trickle of Truth

The day before he called Tina Spear, Devon Tillyard was at the point in his investigation where he had no choice but to confront Sheriff Caldwell. Repeated questioning of the coroner had provided the same answer each time: "Talk to the boss."

"Don't you get it?" Tillyard said, frustrated that the coroner wasn't more in line with the detective's thinking. "The sheriff ordering something doesn't relieve you of your responsibility to the public. This is why we have internal checks on all procedures. How the hell else would I be charged to investigate this irregularity even though, as you say, it was ordered by the sheriff?"

"In that case," the coroner said, "you would be better served to investigate the sheriff himself." A smile like a worm crept across the coroner's lips.

Taking two steps straight at the man, Tillyard stared into his eyes. "You aren't off the hook, Landers. Following orders is a coward's excuse for criminal behavior. I'll be back for you."

"That will be all for today, Detective. Please come back when you have direction from the sheriff and not before."

The two men turned their backs to each other and paced off. Tillyard tried to slam the door on his way out of the morgue, but the hydraulic door closer resisted his force and shut the door with measured calm. He shook off his frustration and walked back to the department.

Caldwell wasn't in the building. Tillyard let out a breath. Works for me, he said to himself. He had a new priority case to occupy his investigative instincts. It was a local drug bust that had happened the previous night in Halfway, a town ten miles southeast of Dahlonega.

The man in custody was a twenty-four-year-old motorcycle repairman, Cletus Birks. He had enlisted right out of high school and served four years as an army private. He and his eighteen-year-old girlfriend had been found with at least two thousand oxy pills and a case of two hundred fentanyl patches. Where in God's name could a young kid in Halfway, Georgia, get his hands on $50,000 of opioids?

Though Tillyard worked alone most of the time, when interrogations were necessary, another detective assisted. He was sixteen-year Dahlonega police force veteran Lance Warren, whose caring manner put people at ease instantly.

It didn't take the two detectives long, tag-teaming Birks and his girlfriend separately, to get a sense of their business. The drug-dealing duo made a rookie mistake by selling to the son of a local lumber magnate. As soon as the transaction was completed, the buyer decided to try the products. Forty minutes later, on a perfect sun-drenched afternoon, the prodigal scion had managed to launch his new Corvette into Lake Lanier from the Lumpkin County boat ramp—the physics of which the police were still trying to understand. Saved from drowning by two local boat owners who had witnessed the airborne sports car, Captain Corvette, as the police named him, was eager to save himself, not just from jail time, but from Daddy's wrath. The police recovered the car and found forty-eight oxycodone pills preserved in a plastic bag in the glove box. Tillyard knew he had a link to a much bigger operation.

Tillyard let Cletus sit alone in interrogation for over an hour before he went into the room and asked about the drugs.

"I swear on my papa's grave, I have no idea where them pills come from."

"How did you get them?" Tillyard asked.

"You see here, Officer, we get delivery from a kid. Comes about every month or so."

"What kid? Where does he come from?"

"It ain't never seen the same kid twice. Sometimes it's a girl."

"How do you connect?"

Cletus shook his head. "I could ... some bad people don't want me divulgin' any ... you know ... information. It might go bad for me and Colleen."

"Seems it's already gone bad, Cletus. Question is, how much worse will it get?"

Cletus hit the sides of his head with both fists and stood up. He walked around the room and talked to himself for a few moments. He addressed the detective. "Say I tell you what you want to know. How does that help me and Colleen?"

Leaning against the wall with crossed arms, Tillyard seemed disinterested. "Better you look at what happens to you and Colleen if you don't. You got busted with major drugs and your bail is going to be high, like $100,000 high. Are you going to post this bond? You're a small fish in a small pond, Cletus. No one's coming to get you out. No big-time lawyer is going to defend you. You don't need to tell me any more than what we already know to put you away for a long time."

Cletus wiped his eyes and sniffled. "You gotta do something for us, Detective. Please."

Tillyard moved to the table and put both his hands on it. "Look, dumbass, you got caught breakin' bad. Got that? You are going down." He let it sink in before he continued. "Here's what I can do. If you tell us everything you know, we'll say you were cooperative, and ask the judge to take that into account. Also, I'll stress you're a first-time offender, et cetera. What the judge will do, I can't say. But this is the best you're going to get. You did this to yourself. You are going to take responsibility, like it or not."

Birks sat down with a thump and, head in hands, nodded. "Okay. I'll wait till the public defender gets here. When he does, I'll tell you what I know."

The public defender, a sturdy woman in her late twenties, arrived within the hour and reviewed the situation with her client. The deal was struck, and information flowed from Birks.

Whenever Birks wanted a new supply, he texted a cell phone number and a week later a shipment arrived. Like the couriers, the cell number to place an order changed constantly, coming to him as a text each week.

Very sly, very whack-a-mole.

"How did you start dealing, Cletus?"

"Buddy of mine in the army contacted me after I got out. I needed the money, so I said sure, send me a text. That's how it started. So fuckin' simple."

"And stupid. What's your friend's name and how do we find him?"

Cletus let out a slight laugh and looked straight at Tillyard. "Ronny Shimkus. And you can find Ronny buried near his parents' home in Fayetteville, North Carolina."

"We'll check your story out. Where was he stationed when he contacted you?"

"Fort McPherson."

Tillyard stopped breathing for a split second and looked at a disconsolate Birks. Fort McPherson is where Jacob and

Carmen Navarro Plyer had been stationed. Suddenly he was collecting his share of dots.

Later in the day when Sheriff Caldwell ambled into the office, he greeted each officer and asked for an update.

When he came to Detective Tillyard, he shook his head and smiled. "Let's get this done and into the light of day, Detective. Come and have a seat in my office. I'll be just a sec."

Tillyard brought a file folder into his boss's office, where he stood for five minutes watching RC work the pit. Who was this man whose size alone would make most men gulp for air? In the year he'd been a detective in Dahlonega, only twice had he heard RC raise his voice. Of course, he had no reason to. Officers and admin staff alike all wanted to please RC. He was more like a tribal chief than a county sheriff.

When RC sat down in his chair he was practically as tall as Tillyard was, standing. RC put out his palm and motioned for his detective to sit, which he did while not taking his eyes from his chief.

"You've been trying to see me for a day or two now. What's on your mind?"

Tillyard cleared his throat. "Boss, this issue with the Plyer kid's suicide? You messed up. I can't say it any plainer or nicer. You ordered the coroner to speed up the autopsy and the report. And you ordered the cremation of the boy's body in about half the time procedures demand. And now, I've got serious questions about how he died. Hard-to-answer questions. Head-shaking questions."

"Like what, Detective?"

"Like, why the report says the powder burns on his head were consistent with a gun held two to three feet away. Not zero to three inches, like you'd expect from a suicide. Like, why no one checked Jacob Plyer for powder burns. It's a mess, Chief, and you know it."

RC pushed back from his desk and turned his head away. He said, "I appreciate you got stuck on this fool's errand, Detective. I don't mean you're a fool. I had the strings on this one way before you started here. It's such a damn shame. Jacob loved the boy, Richard. But here's something maybe you know from your homework, or maybe you don't. Jacob Plyer is my natural son. His mama and I were together for about three years. Back in the late '80s." He turned his head back to face Tillyard, who nodded.

"I thought so," RC continued. "You knew. Good for you. It's not common knowledge around here, but there's no need for it to be secret. Hell, with this coroner report business, my relationship with Jacob will be out in the open in a few days." He shook his head as he continued. "I had no desire whatsoever to let you just swing in the wind for your investigation. But you do have to understand. Jacob, he's not right in the head. Those war wounds don't heal like regular wounds."

"Is that really why you did this, Boss? You went to the trouble of burying this report to spare your son the pain of his little brother's suicide? That's not the Sheriff Caldwell I know. You would have been there to comfort your son and you would have let the due course of the coroner's inquiry play out. Jacob was going to have a rough time with this, no matter how long or short the report took."

"You're probably right. I made a bad decision and it's going to cost me. But what's done is done. All I can do now is take responsibility for it, let the mayor and the county commissioners know, and see what they want to do next."

"With all due respect, I still think you're holding back something material about the boy's suicide. Something Jacob or Carmen told you. Something that scares you. You're thinking maybe it's not material, that it won't change the result. Could be that's true. But keeping it suppressed won't get justice for anyone."

"Don't let your instincts force you onto a path you can't travel, Detective." RC stared at Tillyard with sad, stern eyes. "Like I said, I'm sorry for this mess. I was trying to keep the impact off Jacob. But I screwed up and I'll take my lumps."

Tillyard tried hard to understand his commanding officer. Something else must be pushing him. Did he feel guilt for leaving his son to grow up without him?

"Did you know he had a half-brother, Ricky?"

"Of course I did. And I'll tell you something else. I'm no fan of Ruthann Plyer, but at least she wasn't whoring to pay for rent or dope, like her daughter." RC shook his head. "When I heard Ricky had gone off to the Department of Juvenile Justice, I was sure it was about the best thing could have happened to the boy."

"What happened to Ricky Plyer, Boss?"

RC stood, rolling back his chair. The signal was as clear as plate glass.

"Time's up. You've got all the sordid details you need to write your report and make your case. I got no insight into Ricky's state of mind. Didn't know the boy. You've even got a confession from your sheriff. File your damn report and I'll take the fall. That's all, Detective."

But was it all? He had cleared up the anomalies with a statement from RC. His report would now go to Internal Affairs. Still, Tillyard had a sense, like a song he hated but couldn't dislodge from his head, that the real story how Ricky Plyer died was still untold. He would have to call Tina Spear tomorrow and let her know her mentee's suicide case was closed.

As he ambled back to his desk, Tillyard felt something else poke at his whirring thoughts. This business of Birks getting drug deliveries from kids seemed familiar. Without tidying up the report on Ricky's suicide, he was compelled to look harder at the Birks case. The burner phones were key. He went downstairs to the evidence locker and checked out Birks's cell phone. He brought it to one of the lab techs and asked her to find all the incoming and outgoing phone numbers of the last three months and identify which were burner phones.

Two hours later the list was complete. Tillyard studied it and shook his head. Seven of the twelve phones had been purchased in Florida, between Jacksonville and Hastings. A neat circle right around St. Augustine. He scratched his head and thought about Tina Spear. His thoughts moved to Ruthann Plyer and her drug dealing.

The next morning, Tillyard hadn't stepped more than a few feet toward his desk when a 911 call and subsequent alert came through the department. Jacob Plyer had suffered an overdose of painkillers and was not responsive. The 911 response team was en route and the chief had been alerted. Grabbing his notepad, Tillyard checked for his badge, then his gun, and left for the North Georgia Medical Center.

RC was already at the bedside of his son, as was Carmen Plyer. When the sheriff asked Tillyard why he was there, the detective answered with s stutter.

"I'm working on … on the opioid drug case … from the floating 'Vette in Lake Lanier. Making sure no dots connect."

RC looked at Tillyard as if the detective had lost an eyeball. Tillyard got the message.

"I'll check in with you later, Boss. I need to make a phone call." From the hospital lobby, he phoned Tina Spear.

33

Trying to Learn

Charity was released from prison in June of 2010 and moved back with Ruthann and Ricky. A private transport van left Charity off at the top of the driveway, which she strutted down like a returned monarch. She didn't bother to knock before entering the porch. Her mother sauntered out and greeted her liberated daughter, holding the door for her and taking the one travel bag Charity carried.

"Well, ain't you a sight!" Ruthann told her daughter.

"Yeah, I must be. Though I spent a lotta' time at the gym tryin' to keep these tits from saggin'. No makeup in prison, you know."

"Hmm. Come on in. Your room's waitin' for you."

"Smells like pot, fried okra, and laundry. Can you at least open a window or something?"

"Not here two minutes and you want to change shit around. How about you get settled and we'll get something to eat."

Charity took it all in, trying to see what, if anything, about the house was different from when she'd left three years ago. "Nothin's changed much, has it? You ain't spent much of the money on anything, have you?"

"And call down the eyes of the government, the cops? I don't think so. I kept your car fixed up nice, and Ricky's got decent clothes."

"Ricky? Yeah, where is the little tyke?"

"He's no tyke. They got him spendin' time with some school shrink two afternoons a week. Seems he isn't too good at socializing with the other kids. Not performin' up to his aptitude, 'parently."

Charity said. "Should make him a fine runner for the business. The less he socializes, the better."

Ricky was dropped off at home an hour later. Charity and Ruthann sat at the kitchen table.

Ruthann said, "Your ma's back, Ricky."

Neither woman actually looked at the boy. Ricky glanced at the table as he walked on toward the back of the house.

"Come on over here, son, and greet your mother. It's not like I wanted to be away this long."

Ricky stopped. "You back for good?"

"Umm, maybe. It all depends, doesn't it?"

"On what?"

"Lots a' things. Your gramma and me got a business to build. I'm not sure this has-been shrimping village is the right place for us."

Ruthann looked at her daughter as if she had just spoken Latin. "Huh?" she said.

"I think I need to be in Atlanta."

"Damn, girl, you just got home after three years in prison, and you want to move first thing, lickety-split?"

"I learned a few things while I was away, Ruthann. And I made some contacts. Atlanta is definitely where I need to be."

Ricky turned to go into his room. "Figures," he said into the hallway.

"You hear from Jacob while you was in?" Ruthann asked her daughter.

"Nah. Don't think he wants much to do with me. His life."

"He was in I-raq for more than a year. Came through here two months ago. He's been transferred to Fort McPherson. You know, right there near Atlanta."

"No shit. I will definitely pay my son a visit. First, I gotta check out some options for gettin' and movin' some product. Let's see what you got here."

It took the next three hours for the two women to go over the money, the acquisitions, and the distribution status for the business. Ricky walked through the kitchen at one point, grabbed some water, and made himself a peanut butter sandwich.

He walked out into the yard, eating like a starved lion cub, kicking at plastic buckets, old bales of newspapers, and other debris cluttering the driveway. When he reached Charity's car, he got in on the driver's side and pulled the rearview mirror toward him. There was a smear of peanut butter across his chin, which he wiped away. I look like Jacob, he thought. I sure wish he was here.

He remembered his brother's last visit, listening to his tales of war zone deployment, boredom, and fear stronger than hate. Ricky pounded on the steering wheel, eventually resting his arms and head on it and sobbing. As quickly, he lifted his head and left the car, walking with purpose into the shed in the rear of the yard. An old mattress was propped against a side wall. Without slowing down, Ricky went over to the mattress and hit it with all his might. Then again, and again. He raised his fists and kicked the mattress until he was out of breath. Then he started again, the sweat pouring off his face and arms. When he was spent, he sat down hard on the dirt floor. He wished for Jacob to be back home, teaching him self-defense, going fishing, or just sitting and talking about stuff. The more often Ricky saw Jacob, the larger grew the hole left by his brother's absence.

Later in the year, Charity decided to use Ricky as a runner to a nearby park. He rode his bike and put the delivery in his school backpack. Without telling him, Charity followed a few minutes behind, needing to be certain Ricky could pull off the exchange. The buyer was in his late twenties and a regular customer. At the far end of the last tennis court, Ricky rounded the high chain-link fence and saw a man with thin hair and a small backpack of his own. Ricky came up to him.

"You gotta number?" he asked.

"Fourteen-o-seven," the man replied.

Ricky reach into his backpack and pulled out a plastic shopping bag, which he held at his side. The man took a step toward him, and Ricky took a step back. The man nodded and pulled out a wad of newspaper tied with rubber bands. Ricky put his bag on the ground and walked in a circle to where the man had placed his package on the ground. Each recovered the other's delivery and walked away.

Ricky got on his bike and started out of the park. Before he could get onto the main road, his mother pulled her car out of a parking space and blocked his way.

She got out of the car. "Gimme that pack, Ricky. Lemme see if it all went down like it's 'sposed to."

Ricky handed his mom the backpack. She took it into her car and examined the contents. When she was satisfied, she started up the car and started driving out of the park.

"You come straight home now," she yelled as her accelerating tires flung pebbles and dust into the air.

Ricky stood straight and still as he watched her drive away.

Weeks later, Ricky arrived home from school with a report card and a letter for Ruthann. The two women were arguing about something when he walked in and stood at the threshold. They stopped what they were doing and stared at him.

Ruthann said, "Well? You got nothin' better to do than to stand in the doorway? Off to your room. Go!"

Ricky pulled out the package from the school and handed it to Ruthann.

"What's this all 'bout?" she asked.

Ricky shrugged. Charity went over to her mother's shoulder and looked on as Ruthann opened it.

There were two documents. One was a report card and the other was a letter from the school psychologist. The two women looked at each document, grabbing one or the other, like seagulls fighting over a beached fish. Charity clutched the report card and turned away from Ruthann. Holding it high, at arm's length, she read.

"Looks here like you actually did some learnin'. You got two As, two Bs, and an F. The other side here, it tells a different story, heh, Ricky? You don't get along so good with your classmates, do you?" She handed the letter to her mother.

"What do you care? They're mostly assholes, anyway."

Ruthann read the letter from the psychologist. When she finished, she looked at Ricky. "You're still fightin' in school and sassin' your teacher. Says here you need your momma and me to spend more time teachin' you right from wrong. Teach you self-control. Ha!"

"Let me see that," Charity snarled, snatching the letter from Ruthann. She read it again and then looked over at Ricky. "Goddamn it, boy. You got brains! Why you have to be so ornery. Nobody likes you, do they?"

"Shut up!" Ricky said and started to walk toward his room.

Charity pulled him around and slapped his face. "You don't talk to your momma like that, you hear?"

"You ain't my momma," Ricky screamed. He pulled away from Charity. "I ain't got no momma, and no daddy neither." He ran to his bedroom and slammed the door.

After a short silence, mother and daughter resumed their conversation.

"See? You gotta take him with you to Atlanta. End 'o story," Ruthann said.

"Bullshit. You got legal custody. You keep the kid and the welfare. I gotta work on the trade. Can't have no kid to worry about."

"Jacob's in Atlanta now. Might be good for the boy."

"Jacob's in the military. He ain't gonna find time, make time. He loves the boy, all right, but he's got his own shit. Besides, I may need him back in the business."

Ruthann took her time to say, "What? Like you gotta chance gettin' him to agree."

"You just worry about the local trade and keep the boy workin'. I need to get to Georgia and consolidate our suppliers. Build up the distribution."

"You some drug lord now, all business and know-how? Girl, you're gonna get swallowed up again, you get too big for them honey britches o' yours."

"You worry about yourself and the business here."

34

Surrogates Falling

PRESENT

It was not a conversation Charity Plyer would have relished in the best circumstances. And fuck knows, these were as far as one could get from the best of circumstances. RC was phoning her from the North Georgia Medical Center Hospital Emergency Room. She strolled through the heavy plexiglass doors with the imbedded iron X. A prison guard took her to the incoming phone room, where she leaned against the wall and covered the phone's speaker with both hands.

"This had better not be fuckin' bad news, RC. I mean it."

"Shut up for one goddamn minute, Chare! Listen to me. Jacob has just been brought to the hospital in an oxy overdose coma. They're pretty sure he'll pull through, but there's no doubt Carmen saved his life. At least for the moment."

"Nurse Carmen knows her shit, she does. Damn it all! This has nothing to do with you coming down here on Tuesday, RC, and testifying at my hearing, right? We have an agreement."

"You don't get it, do you? Our son—the one remaining son of yours—is fighting for his life in a hospital bed, having his stomach pumped, hooked up to an IV, and barely breathing."

"Look, you've never understood how I love, but God strike me dead if I don't love our son. Don't you even think for one fucking minute I don't care. But do tell me, what can I do, trapped in this rat hole of a prison? It ain't like I can get a leave of absence. And if I was out and up in Dahlonega, would you help me to see my son?"

"It's me you're talking to, Charity. I know all Jacob is to you and what he isn't. I'm telling you about Jacob because maybe, just maybe, there's a shred of motherhood that actually cares and loves the man. And I need to let you know if anything worse happens to Jacob, our deal for me to testify is off."

"Now that's just fucked up, RC. You testifying for me is in everybody's best interests, and Jacob's, especially. Me moving in with him, Carmen, and the baby, is gonna make me a kinder, gentler person than the old messed-up criminal you wanted to marry twenty-five years ago. Ain't you glad I turned you down back in the day?"

"Sure, Chare. I'll always be grateful to you for screwin' Bart Epson right after I asked you to marry me."

She heard RC spit onto the phone, followed by static as he likely cleaned the speaker with his sleeve.

"Look, I'm calling to let you know Jacob's condition. It shouldn't affect my driving down in five days to testify at your hearing. But if Jacob takes a turn for the worse, things could change. They could. Simple as that. Jacob's my priority. It sure as hell ain't you."

Charity's face turned red as she fought down a desire to hit the wall with the phone receiver. "I understand," she said. "I can't get the hearing postponed or nuthin'." As she said this, another thought struck her. "Maybe this could speed it up. I mean, when a mother's son is in a bad health condition, couldn't, you know, the process move the hearing up a few days? A few days early. For humanitarian reasons."

Charity's smile at this thought bled into her voice. Her mirth was lost on RC.

"I can't do anything 'bout the hearing."

But I'll bet I can, Charity thought. "Thank you for calling me and telling me about Jacob. You need to let me know as soon as anything changes. I wish I was there already, by his side. Say it, RC. Say you'll call me when Jacob's condition—"

RC hung up the phone.

It was worth a shot. Charity walked up to the guard and said, "Officer, I just learned my son has had a horrible accident and is fighting for his life in a hospital in Dahlonega. May I please speak to the warden right away?"

"Warden won't be in until ten tomorrow morning."

"I understand. Then, please, may I speak to the deputy warden? It may actually be a matter of life or death, Officer. I'm not joking. Listen to the recording if you think I'm lying."

The guard spoke into her walkie-talkie to ask if she could bring prisoner Plyer to see the deputy warden. Charity used the time to consider how to word her "proposal."

The deputy warden agreed to give Charity five minutes.

She stood, facing the big desk in the small office of the woman who was second in command at the prison. Charity spoke calmly with a quiver in her voice.

The deputy warden pursed her lips and nodded. "I'm sorry about your son, Miss Plyer. But your hearing is early next week. There's no way we can reschedule earlier."

"I … I understand. I had to try, you know. My son could die, and I wouldn't have even been able to say goodbye." She sniffed back tears as she turned to leave.

"But what I might be able to do is accelerate your release date, *if* you receive parole."

Charity brightened a bit. "So if the hearing goes in my favor, instead of a release date, say, in two weeks or a month, I might be able to leave sooner? I can't tell you how important it could be, Warden. Thank you so much."

"No promises. We'll check out your request. The warden will let you know on the day of your hearing—again, if you are paroled."

"Yes, ma'am. I understand." Charity looked up at the ceiling as she left the deputy's office, put her palms together, and raised them toward the sky. God loves a basket case, right? Shit could turn around if You make this happen, God. I swear.

Deciding it was time to get back in touch with her mother, Charity recalled the conversation of two days ago, when it took her ten phone calls spaced over thirteen hours to reach Ruthann. Ruthann had just been released from the hospital after the beating and was nursing her wounds. As she had listened to her mother curse her assailant, Charity couldn't believe the soft, privileged woman who had visited her in prison was the same person who had put Ruthann in the hospital.

"I cannot stand that woman," Ruthann complained to Charity. "Never thought she'd go all psycho on me. Fuckin' bitch."

"Did you let Virgil know?" Charity had asked.

"Course, I did. Called him from the hospital. Had no choice. I—"

"Stop talking, Ruthann. So long as everything is all normal, we're good. You awright?"

"Hell no, I ain't awright! You think I'm all healed in a day?"

"Okay, calm down. We've got work to do. My hearing is next Tuesday. Are you going to be here?"

"I don't know. Should be in better shape after the weekend, so's long as I can rest up. I need transportation, though. I ain't takin' no bus, in my condition. And it's too damn far for a taxi."

"Call Dodd or Virgil and see if they can help."

"Virgil ain't gonna risk showin' up at your parole hearing."

"I'm not asking him or Dodd to show up. Just to see if they can get you here. A mother's testimony at her daughter's parole hearing will be a good ... I need you here."

Ruthann grumbled some more, said she'd look into it, and hung up.

Now, two days later, inspiration again visited Charity. Using her one last phone privilege for the week, she phoned her mother. Ruthann picked up after the fourth ring.

"You any better today, Ruthann? Them bruises fading and all?"

"Hell! It's the other way round. My face still looks like I ran into a hornet's nest. And my back is sore all the time. Tina Spear's goin' pay for my chiro-practioneer, for sure."

"Were you able to get a ride up here Tuesday?"

"No, no. Nothin'."

"I want you to consider something."

"I ain't gonna like it, am I?"

"Just shut up and don't think like that. Open your head and hear me out."

"I'm listenin'."

"Suppose you were to ask Mrs. Spear to drive you up here?"

"Now I know you jus' fuckin' with me. Unless you are a one hundred percent mean, ungrateful bitch of a daughter."

"The Spear woman owes you, right? I'll bet you she's all guilt ridden and feeling sorry for herself. This is her chance to make it up to you."

"You are outta your little mind if you think I'm gonna get in a car with … with …!"

"Ruthann, you need to calm your ass down. This is a perfect opportunity. RC will be here, and—" She needed to choose her words carefully; the prison had ears. "—it would be good for me, I believe, if a professional woman from Florida, one who worked with my son Ricky, showed up at my hearing. Besides, you making up with her will take some wind outta her sails. She needs Jacob too. She knows she needs to help us out, help Jacob out. You know what I'm saying."

Ruthann was silent for a few seconds, after which she renewed her argument against Charity's suggestion. However, Charity's belief in the exquisiteness of her idea was stronger than her exasperation with her mother. She pressed and pressed again, ending with "I may be able to get out like the same day or a day later 'cause of Jacob. My last remaining son."

"Say what? What about Jacob?"

"Noone told you, heh? Well, looks like my son managed to overdose himself on them painkillers he been takin' for his leg an' all."

"Shit, Charity, is he all right? Is Jacob alive?"

"Yeah. Yeah. I think so. RC called me this mornin' and told me it happened last night. I could be outta this ho— institution next week. You get what I'm telling you? I could start my rehabilitation by helping nurse my son back to health."

Ruthann was working hard to process all this without speaking. She knew as well as Charity that prison phone conversations weren't private.

"You still there, Ruthann?"

"Hush a minute, will you? I'm trying to get my head around all this."

"Don't take too long, I got no more than five minutes left."

"I'll do it. I'll call the Spear woman and get her to take me to Pulaski in three days. But what then?"

"I'm still workin' it all out. Besides, there's lots of moving pieces. First is, I gotta get paroled. Second, I gotta get released. But if we get to that point, I'll be sure there are some options."

"Poor Jacob. I sure wish he hadn't done those pills, Charity."

"Me too, me too. He was such a good son."

"Don't be talkin' 'bout him like he's already gone, like you was in his life an' all!"

"I'm not, I'm not. I don't want Jacob gone. I'm remembering the way it was when it was only him and me. When we were each other's world. Can't ever go back, though, can we?"

"Call me tomorrow night. I'll talk to Spear and hope she's just as crazy as you are."

Charity laughed. "You'll have to call me. And call Virgil. Don't tell him I might be gettin' out early. Let him know I could, umm, use his support later if I'm able to get out."

Ruthann said she would and hung up. Charity had a lot to think about. Jacob in the hospital wasn't good, but she was sure she could turn it into an advantage at her parole hearing. What consumed her more than her son's overdose, more than Ruthann's attendance at her hearing, even more than getting back control of her dealing network, was how to finish the business with Captain Virgil Lapis. Jacob's former commanding officer and Charity's former partner had a reckoning in his future. He just didn't know it yet.

35

In Bed with the Enemy

Every purchase of oxycodone, fentanyl, and crystal meth relied on meticulous planning and a paranoid approach to security. Jacob was the perfect go-between for Charity's supplier at Fort McPherson. It had been easier than Charity thought to leverage Ricky's well-being to secure Jacob's small but critical role in the trade.

As soon as she moved to Atlanta, Charity planned to visit Jacob every week. During her visits Charity greeted soldiers she met along the way, engaged him or her in conversations, and remembered their names. She visited her son regularly at his station between his assignments, giving her all the access she needed to become known to the base security. Every fourth visit Charity carried her large purse through the fort's security gate and to the visitor center, where she met Jacob. Sometimes her gifts for him were clothes, sometimes food, always presented in a box or an opaque container. Whatever the vessel, it always held bundles of cash and a hand-written sales journal. The containers were exchanged for similar, empty vessels from her last visit. Except they weren't empty. Any of them could contain tens of thousands of street-dollar-value opioids in pills or patches. It was all so straightforward, without so much as a surreptitious wink.

After a year of this operation, Jacob received the notice of his second deployment to Iraq. A new method to exchange merchandise and proceeds was needed. The officer who had hatched the lucrative scheme couldn't trust another under his command for the meetings, so in the last gift exchange before Jacob shipped out, Captain Virgil Lapis put a typed message in one of the return containers, stating a time and place for Charity to meet him.

Arriving by taxi to an upscale bar in East Point, not far from the captain's off-base residence, Charity Plyer stepped into the noisy establishment dressed as she hadn't dressed in years: a low-cut navy dress clinging to her figure like cellophane, makeup, a touch of perfume, and three-inch heels in which she had practiced walking for two days. As if on cue, every male head swiveled toward the entrance to glimpse or gawk, depending on whose company they were keeping. She found a seat at the end of the bar, ordered a whiskey soda, and waited for Captain Lapis to find her.

He was a good-looking, solid man, she noted as soon as he walked up and stood next to her. Nothing about him was soft, from his tight haircut to his knife-creased khakis.

"Mrs. Plyer, thank you for meeting me," Captain Lapis said.

"I could hardly refuse, now, could I? With Jacob heading to Iraq, we have a business issue to resolve."

"Very true. Getting our merchandise off-base and into your distribution has become … problematic."

"Oh, I know. Got any ideas?"

Lapis glanced around the bar. "I have a table in a corner in the back. Why don't we discuss this with a little more privacy?"

"I'm all in, sweetie," she said, rising slowly from the bar stool, stretching her torso and legs as she placed her heels on the floor. "Lead on."

Lapis looked behind him a few times to be sure Charity was following close. He needn't have worried.

Having foreseen this dilemma months in advance, she had formed a plan. Two of her runners went to a high school attended by several military sons and daughters. She had asked her boys to identify a few and befriend them. One of them was already dating one of the military daughters and exchanging small tokens of affection. Lapis thought the idea foolish and risky, but Charity assured him her boys were smart, careful, and loyal. When they left the bar, they had worked out most of the details, including a trial run and regular assessment of the risks.

On the curb, before hailing a cab for Charity, Lapis said, "I have to say, Mrs. Plyer, you look a whole lot different tonight than you did on any visit to your son."

"I never saw you there. So, you were watching me, were you?"

"Now, what kind of businessman would I be if I hadn't?"

"And does this …" she paused and outlined her silhouette with her arms and hands, "make you more interested in staying in business with me?"

Lapis took a step closer to Charity, who smiled and looked directly into his eyes. "So long as we are under the radar and making money. Yes, Mrs. Plyer it does."

She grabbed hold of his wrist as she leaned in and kissed him on the cheek, moving quickly to his mouth. Lapis stiffened at first and then let himself be drawn into the long, hungry kiss.

"Let's go to your place," Charity whispered.

"Let's go to yours," Lapis said in her ear.

She rubbed her cheek on his and said, "I'm sure your place is closer." She kissed him again.

Lapis nodded. "I know a place even closer," he said, pointing with his eyes and head to a neon banner down the street. The Forsythe Hotel.

"Your treat," she stated, pulling him by his elbow.

* * *

Over the next year, Lapis noticed a marked decrease in the proceeds coming back to him, even though the volume of drugs going out had continued to go up. He even had to make adjustments in his supply chain to keep below the scrutiny of higher-ups.

During one of his trysts with Charity, Virgil confronted her. He knew she was skimming hundreds and sometimes thousands of dollars. Did she not think he'd notice?

"Virgil, honey. My expenses keep going up. The runners are getting older and expect to be paid better. My mama's business in Florida needs more security, and I can't jeopardize that stream of cash, can I?"

She hadn't even denied it. Lapis sat up in bed. "Are we in business together, or aren't we? You can't just decide on your own to change our arrangement. I'm working with some heavy hitters on the supply side. Foreign nationals who aren't going to accept a haircut on their take. Do you get what I'm saying?"

"Well, your hair's a bit longer than it needs to be, sweetie." She rubbed her palm over his head and mussed his hair.

Lapis jumped out of bed. "Don't you fuck with me, Charity. Starting today, you make sure our original split makes it back to me every time. Now get up and get out of here!"

Without showing a shred of concern, Charity went into the bathroom. Five minutes later she came out dressed and headed for the door. "Keep your eyes on the prize, Captain. You'll be fine." She gently pulled the door closed.

* * *

Less than two months before Jacob's return from Iraq, Charity was hard at work in her rented Decatur bungalow. Noble Dodd was there to take a shipment, by bus, back to St.

Augustine for Ruthann. Two other runners were taking smaller caches of pills north and west. That left half of the latest exchange package to be distributed locally. After all her runners had departed, Charity set herself to make the detailed notes: how much oxy, how much fentanyl, and meth, the prices they should bring, the comparison to last month at this time. She entered the payments to her runners and to her security. It always surprised her how much she enjoyed this part of the job. Here she had the most control.

The shock of the pounding at her door sent a bolt of electricity through as she had rarely experienced. She knew without doubt what was happening.

"Charity Plyer, this is the DeKalb County Police. We have a warrant to search your apartment."

She had prepared for this moment with myriad bank accounts, burner phones, and a go bag; safety protocols for her runners; and an alert to Ruthann and Lapis. What she could not have prepared for was the speed with which she was overtaken. With only enough time to rise from her chair, the police burst through the door. On her dining room table, the police found many dozens of oxycodone and fentanyl pills and patches in plastic bags and vials, eight bundles of cash, and a ledger to manage her business. As she was lowered onto her own floor in handcuffs, the police took photos of it all. A forensic team was part of the raid, ready to sort it out. She'd been set up. There was only one person who had the ability, the balls, and the motivation for such a move. By the time she was placed in the back of the squad car, Charity was already thinking hard how she would take her revenge on Captain Lapis.

36

Something Like Addiction

Speaking to Detective Tillyard was like an out-of-body experience for Tina. After he delivered his news about Jacob, his voice became distant and muffled. Tina's eyes struggled to focus for a few moments. Catching herself slipping away, she fought back. This is no time to be weak, she told herself. "Detective, please. Start again."

Tillyard explained the burner phone information. "I'll be contacting someone at the police department in St. Augustine, but I wanted to be sure you knew. It's possible Ruthann Plyer and others are connected to an opioid trade based in Atlanta."

"Of course." She exhaled and told him about the assault on her husband and the message she'd been sent.

"It doesn't make sense, ma'am. Forgive me, but you're just a private citizen asking about a boy. It may have put you in touch with some bad actors, but why would they take the risk by hurting your husband?"

"I think by putting Ruthann out of commission for two days, I messed up worse than I knew. I can only guess I was getting close to something I never intended to find." Tina took in a stuttered breath and held it before she exhaled. "I thought I needed some truth that Ruthann and her family could unlock for me. But the more I think of it, I just want it all to stop. It has to stop here. My husband was beaten badly for no reason other than my stubbornness. His assailants may be found or not. But I'm done. I need to let Ricky rest. And I need to rest."

"This is not your fault. When a bad person does a bad thing, there's no justification. You should stop feeling guilty. I know words don't mean much in a situation like this." After a long pause, Tillyard went on to tell her how the chief had confessed to ordering everything associated with Ricky's death to speed up. "The chief's going to fall on his sword."

"I know. You told me about the GSR on Ricky's hands but not on his skull, where the bullet entered."

"And the report on the weapon?"

"You haven't mentioned any weapon report to me!"

"Wasn't public information. Now it is. Anyway, the lab confirmed it was the gun that killed Ricky. But they only found Ricky's fingerprints on the barrel, not on the handle. Jacob's fingerprints, not surprising, were everywhere on the gun. Prints on the trigger and most on the handle couldn't be made."

Tina's eyes widened. "Are you going to speak to Carmen Plyer or anyone else about this? What the hell does this mean?"

"The sheriff will make the full report to the commission next week. I'm working other cases now. Honestly, the report isn't conclusive. There are no new theories. Maybe there was a struggle, maybe there was an accident. Maybe neither of those. There's no way to know. As soon as the sheriff submits his report, it's over. For all intents and purposes, Richard Plyer's death will be ruled a suicide."

"I have to get to Dahlonega, Detective. I have to talk to Carmen Plyer. With Jacob in a coma, she's the only one who can possibly know what Ricky's fingerprints on the barrel could mean."

"Look, if you come up here, you're going to be on your own during the day. I'm not working Ricky's case anymore. You understand?"

"I understand. I won't bother you for any favors. At least, I won't plan to." A scorch of electricity burned her skin. She realized leaving Walter alone wasn't such a big concern for her. Did she even love her husband anymore? "Thank you, Detective. Thank you for all you've already done."

Hearing a change in Tina's voice, Tillyard was slow to respond. "Take care of yourself, Ms. Spear. Be careful, and let me know when you get to town." The detective hung up.

Tina was shaking. Ricky's prints were on the barrel, not on the handle. The more she learned, the more she believed Ricky had not taken his own life. But nothing, goddamn it, no evidence of any kind could faithfully reconstruct what had happened. Her emotional seesaw bounced up again.

Tina started planning. She called a Spearhead Design team meeting. Each staff member made a short list of their top three priorities as Tina wrote them down on the whiteboard. Together they determined on which ones Tina would focus on. This exercise buoyed the office like a sea breeze.

"Glad to have you back, boss," said a smiling Dale as the team dispersed.

Tina took a deep breath. "Thank you, Dale," she said. Her face went rigid, her eyes looking at a distance, like a sailor who assesses the far horizon for weather.

Dale nodded quickly, his smile drooped, and he returned to his desk. Tina was again focused elsewhere.

The Spearhead Design office remained buzzing with energy into the early evening. When the light outside faded, Tina told everyone to go home. The perfunctory refusals gave way one by one. At seven o'clock, Tina was alone at her desk. She called the hospital. Walter was out of surgery, still under sedation. All his vitals told the surgical staff he was doing well. Tina could take him home in two days. She started putting away her work, intending to go to the hospital. It was her duty, after all. She had no thought of dinner. Her cell phone rang. It was Ruthann Plyer. What in the world?

"I need to see you in person," Ruthann said.

"Oh, for God's sake, Ruthann, can this please wait until morning?"

"Don't think so. You and I need to talk."

Now? I can't get you to return a phone call for days at a time, and now you have to see me? She said, "I can't come over for at least another hour."

"No need. I'll come to you. Where do you live?"

Not on her worst day did Tina want Ruthann to visit her home. "Come to my office." She gave Ruthann the address.

"I'll be there in thirty minutes." Ruthann hung up, and Tina looked at her phone as though it had betrayed her.

Forty-five minutes later she heard the ding of the elevator. A small figure emerged, slightly bent over, wearing a brace of some sort around the waist. Every time Tina wanted to see Ruthann Plyer over the course of the last three years, the meeting took place only at Ruthann's residence. Now, when the older woman was racked with injuries—injuries Tina had inflicted—Ruthann insisted on coming to Tina. Again, up had become down.

Tina walked into the main work area. "Ruthann. I'm leaving for the hospital soon. My husband has just had surgery. Did you know he was beaten very badly at his office?" Tina stiffened her body and walked in slow, determined steps toward Ruthann. The older woman was looking around the office and saw Tina in her peripheral vision. She turned and put her hands up to fend off her one-time assailant.

"I ain't here to cause you or anybody any problem. I just need to talk to you. You okay if we talk? Don't you go crazy on me again. No, no, no!"

"My husband's jaw is broken, and he has a concussion because of you. I should—"

"What? Hell, no! None of that's 'cause a' me! You should recall darn well I was in the same hospital myself not two days ago. And do you remember why? 'Cause you put me there, that's why! I got nuthin' to do with your husband gettin' hurt."

Tina stopped her march toward her nemesis. It was possible the people for whom Ruthann was working made their own moves without her. But it was irrelevant. She was part of a loathsome criminal enterprise that used violence as easily as most people use a copy machine—violence that had damaged her family, compounding the rubble around her. "Why are you here, Ruthann?"

"I'm here, like I said, to talk to you."

Tina crossed her arms. "So talk."

"You think I'm a bad person." Ruthann lowered her head as she shook it. "I ain't near as bad as you make me to be. My family has been on hard times for generations. Do you, Mrs. Spear, have any idea what it's like? Was you raised in a fallin' down farmhouse with a dirt floor?"

"Is that what you want to talk to me about? Poverty and strife ripping through the generations of your family? Get a grip. Your son Ricky was about to change the trajectory of your whole family, and you didn't even have the decency to attend his memorial service."

"Look. I ain't been a great mother to any a' my kids. I did what I had to jus' to put food on the table, keep a roof over our heads."

Tina remained a totem of indifference.

Ruthann continued. "I come here to ask you a favor."

Tina clapped her hands together and laughed. It startled Ruthann. "A favor of me? Oh, you must think me a world-class fool, Ruthann Plyer." Tina tried to stop laughing but couldn't. Something in her heart had unanchored. Her laughter turned into shrieks. She steadied herself with a big breath as she wiped away tears of a new kind.

Ruthann winced like a struck puppy. "You got no right to make fun a' me like that. I come here in good faith, and God knows I sure didn't want to."

"Take it easy, Ruthann. The fact of you asking me for a favor struck me as absurd."

"Forget it! Jus' forget it!" The older woman turned to leave.

"Hey! You came all this way in a taxi to ask me something. Are you going to leave before you even ask? All I can do is say no, right?"

Squinting to get focus, Ruthann stopped short of the elevator. "My daughter is up for parole on Tuesday, and I want to say a few words on her behalf. You met Charity. She's a bit like me, smarter by half, but she's served a lot a' time. Now with Jacob in the hospital with an OD an' all, Carmen with a baby, Charity's fixin' to go up to Dahlonega and help out. I … I need a ride to Pulaski Prison on Tuesday."

Tina shook her head and put her fingers in her ears. "Did I hear you ask me to help you get to Pulaski Prison in Georgia? Let's see. The prison is about four hours from here. Should cost around three hundred dollars by cab. Of course, you could take Uber or Lyft, but you'd need a credit card for that, wouldn't you?"

"You had no call to put me in the hospital the other day. You owe me."

"Yes, and I'm paying for your hospital visit to the tune of … let's just say it's a lot of money. It's what I owe you and it's what you're getting. You can take a bus or rent a car, or I don't care what. You aren't getting any money from me for a ride."

"Wasn't askin' for money. Was askin' for you to drive me there. RC's goin' be there. Maybe he knows something about Ricky like yur lookin' for. You ain't seen him since you found out he's Jacob's paw, have you?"

Tina thought, Oh my fucking God! Here she was planning to drive up to Dahlonega Monday or Tuesday anyway, and one of the key people with information was going to be at Pulaski Prison. She couldn't decide if this was serendipity or cruelty. Ruthann may be a lowlife, but she knew how to get what she wanted. It infuriated Tina that her needs and Ruthann's converged.

"I won't say yes or no right now. I need to think about it. If I say yes, Ruthann, there had better be something in this for me. Particularly if I'm going to be leaving my husband, who will need me when he gets out of the hospital. You swear Caldwell will be there?"

"Sure," Ruthann said.

"I don't like this. If I need to call you, you have to answer your phone. You can't put me off like you're used to doing. Understand?"

"I get it."

"You need to say it. Say, I will answer my phone if you call."

Ruthann's face shrunk under the force of her anger and turned dark red. "I ain't no damn child," she yelled. She made an about-face and stood in front of the elevator.

"Say those words if you want this ride."

With her back to Tina and barely opening her mouth, Ruthann uttered, "If you call me, I'll answer."

"Goodbye, Ruthann."

The older woman stepped into the elevator. The two stared at each other as the noise of the closing metal doors echoed through the office.

37

Going Away

"Hell, no, you can't have no new skateboard." Ruthann told Ricky. "You earn money from the runnin'. You gotta learn to save it up." She turned back to her ledger.

"You treat me like a slave and pay me shit! You're supposed to be my ma!"

"You're not even thirteen and yet you got it all figured out, do you? Mister, you got lots to learn."

"You said I could get a new one when this here board I made wore out. I can't fix it no more and I need a new one."

"Manage your allowance better and buy yourself one. Now get out of here while I work on these books. Go."

He went to the shed in the back yard and flung open the door. Racing inside like a battering ram, Ricky launched a full-body slam into the filthy mattress. With a large thud the shack shook and creaked. He hit it again with all his might. And again. Three roof joists fell onto the floor as half the roof caved in. Ricky raised his arms to shield his head as he ran out the wobbling door and a small carpet of asphalt shingles hit his legs. He fell forward, yet was able to break the fall with his hands. He turned over and looked back at his crumbled refuge. It was no longer a small building. It was a derelict of another time. He picked himself up and trudged toward the house to tell his grandmother.

The noise of the collapse had broken Ruthann's concentration. She looked out the kitchen window in time to see Ricky, face down on the ground, and her tool shed in shambles. "What the fuck?" she said and headed through the porch.

As Ricky rounded the corner of the house, Ruthann appeared and grabbed him by the collar. "What the hell have you done, boy!" she yelled, and slapped him hard.

Without a thought Ricky took a step back and plunged his head forward into Ruthann's diaphragm. All the air left her body at in a whoosh and she slumped to the ground. Ricky remained standing with clenched fists, panting.

"I didn't mean to do it. I didn't! I just wanted to … I …" Seeing his grandmother on the ground, gasping for breath, Ricky put his hands to his head and yelled, "Shit!" He ran to the side of the house, picked up his bike, and pedaled as hard as he could into the neighborhood.

Ruthann rolled over onto her knees and rose with difficulty. She held her stomach and hobbled back into the house. At the kitchen sink she splashed water onto her face. Feeling recovered, she leaned against the counter and shook her head. "Boy's nuthin' but trouble. Ain't hardly worth five hundred a month," she muttered. She brushed off her clothes and returned to her work.

The sun was settling below the horizon when Ruthann heard a knock on the outside door. She put away her work and yelled, "I'm comin'."

Two police officers greeted her. She peered outside. There was a squad car in the driveway.

"Are you Mrs. Ruthann Plyer?" the woman officer asked.

"Could be. What's the problem, Officer?"

"Ma'am, we have Richard Plyer in custody. He was caught stealing a skateboard from Ron's Sporting Goods. He punched the retail clerk who tried to stop him, and he resisted arrest when we caught him leaving on his bicycle."

Ruthann touched her stomach, still sore from Ricky's headbutt. "Boy's a bad seed," she said.

"The store owner intends to press theft and assault charges, ma'am. Seeing as the boy's a juvenile, apparently under your guardianship, you and he will be required to appear in court. If you'll come down with us to the JAC—that's the Juvenile Assessment Center—we'll process him. Since he has no prior record, we expect he'll be remanded to your custody until the hearing."

"Ain't no way you all could keep him in jail for a spell?"

The two officers looked at each other. "Not for us to say. It will be determined at the JAC. They'll explain everything to you there. Please follow us now if you can."

"Sure, sure. Gimme some time to tidy up. I'll meet you there."

"Would you like to speak to the boy, Mrs. Plyer?"

"Don't think so. I'll be right out."

At the JAC building, Ruthann followed the officers holding Ricky. An Assessment Officer was assigned and the interviews began. It was already 7:00 p.m. Ricky was interviewed alone first. After ten minutes, Ruthann was called in. She took a seat against the wall, but the officer indicated she needed to take the only other seat available—next to Ricky. After the officer completed the informational questions, he asked Ruthann why she thought Ricky should stay in custody.

"'Cause he assaulted me, that's why!"

The officer shook his head.

"You don't believe me? Go ahead. Ask the boy." She turned to face Ricky. "You tell this man straight. Did you or did you not knock me to the ground today and I nearly passed out?"

Ricky jumped out of his chair. "I didn't mean to, I didn't. You started it!"

"There. You see, Officer. The boy is violent and I'm … afraid for my own safety."

Ricky sat quietly in a soup of remorse, anger, and fear. He whispered, "I'm sorry."

"Too late for your sorrow, boy." She looked at the officer. "You gonna keep him here?"

The officer crossed his arms and leaned over the desk. "Sure, Mrs. Plyer. We'll take care of Ricky for now."

Two weeks later, at the Detention Risk Assessment hearing, the avalanche of witnesses bore down on Ricky. His school psychologist, a teacher, the sporting goods store clerk, and Ruthann herself, all testified to Ricky's violent outbursts, his lack of self-control, and lack of care for others. It was a surprise to no one, least of all Ricky, that the hearing concluded with a judgment for juvenile incarceration.

38

Silence of the Wolves

It was no blessing to have Walter home after his surgery. His jaw was wired, so he could have only liquids for the next five days. Though his left arm was in a dry cast, requiring a sling from time to time, right-handed Walter could walk and fend for himself for the most part. Even so, when Tina and Walter communicated, they engaged in a stilted ballet of text, speech, and body language.

"I may go to Georgia for two, maybe three days," Tina said.

Walter's eyes flashed in a scowl. He shook his head and then punched words into his cell phone. *WTF? I can't talk, drive, cook!*

"I'll have meals ready for you. And you need to rest." She looked at the man she had loved, who was now a misshapen stranger. The little guilt she harbored for his injuries had become lost in the gray of her emotional disconnection from him. A part of her wanted to do more for him, wanted to take all those neglected steps of the past six years so the two of them might hurt and heal together. But she couldn't find it within herself to want it more than she wanted to leave. She felt sad and resigned. Walter saw this in her facial expression and involuntarily clenched his jaw, which drove a steel wedge of pain through his head. He growled and bent over. Tina moved to his side and patted his back.

"I'm so sorry, Walter. So terribly sorry. You should lie down, and I'll bring the soup to you."

He looked at her and shook his head. When he righted himself, he walked into the bedroom.

Tina thought hard to convince herself to make the trip. Sheriff Caldwell certainly had the answers Tina needed, even if his knowledge was not firsthand. Or was it? Whatever the truth, RC was sure to possess it, and Tina needed to pry it from him. Since RC had all but turned himself in, would he now, with little to lose, tell Tina the whole truth? It was worth a try, even if it meant four hours in a car with Ruthann.

The next day, Tina confirmed to Walter her decision to travel. Unable to convince her to stay, he tried to convince Tina to take him on the journey with her. This did not tempt Tina in the least. Walter's eyes, questioning and wide, told Tina he had doubts.

Ruthann can't be trusted, he texted. *You could be in danger.*

"Walter. You need to stay here and rest. Taking you on this trip would definitely set you back, and possibly set me back. You will want to do more for me than you should, and I will want you to do as little as possible. And I need to be totally honest with you: I need the flexibility to change plans. I have no idea how things will unfold. This may be my last best shot at understanding why Ricky is dead."

On Sunday, just as Tina considered giving Ruthann the thumbs-up—against a chorus of warnings going off in the back of her mind, her phone rang. It was Sergeant Wilmot.

"Sorry to bother you, Ms. Spear. I have an update on our investigation into the assault on your husband."

Tina let out a breath. "I'm listening. Please tell me."

"We were able to locate a vehicle as you described and trace it to a local residence before it crossed over into Georgia. This vehicle is a rental from Hartsfield International Airport. It was paid for in cash, using fake IDs. We'll confirm all this by tomorrow. Even if we can't identify the folks in the car, we hope to find out which flight they took—if any."

"None of this sounds terribly promising."

"The vehicle stopped at the residence of Cole Hart. We have the camera shot and time stamp. This is only a circumstantial connection to the assault on your husband. We'll question Mr. Hart, but at this point, we have to wait on the Georgia Bureau of Investigation to give us whatever they can."

"I'm not surprised by any of this, Officer. Good luck with Mr. Hart."

Tina decided not to share this scant information with Walter. This could be added to whatever she learned in Georgia, when she was back in St. Augustine. She noted that keeping information from Walter had become uncomfortably easy. She deliberately truncated her conversations with him, convincing herself there was nothing to be gained by sharing what she knew and thought. She avoided Walter as much as possible. Soon the guilt of leaving him alone and losing her love for him seeped in like swamp water, filling her mouth with saliva and stuttering her speech.

Walter could see she was in a bad place, believing he knew why. He texted her with the same message over and over: *You shouldn't go tomorrow. You may be putting yourself in danger.*

"No, I'm not," she said. "I'm pissed to be doing that horrible woman any favors. But because I'm doing her a favor, I'm safe. From her, at least. The reason I'm doing this has nothing to do with her. Think of it this way: If I learn the truth about Ricky, we will all be able to move on and I'll never have anything more to do with Ruthann Plyer and her … cesspool."

The text came back: *This is a BAD idea. I can't stop you, but I want to.*

Tina sighed. "There's nothing more to say on this, Walter."

In the evening Tina called Ruthann and told her the plan. The parole hearing was set for 2:00 p.m. Tuesday afternoon. They would need to leave no later than eight thirty in the morning. When they arrived, Ruthann was on her own, including how she would get back.

"That don't make no sense!" protested the older woman. "How the heck am I supposed to get back to St. Augustine?"

"Not my problem," Tina said. "If our plans converge after the hearing, I'll consider it. But if they don't, you will still be on your own to get back."

"Why would you take me all the way there and just leave me like a pile a' trash?"

Tina thought of many answers for this question. Her reply contained none of them. "If I don't get what I need from RC, I may need to continue to Dahlonega. If I do get my answers, I'll come back right away. I won't know until I have time with RC. What I'm telling you is you asked me for a ride to the parole hearing. That's as far as I'm committing myself to your travel. You can take or leave it."

"You ain't never easy, goddamn it. Not one time. I'll take it."

Tina allowed herself a slight smile. "I'll see you Tuesday, Ruthann." She jabbed the red button on her phone to end the call.

Tuesday morning Tina honked her horn in Ruthann's driveway. Two minutes later Ruthann pushed back the untethered screen door of the back porch and stepped quickly toward Tina's Audi. Not since Ricky's graduation had she seen Ruthann in a dress or wearing makeup. Today the older woman was in a gray skirt and matching jacket, and a yellow blouse. Her hair was done up with barrettes on either side of her head, giving her the look of a schoolteacher. Tina kept mum when Ruthann opened the rear passenger door and flung in an overnight bag. She climbed into the shotgun seat and didn't give Tina a glance. As soon as they were driving away, Tina tuned her radio to a morning talk show.

After three hours without a word spoken by either woman, Tina announced, "I'll be stopping for coffee, gas, and a pee at the Adel exit up ahead."

"Suits me," Ruthann replied.

These words were the full extent of their interaction until reaching Pulaski Prison.

The visitor lot was overflowing. Tina saw three cars circle the lot twice, looking for parking. She wondered how many hearings were taking place today. After a long quest herself, both women kept a healthy distance between them as they walked into the reception area. A shudder whipped through Tina when she recalled her only other prison experience two months ago. For the first time Tina wondered if it might be a good thing if Charity Plyer were paroled. But as quickly as the question popped into her mind, she dismissed it as insane. She cringed, wondering why in the world she ever consented to this desperate errand. RC had better show up. Tina picked up her pace, getting to the door before Ruthann. Holding the door open for Ruthann to walk through was mere reflex. Tina shook her head.

The hearing room was in an annex away from the prison proper. They received visitor badges after they put their identification into escrow with the attending officer and were escorted to the waiting area. Visitors could attend only the hearing they had specified. With an hour before Charity's hearing and limited lunch options, Tina decided on lemonade and oatmeal cookies from the vending machines. As she withdrew her snack, the ceiling lights seemed to dim as she felt a shadow like a wall behind her. She turned around with a lurch.

39

Choose Your Relatives Wisely

PAST

Jacob needed oxycodone every day when he returned to the US, after his second duty tour in Iraq. With a torn-up leg and deep wounds not only over his body but lodged in his psyche, his days as a soldier were nearing the end. Back at Fort McPherson for three scheduled operations and rehabilitation, Jacob Plyer was not looking forward to getting reacquainted with his former commanding officer and his mother's business partner. But Virgil Lapis thought differently. The captain's courtesy calls on his recovering former subordinate seemed entirely appropriate.

Lapis knocked on the door of Jacob's room in the infirmary and walked in. "At ease, soldier," he said to Jacob, who was sitting in a wheelchair and staring out the window.

"Captain," Jacob acknowledged without turning his head.

"You got beat up pretty badly over there, son. We'll be taking good care of you for the next few months. Keep your head high and your nose clean, and everything will work out for the best."

Jacob wheeled his chair around and headed for Lapis. "Keep my nose clean? Yes, sir, Captain. Whatever you say." He went back to the window.

"Corporal, the management of your health is now the obligation and commitment of this facility. This includes your evaluations, surgery, and pain management. Let us take the lead, and you'll be able to go back to civilian life with dignity and self-reliance. You understand?"

"Frankly, sir, no. I don't understand. I shoulda' bought it over there, like Casey and Jefferson. No rehab for them. No return to civilian life. Just the big void and a flowerpot in a cemetery."

"Where there's life, son, there's hope."

"You sound like my pa. You ain't my pa. Sir."

"That's true. Have you been in touch with your father since you got back?"

"Sure. He's comin' to visit next week."

"Good. RC was a good soldier. I hear from your grandmother he's doing well for himself upstate."

"You talk to my grandmother?"

"I do, Jacob. We have mutual interests going back to when your mother was living here. I'm sure you recall. I'm going to leave you alone now, son, but I'll be checking up on you regularly."

"I don't need no special favors, sir."

"Oh, I think you do, soldier." He closed the door softly behind him.

In the infirmary corridor, Nurse Carmen Navarro pushed a cart full of patient care items toward Corporal Plyer's room. Lapis stopped her.

"Lieutenant, what's your assessment of the patient in 106?"

"He's physically improving but in constant pain, sir. His next surgery is scheduled in two weeks. His surgical lead believes it will be that long before the results of his last surgery are set and strong enough to support the next set of procedures."

"How about his pain medication?"

"What about it, sir?"

"His prognosis for returning to a decent civilian life is good, yes? But he needs to keep his mind sharp. He's got a fine line to walk, Lieutenant. He can be very … useful after he's released."

Lieutenant Navarro looked at her captain directly. "He needs to heal, sir. This is our priority for his future health, sir."

"Carry on, Lieutenant." Lapis left Nurse Navarro to continue her rounds.

When Carmen was finished taking Jacob's blood pressure and all the other measurements connected to his vitality, pain, and healing, she put her hands in her lap before administering the prescription medicine. She looked at him, willing herself to connect with his pain, his anxiety, his need to envision a future. She believed her empathy was important fuel for his recovery.

"You have only one more surgery ahead of you, Corporal. You're strong, I can see. You'll be back on your feet before the end of the month."

Jacob looked at her with watery eyes and a stern face. He nodded.

She said, "Captain Lapis tells me your father was stationed here at Fort McPherson some years back."

"Yes, ma'am. My daddy was a military man and now he's a sheriff up in north Georgia."

"He's on the visitor's log. He's been at your side a few times."

"I know. Seems always when I'm just outta surgery or overrun with pain meds."

"We can make sure you're in your best form the next time he visits."

"I appreciate that, Nurse …" He squinted to read her name tag. "Lieutenant Carmen Navarro."

"Yes. In this room I'm Carmen."

"And in this room, I'm grateful you're a regular visitor."
He smiled. "Carmen, you gotta be real careful around your captain."

This surprised Carmen. She knew only too well Captain Lapis wielded power well above his pay grade, inside and outside the military base. Lapis had coerced her to introduce him to her cartel cousins. The less she knew of their dealings and the less she saw of her captain, the safer she felt. But how would this wounded soldier have any idea about that?

"I'm afraid I don't know what you mean, Corporal."

"I'm Jacob in this room, Carmen. And I know this man from when I was stationed here. Three years ago. Just watch your six. Thas' all I'm sayin' for now."

"It's time to take your medicine, Corporal. And I'll see you in a few hours."

"Go easy on me, will ya? I don't wanna be a sad lump the rest a' my days. The pain's bad, but the drugs, they scare me."

"Your pain management is critical to your recovery. We'll go easy on you, I promise."

Leaving the room, Carmen looked back toward her patient, who was slowly falling asleep. Jacob managed a wave of his hand and, did she see it? A wink.

40

The Chief and the Soldier

"Mrs. Spear. I have to say I'm less surprised than I should be to see you here."

"Hello, Chief." Tina extended her hand, which RC scooped into his as if picking up a baby bird. "I was told you would be here."

"Bad news travels fast."

"Please tell me, how is Jacob?"

RC's face morphed into a soft smile. "I appreciate you askin'. Jacob will be ... back to his old self any day now. He's back home with Carmen."

"You probably know this, Sheriff, but I didn't come here for Charity's parole hearing. I brought Jacob's grandmother up for only one reason."

"Let me guess. You wanted to interrogate me about the night Ricky died."

"I-I wouldn't say interrogate. Please tell me if I'm wrong, but you know more about what happened that night than you have ever made part of the public record, am I right?"

RC looked down at Tina, expressionless.

"There are just too many inconsistencies in the notion of Ricky killing himself. Even your detective—"

"Detective Tillyard did his job, Mrs. Spear, and he's working on other cases now."

"I understand. What I don't understand is why the truth needs to be hidden."

RC looked to the ceiling. "Why must the truth be hidden? The truth is not hidden. It visits us every day like a plague. It shows up in an overdose, a jail sentence, in a tragic death. The truth presides over every aspect of our lives. We are just not smart enough to figure out what it means or what it wants from us."

Tina squinted at the police officer turned existentialist. Her anger rose, then ebbed. "The reality at the core of Ricky's story is that he was a bright, motivated young man who had turned his life around. Maybe Ricky was complicit in his own death. Maybe it's a piece of the truth. But only a piece. It's not the whole truth, is it? I want the whole truth. Not some crumb to keep me in the dark and guessing. Please."

"Why don't you believe you already have it?"

"Stop talking in circles. Ricky did *not* take his own life on purpose. He did not. He would not!"

"What do you know of sacrifice, Mrs. Spear? Don't worry, that's a rhetorical question. I'll tell you a little bit of what I know. I was a soldier, and after me, Jacob was a soldier. And soldiers know they could be called upon at any moment to give their lives for something bigger than themselves. They put themselves in a position to sacrifice their lives for a higher purpose. Most people are not called in this way. To most people, the notion of sacrifice at its highest is maybe raising a child. But in those cases, if you're lucky, you get rewarded for the sacrifice after a time. Do you see?"

"Are you going to tell me or aren't you?" Tina yelled. She stopped herself and stepped backward, stumbling into the vending machine. Those waiting for the next hearing,

Ruthann included, looked at the pair with surprise and unease.

"Whatever you're looking for, Mrs. Spear, whatever it is you need, I don't even know if it exists. But there is one person who does know. It's his story to tell if there is one."

Tina nodded. A visit to Jacob and Carmen in Dahlonega would be her last best chance to confirm what she believed. Her eyes softened and her shoulders drooped slightly as the wave of her frustration subsided. She looked around the waiting room. Heads turned away, back to magazines or into laps or to a poster on the wall about safety. Tina's cheeks flushed.

"And this thing today, Chief, this parole hearing for Charity. Will it …" Tina didn't finish her sentence. She had lost the chief's attention.

He moved to the center of the waiting area. A man had just entered the waiting room. Six feet tall, trim and straight, he wore jeans and a blue blazer over a camouflage T-shirt. He walked up to RC and put out his hand. RC took the hand and held it steady in a grip like the bite of an alligator. RC said something in the man's ear and then released the hand. The man turned and walked over to Ruthann. The old woman jumped up from her seat as if it had been set on fire, stealing a glance at Tina. Ruthann's face went from tight-lipped red to ashen. The man looked over at Tina and smiled in a way that was both generous and terrifying. He walked over to her.

"Hello again, Mrs. Spear. I want to thank you for transporting Ruthann to this hearing." He extended his hand. "Captain Virgil Lapis, as you may recall. We met some weeks back when you were leaving Jacob and Carmen's house. I was Jacob's commanding officer at Fort McPherson."

"Nice to see you again, Captain," she said as she shook his hand. Captain Lapis held Tina's hand longer than another stranger might. She pulled away with difficulty.

"It's important Jacob's mother get every opportunity to make up for all she's done in her past. She has a chance to make peace with her son."

Tina stared at the captain and nodded. She thought, but only one of her sons.

He smiled and walked back to Ruthann.

Tina took advantage to recover the attention of RC. She pulled him by the elbow. RC looked at her with a grimace.

"Sheriff, do you have any idea why Jacob's commanding officer would come to a parole hearing for his mother? Do you think Jacob asked him to?"

"Frankly, I'm surprised to see him here. He did come to the service we had for Ricky because he was already in Dahlonega for a training at Camp Merrill."

"He gives me the feeling of a lion prowling a campsite, looking for dinner. It's eerie. Does he have an interest in seeing Charity paroled?"

"The captain and Charity have some history. He uses people. My guess is his motives here are purely selfish. I need to speak to him. And to Charity's mother."

RC walked over to the captain. Tina felt deliberately uninvited. She scratched her head and looked around for the ladies' room.

Tina's mind whirred. For the next five minutes she struggled with what she should do next. It made no difference to her whether Charity was released today or in two years, after a completed sentence. She had no reason to remain for the hearing. Tina walked to where RC and Ruthann huddled. They halted their conversation.

"Ruthann, I'm going to head up to Dahlonega and meet with Jacob one last time. And Carmen. Right now."

"Why don't you wait for the hearing to be over?" Captain Lapis suggested from behind her shoulder. "If the vote to parole goes in Charity's favor, there's the possibility they may let her out today or tomorrow because of Jacob's situation."

This made Tina shudder. "In that case, I'd best be going now!" She turned to go when the captain reached to stop her. RC stepped between them. The soldier's eyes flashed. He stiffened, ready to fight.

"Mrs. Spear just wants Jacob to tell her the details of his brother's suicide, Captain. I think it's up to Jacob to give her what she needs, or not."

"Jacob isn't a well man these days, Mrs. Spear. He could have difficulty remembering something so painful."

RC had had it. He pushed Lapis enough to make him take a step backward. "If you want this to be the place of reckoning," RC growled at the captain, "then you go ahead and come at me. Otherwise, sit the fuck down."

Lapis took a step toward RC and looked at him with curiosity. "Reckoning isn't yours to administer, RC." He turned toward the chairs along the far wall and stood in front of one of them. Ruthann remained seated, looking into her lap, shivering.

Tina couldn't help herself. "You sound to me, Captain, like a man who wants everything buried." She turned and walked out without looking back.

41

Recovery

RC drove down to visit his son in the Fort McPherson Hospital the day after Jacob's final surgery. He was on autopilot through the Atlanta-Decatur traffic and up to gate 4 at the army base. The condition of his son occupied his mind, as did the gift he was bearing.

He knocked and entered. Room 106 was bathed in light. It was a good sign, he told himself. Jacob was sitting up in bed, reading the book *The Occupation of Iraq*, by Ali A. Allawi.

"Trying to make sense of the war?" RC asked. He strode to the edge of the bed.

"Actually, trying to make sense a' the peace. I tell you, RC, there are some things over there I will never understand. And why we spend all those lives and money ... it haunts me, ya know?"

"I do, son. How are you feeling? What's the latest prognosis for your leg and all?"

"Carmen should be here soon. She can give you the details. All I know is I'll be gettin' out by the end of the month or so and heading ... well, that's a question, ain't it?"

"I've got an answer, Jacob. I want you to come live with me. Actually, not with me."

Jacob turned his head and leaned toward his father. "Me? Come up to Dahlonega? I can't live with you, RC. I mean ...

I'd love to and all, but I'm gonna need some convalescent care for some time, I reckon, and you're a full-time county sheriff."

"You like my place in Auraria, don't you? I've had some work done to the place and it should be everything you need."

"Yeah. Except it ain't near nuthin', is it? Kinda isolated, right?"

"It will be a while before you're walking and driving. I don't think it matters much how far it is from anything, so long as you can get deliveries. Besides, it could be a great place to raise a family."

Jacob started to laugh, but stopped, let out a groan, and grabbed for his leg, which was still wrapped and bound from the surgery. "Christ. Shit," he said. His breathing started to labor and his face contorted with pain. "Them pills!" he yelled at RC.

Rather than reach for one of the three bottles on the bedstand, RC grabbed the nurse-call control and pressed it hard. In thirty seconds, Carmen Navarro came through the door and over to Jacob's bedside, acknowledging the giant in the room with a slight nod as she brushed by him.

She could see the pain across Jacob's face and his quivering body. Reaching up to a valve on Jacob's IV, she gave it a turn and then took Jacob's pulse. His shivering stopped and his eyes became glassy as he turned his head toward her and smiled. She put a hand on his forehead and rested it there.

RC patted his son's arm. "Is he going to be all right, Lieutenant?"

"I'm going to be just fine," Jacob answered. "Don't be talkin' about me like I ain't here."

RC smiled. "I know, son. I merely wanted to ask the professional, here."

"Jacob understands his own body, Mr. Caldwell," Carmen told him. "He's healing. Getting stronger each day. Aren't you, soldier?"

"Only 'cause I got the best care on earth." Jacob grabbed Carmen's hand and rubbed it on his stubbled face before letting it go.

"I was just telling Jacob I want him to come and live near me in Dahlonega, and I have a house ready for him … and anyone else he considers family."

RC and Carmen both blushed a little. Jacob closed his eyes.

Carmen pulled RC aside. "The sooner, the better. This isn't a great environment for him. I can't push his discharge any faster, but between the painkillers and the command, Jacob's anxiety continues to peak every day. He's got another three, maybe four weeks of rehab and he'll be discharged. I've looked into the rehabilitation facilities at Camp Merrill. It's only a few miles from Dahlonega, and I've put in for a transfer there. I need to leave this installation myself."

RC nodded. "Had I known what your captain and my ex were doing back when I was stationed here, Carmen, I'd have put a stop to it. Sure as damn I would have."

"The captain seems about as untouchable here as anyone you can imagine. I swear he must have a picture of every brass on base screwing something they shouldn't. We all need to save ourselves and be done fearing this man."

"He won't stop your transfer, will he?"

"He wouldn't be that stupid. I introduced him to my vile cousins, and it would be too easy for me to wreck his little enterprise. But I know he could make life unbearable for me and for Jacob. So, we have this … understanding."

A knock on the door overtook their conversation. Captain Lapis walked in slowly, and the door closed. He stuck out his hand for RC. "Good to see you again, RC. I was told you were visiting Jacob."

RC took the captain's hand and shook it, staring grim-faced at Lapis. The captain's eyes were calm to the point of being blank.

"Captain," RC muttered.

"And how is the patient, Lieutenant?" Lapis said to Carmen.

"He's still in a great deal of pain, which we're managing," she said. "His recovery is moving along well, according to the surgeon."

"He'll be back on duty before you know it."

Jacob stirred, looked over at Lapis, and slowly raised his hand, middle finger first.

Lapis smiled.

"I won't be stayin' in past my rehab, Captain. Paperwork's already filed. But you already have the information, don't you?"

"I do, soldier. Duty can be many things. I'm thinking what will be best for you in the long run."

Jacob, Carmen, and RC all stared at Lapis.

"Protecting your family is the highest call to duty, isn't it, RC?"

RC walked to the door and held it open. "A quick word, if I may, Captain."

In the corridor, RC closed the door to the room. "I'm not sure what you were getting at in there, Lapis but here's—"

"I was trying to direct your son's outlook to the future. What are you—?"

"I'm talking now. Hear me good. Whatever shit you had going with my ex, it's between you and her. Society already rewarded her with a five-year hiatus. Jacob caught in the middle is way in the past. It's got nothing whatsoever to do with his future. I'm his father and I have his back. Do not ever think otherwise."

"RC. Don't work yourself up over nothing. I've approved Lieutenant Navarro's transfer and, like you, I expect the future to be steady and calm for the two of them. Have a pleasant rest of your visit." Lapis turned and walked toward his office.

Back in Jacob's room Carmen was holding onto Jacob's hand as he spoke in a low voice.

RC went to the bedside. "Lapis told me he already approved your transfer, Carmen. Let's all take one step at a time and get Jacob healed."

"Sounds good to me, RC," Jacob said. "I gotta let Ricky know soon as I'm in Dahlonega. Last time I talked to him, he had some mentor from the juvy program. I can't tell if this is good or not but can't be worse than Ruthann pretendin' to be Ricky's ma."

Carmen said, "Get some rest, Jacob. Get in touch with Ricky when you're rested."

Jacob replied, "He's had it bad, RC. He needs to get outta St. Augustine."

His father said, "We're gonna save one brother at time, Jacob. You first."

42

Connection

It had taken Devon Tillyard all his time over the last five days to gather and assemble the pieces. The connection to Atlanta confirmed several burner phones had been purchased there. Other phones showed up in Alabama, Georgia, Florida, South Carolina, and Tennessee. Tillyard knew he needed help.

Having worked closely with the Criminal Interdiction Unit during his tenure in Decatur, he called CIU Investigator Levi Horwitz. After a few moments of catching up, Tillyard made his request.

"Levi, I've got an opioid bust up here, looks like it's got an Atlanta connection. I'm hoping you can shed some light for me."

"If I can, Till. What you got?"

Tillyard did a data dump on his case, tracking drug runners in five states. The nexus seemed to be Atlanta, with a possible secondary point south of Jacksonville, Florida.

"There's nothing on my desk like what you're telling me. I'm still working with the Coast Guard in Savannah, looking at small airports and landing strips. Let me check a few things in the system."

The arrhythmic tap of the keyboard sounded like Morse code through the phone. After a few minutes Tillyard heard, "Yup. I have something here. Looks like there's an active investigation into soldiers, mostly vets, who've been questioned but not charged. Evidence doesn't support arrest. Says here these vets were supporting juveniles after their time in detention and at least six of these kids were caught transporting meth, fentanyl, or oxy. They were using burner phones the vets had purchased."

"Any of them still active military, by any chance?"

"One. A captain out of Fort McPherson."

"Anything about the sources of the pills?"

"Let's see this link here. ... Ah, here's something. It looks as though there is an active investigation at the base. But the military is handling everything internally. Doesn't look like it's coordinated with our investigation."

"Thanks, Levi."

His next phone call had to be to someone in St. Augustine or Jacksonville. He had no personal connections with the police there, but he had the name of the person who had purchased at least a dozen burner phones over the last six months, all linked to the ones he was tracking. A man living in St. Augustine named Cole Hart. Tillyard realized Tina Spear was working with a St. Augustine police officer investigating the assault on her husband. This officer seemed a better starting place than a cold call.

When Tina saw Detective Tillyard's name flash on the touch screen of her Audi, electricity shot through her body. When it subsided, a sense of calm rose in her. She pushed a button on her steering wheel and took his call. "Detective, I'm heading your way at this very moment. But not to see you, of course. How can I help you?"

"You're going to Jacob Plyer's home, I presume. You need to know he just got home from his overdose recovery. Not sure what shape he'll be in."

"This has to end, Detective. It just has to. I'm not sure I have the stamina to keep this up. And it's time Jacob came clean. Maybe if he feels vulnerable and as tired as I am, it will make it easier for him to tell the full story. After my visit with your boss just now, I know for certain there's something he needs to come clean about."

"Don't let this get sideways now. You may be on a mission, but we both know you are not a trained interrogator. But I called you for a different reason. I'd like you to put me in contact with the police officer looking into the assault on your husband."

"I will, Detective, though not right at this moment."

"Are you on the interstate? Please get off at an exit and call me back with his name and number."

They hung up. Tillyard considered how odd it was that this case of his was leading him back to Christina Spear. His phone rang within minutes.

"I'm at a gas station, Detective, searching my contacts for the officer working my husband's case."

"Thanks."

"But I want to know why you want the officer's contact information. Have you discovered something that could help the police here apprehend whoever did this to Walter?"

"I don't think so. I'm working a drug traffic case that has ties to St. Augustine. I want to speak to someone who can point me in the right direction."

"If you get any information remotely relating to Ricky, or Walter's attack, please contact me."

"The investigating officer will take care of any calls."

"Officer Wilmot is, no doubt, a dedicated public servant. But he doesn't know me, or Walter, and he certainly has no connection to the Plyer family that I'm aware of. Except maybe to Cole."

Tillyard sat up straight. "Who?"

"Cole Hart. He is one of Charity Plyer's exes. Ricky lived with him for a while, off and on. He may have been involved with the men who assaulted Walter. But we don't know. Anyway, that's what Officer Wilmot told me."

"I see." Tillyard wet his lips and slowed his speech. "If I discover anything linking to Ricky or Walter that I'm allowed to share, I will."

"That's all I ask, Detective. I'm texting Officer Wilmot's contact information to you."

"Thank you. I have to run."

"Me too."

Tillyard dialed the number and reached Sergeant Wilmot.

"Hi, Sergeant. This is Detective Devon Tillyard of the Lumpkin County Georgia Sheriff's department. I understand you're among the investigators on the Walter Spear assault case, is this correct?"

"It is, Detective. What can I do for you?"

"I'm working a drug trafficking case up here. Seems to connect directly to Atlanta and to St. Augustine. I would appreciate if your department could help me locate one of the bulk buyers and perhaps question him."

"I presume you have a warrant for us to bring him in."

"I'll give you his name and maybe you'll know if I still need one. His name is Cole Hart."

After a pause, Wilmot said, "Mr. Hart is about to be questioned regarding knowledge he may have on the assault case you mentioned."

"The assault on Walter Spear—"

"I think you'd better—"

"I've worked with his wife, Christina Spear, on an apparent suicide case here in Dahlonega. She came to me for some assistance and we were able to help each other. This is how I came by this information, Sergeant. But I'm starting to see a connection here that wasn't apparent last week. We have store security video confirming Hart was one of the people who purchased burner phones that showed up in the hands of four drug mules. I'm pretty certain I can get an out-of-state warrant for my investigation."

"You do what you need to do, Detective. We don't expect we'll need a warrant to get Mr. Cole to answer a few questions. But we haven't any solid evidence linking him to the assault. If he won't come in voluntarily, I may be back in touch with you. I'll alert the St. Johns County Sheriff's office, which handles drug enforcement here. You may want to call in if we get the opportunity to question Mr. Hart."

"You can bet I will if things go there, Sergeant. I'll work on my warrant straightaway. If Hart doesn't lawyer up too fast, we could both get enough to make our cases. I want to take this drug operation down."

Tillyard hung up and leaned back in his chair. He knew in his gut this case was going to break open. But what happens between now and then? Whether Tillyard went to St. Augustine in person or joined the interrogation by phone, he had to secure his out-of-state warrant now. He jumped up and rushed into the office of the chief deputy. They reviewed the case and the second in command agreed to get the warrant. The urgency of the matter was not lost on the assistant district attorney. She scheduled a meeting with the judge in an hour. Tillyard and the chief deputy discussed the next steps.

A call back to Sergeant Wilmot came next. Wilmot liked the idea to question Hart jointly, particularly if Tillyard could show up with a warrant.

He couldn't tell Christina Spear anything about the cross connection of Cole Hart to the assault and the drug mules. But what if the drug trafficking had more to do with Ricky Plyer's death than any of them knew? Could Tina Spear unravel something at Jacob Plyer's home that didn't want unraveling? Carmen Plyer was so hard to figure. She was the niece of a Mexican drug lord, after all. What the fuck? He grabbed his phone and dialed Tina's number.

"Now I'm concerned," she answered. "Two calls in one afternoon."

"Ms. Spear, maybe you shouldn't go over to the Plyer residence right away. Do you have a plan or are you just going to stir things up and see what falls out?"

"Seriously, Detective. You're the one who said I was going to be on my own."

"I know what I said. And I think there are too many unknowns. You shouldn't go down a path no one knows where it ends."

"Jacob Plyer knows."

Exasperation evoked a grunt from Tillyard. "What you also don't understand is no one has figured out if Carmen Plyer's drug family is in any way involved."

"Well, that's for you to figure out and prosecute. But for me, it's irrelevant."

"It may not have been irrelevant to your husband or maybe not even to Ricky."

This made Tina seethe. She took a few moments to calm herself. "And since the St. Augustine police don't work up here and since I'm on my own, as you made clear, I'll be the one who gets to the bottom of this, Detective. If Carmen Plyer had anything to do with Walter's—"

"No, no, ma'am. That's not what I'm saying."

"For God's sake, what are you saying?"

"Look, why don't you meet me in an hour."

"This is exhausting, Detective. You don't have to—"

"One hour. Are you staying at the Days Inn?"

Frustrated, Tina smacked herself on the forehead, making her car swerve. She shrieked.

"Ms. Spear?" Tillyard yelled into the phone. "Ms. Spear?"

PART 3

RECKONING

43

A Short Lease

Charity Plyer's parole hearing was not the first time she relied on the discrepancy between her appearance and her personality to steer events her way. Sitting in front of the five-member parole board, her head was bowed, her hands folded, her hair combed but not done up. A pretty woman, soft-spoken, and appropriately contrite. Charity knew the drill.

"Why do you think you should be paroled?" the warden asked.

"Well, it's really you all to determine if I should be paroled. I can only tell you why I want to be. I've had a very long, very hard six years inside this facility. It's given me more time than I ever had in my life to think about who I am, who I was, and who I want to be. Let me just say that who I was, the woman who dealt drugs and ..." Charity choked up and tears rolled down her cheeks. "... and prostituted herself, the Charity Plyer who got herself locked up? I have to own that person. I was that person. I was very messed up and I'm sorry in a way I can ... I can't ever fully describe to you. I am sorry, down to this torn-up heart. I know I can't undo all those bad things. I would if I could. But you know, like I know, you can't go back and change the past. You can only learn from it and commit yourself to doing better. I had two boys when I came in here. Now I only have one, and he's not doing so good. I owe him a better me. I owe my son a mom he never had. I want to be a real mom for him."

The questioning of Charity lasted only ten minutes. Lumpkin County Sheriff Rutherford Caldwell was asked to come forward to speak on behalf of his ex-wife.

Every pair of eyes in the room was locked onto RC as he towered up out of his seat and took the chair in front of the panel. He read a prepared statement highlighting his communication with his ex over the years and believed she cared for her remaining son, Jacob, the son they had together. He stated she needed now to be at his side to nurture him in a way she never did, never could, before.

The board asked Charity Plyer's mother if she had anything to say on her daughter's behalf. She nodded and limped up to the witness chair.

"I ain't good at public speakin'." She coughed and steadied herself. "My daughter ain't had much of a life. My husband ran off when she was a little one, and I scraped by best I could. I couldn't give her all what she needed. Hell, I didn't even know what she needed. But now, I seen her pain. I seen her change. She gives herself, in this here prison, more than I gave her as a mother. God knows I ain't proud of such a thing. But for the first time I can think of, I am proud of my daughter." Ruthann's lower lip quivered. "This is all what I got, Your Honors." She walked back to her seat.

The commissioners said a few words among themselves and then adjourned the room to make their decision.

In the waiting room, RC and Ruthann rejoined Captain Lapis. He asked how the hearing went. Both shrugged.

"Will they at least give Charity an up or down today?"

RC answered, "Hard to tell. No one was here arguing for her to stay in for her full sentence."

This made Captain Lapis snigger. "No kidding. They're either dead, or don't want anything to do with her."

RC narrowed his eyes. "Could be true. Sounds like you might know my ex better than you let on, Captain."

"Well, there is no need for me to stick around here. Ruthann, would you give me a call …"

The door to the hearing room opened and the administrative officer called everyone back in. As RC went ahead and took his former seat, Captain Lapis held Ruthann by the elbow. He pulled something from his pocket and handed it to her.

"Here's a phone. I want you to call me as soon as you know what's going on with Charity. You got that?"

Ruthann took the phone and put it in her purse.

"Do you have enough cash to get a taxi back to St. Augustine?"

Ruthann nodded.

"Are you going to take her back there with you?"

"Hell if I know! She ain't even got her pardon yet!"

"Fine. If she gets out and you're still here, do what you can to make sure she gets back to Florida. Get her out of Georgia. You understand?"

"Let go my arm. Look, Virgil, I may work for you, but my daughter, she makes up her own mind 'bout shit. I'll let you know what happens."

The warden addressed the room. Charity Plyer was granted a parole under all the restrictions and regulations governing parolee behavior. In addition, given the extenuating family circumstances, she would be released the next day.

Charity exhaled deeply and bent over.

RC said to Ruthann, "She's all yours." When he approached Captain Lapis at the doorway, Lapis unfolded his arms perhaps to shake RC's hand, but the big man was past him in a flash and out through the exit. Lapis walked over to Ruthann.

"Better get yourself a hotel. Find out what time they're letting her go tomorrow and get the both of you the hell outta here."

"I'm … I think I'll wait right here until they tell me when she's s'posed to be released."

"I have to return to Atlanta. Remember what I said. Call me when you know what's happening."

Out in the parking lot, Lapis got into the brown Chevy Malibu he had borrowed from a friend at Fort McPherson. When he reached the highway, he headed north for Atlanta. When he approached the exit for Fort McPherson, he passed it altogether, went up and around the perimeter, and took Route 19 to Dahlonega.

* * *

After two hours of waiting, Ruthann was able to visit her daughter.

"Now, what the fuck am I s'posed to do, Charity?"

"Keep your voice down and stay calm. We got what we hoped for."

"You got what *you* hoped for. I got no ride and no place to stay."

"Hush. You got plenty a' cash. Get a taxi, find a cheap motel, and get back here by eight tomorrow morning."

"That's when their lettin' you out?"

"Sure looks that way. I gotta be ready at seven to get the whole process rollin'."

"Virgil's gone back to Fort McPherson. Wants me to call him when we know what time we're leavin'."

"Figures. Controlling prick. All right, Ruthann. You call him and tell him exactly what he wants to hear."

"He wants to be sure we go back to Florida."

"Course he does. Then that's what you tell him. He's gotta pay for what he did to me, Ruthann. We gotta take care of this asshole once and for all."

"You are so sure he's the one set you up? How do you know? Coulda' been Noble. Could a been Cole, maybe even Carmen."

Charity laughed. "First, Cole or Noble ain't got the brains or the balls to take me down like that. I'm willing to bet, though, Noble helped Virgil. Second, Carmen doesn't know shit. Her family loves me. Well, loved me. Not sure how they feel now. And as much as Carmen wants me to stay away from Jacob, she's not the conniving, back-stabbing type, you know. Uh-uh. Captain Virgil Lapis, our too-smart-by-twice Atlanta partner. He did this to me. And he will pay. He will. Now, we gotta get ourselves up to Dahlonega first thing tomorrow. See what it'll take to get a taxi or a shuttle or something. I wanna get on the road as soon as I'm out."

Ruthann nodded.

"By the way, how'd it go riding up here with the Spear bitch? Must o' been some fun, right?"

"We didn't say two words the whole ride. I think she's headed up to Jacob's. May even be there by now."

"Fucks sake! Why does she not know when to quit? Didn't RC set her straight? Shit. What do you think Jacob's gonna tell her?"

"Why is it people are always askin' me stupid questions I can't answer! I got no fuckin' idea. I do know it's where she's headed. Her husband was beat pretty bad, but it just made her worse, you know. She's a fuckin' hornet."

"What do you know about the beating of the husband?"

"Since I couldn't coordinate any deliveries for a couple of days, I had to call Virgil and let him know I was laid low. Whatever he decided afterward, he chose not to share with me."

"Dumbass. Makes no sense to scare her. She doesn't give a shit about us or our business." Charity paused. "Ricky did actually off himself, right?"

"I only know what RC told me."

"Well, well. I wonder if Mrs. Spear thinks Ricky's dyin' had somethin' to do with the trade. If she's still drivin' up to see Jacob, it's gotta mean she doesn't believe Ricky killed himself. That's why she's trouble. Do you get this, Ruthann? But what if she's right? Do you think Ricky was killed and this whole thing is a cover-up?"

"Jesus H! This is just you makin' shit up. This is RC you're talking about, the straightest arrow I ever known. Hell no, I don't think Ricky was killed. But I do know Mrs. Spear is trippin' over all kinds a' shit, makin' everyone crazy!"

"I get it. This is why Virgil's gettin' nervous. That and my parole. Hard to make sense of it all. We should give Cole a call tomorrow. He's gonna know what Virgil's up to."

Charity went silent for a few moments. "Sort it out, Ruthann. Eight o'clock here, with transportation. I'll be ready."

44

Not What She Wanted

PRESENT

"Shit!" Tina yelled into her phone. "Yes, Detective, I'm still here. But I blew a tire, I'm pretty sure." She let out a long sigh. "I'll get to the hotel after I get someone out to fix my tire. Probably won't be for another couple of hours."

Tillyard shook his head. "Okay. Glad you're not hurt. Do what you have to do and call me when you're checked in."

Tina agreed and set about notifying roadside assistance. Among the cars whizzing by her was a brown Chevy Malibu. It was just another of the hundreds of cars to Tina. But the driver of the Malibu recognized the disabled Audi. It had been parked in Jacob Plyer's driveway when he had visited a few weeks ago.

Collapsing on the hotel bed later, Tina pushed her shoes off and curled into a fetal position. No one gets this, she said to herself. Not a soul. Maybe I'm the crazy one. And why would Detective Tillyard want to speak to her before she met with Jacob? Did the conversation promise resolution, or a warning or just another rabbit hole? She went into the bathroom to freshen up, and then went downstairs to order a glass of Chardonnay. Maybe two. Midway through the first, she called her detective.

She met him in the lobby of the hotel. The lighting was low, as if to discourage reading. The furnishings were spartan.

Tillyard shook her hand. "Thanks for agreeing to meet me, Ms. Spear." They sat at a small table.

"I think it's time you called me Tina, Detective."

"Okay. Tina. When you mentioned an individual possibly connect to your husband's case—"

"Cole Hart."

"Yes. Well, his name surfaced in my investigation. I'm not sure what it means, but this was too much of a coincidence. It also occurred to me that Ricky's death may not have been an accident. If it's true, it would mean you could be in more danger than either of us realized."

Tillyard sat back to observe Tina as she processed this. For a few moments she didn't move, she didn't blink, and Tillyard couldn't tell if she was still breathing.

Finally, Tina said, "You don't think your boss would have covered up Ricky's murder, do you?" She rubbed her arms to get warm.

"No. I don't. What I do think is the risk for your conversation with Jacob is observably greater than it was yesterday."

A lone tear fell slowly down Tina's cheek. "I'm not a threat to anyone, I swear."

"And you don't want to become the loose end of a crime someone may be trying hard to cover up."

Tina nodded. "I am too invested in this to turn back now."

"I figured you'd say that. I propose you and I go to the Plyers together."

"Hmm. This sounds like a decent idea, Detective. I was originally thinking I'd go there this afternoon. But after my flat tire, two glasses of wine, and three wasted hours, it is not going to happen today. Can we go over tomorrow morning?"

"I've got some plans to rearrange, but I'll make it happen. How about I meet you here at ten, and we'll go in my car."

"See you tomorrow," she said.

Tillyard and Tina stood at the same time, finding themselves inches apart. She looked up at his face. As another tear formed, she threw her arms around him, pressed her cheek into his neck, and held tight. Her voice was calm. "Thank you for thinking of me. Thank you for having my back. You've been the most solid thing in my life for the past two months. Maybe the only solid thing."

For a few seconds Tillyard kept his arms suspended in the air, and then slowly brought them around Tina's shoulders.

"You're a determined woman, Ms. ... Tina. And everything you've done has come from a good place in your heart, I'm sure. Let's take these next steps with as much caution as we can. Okay?"

"Tomorrow might be more interesting than I'd hoped for," she said, and stepped away from Detective Tillyard.

* * *

Tillyard was back at his desk when RC returned from Pulaski.

Before the sheriff could walk into his office, Tillyard sprang from his seat. "I know this may not be a great time, Boss, but there's some things you need to know."

"Can't wait till tomorrow, I take it."

"No, sir."

"All right, Detective."

Tillyard brought RC up to speed on his case, and its connection to Ruthann and the attack of Tina's husband.

RC put his hands to his mouth then wiped them on his shirt front. "God damn it. God damn it to hell."

"Boss, what's wrong? I got this covered. I was going to be in St. Augustine tonight, but I need to stay here until noon tomorrow. I'll fax St. Augustine police the warrant, and I'll join the questioning by phone. What's the problem?"

"The problem is Charity was paroled today. She'll be released tomorrow. She and her mother will be coming up here to stay with Jacob for God knows how long. Depending on what you get from Mr. Hart, I may have to arrest my ex-mother-in-law."

"Jesus Christ. Can this get any weirder? What can I tell you? You probably know about Carmen's family and all."

"More than I'd like to, God knows. But I'm also one of the reasons they let her be. Okay. I want to listen in on the call, Detective. What time tomorrow?"

"Sure, Chief. After they pick him up. My guess is first thing in the morning."

45

Harvest Time

PRESENT

The next morning Ruthann used the phone she got from Lapis and called him. It was eight fifteen. "We's on the way to Dahlonega, Virgil. I want to call RC and let him know to tell Jacob and Carmen."

Charity looked at her mother, eyes ablaze. Mouthing the word 'no." Ruthann shrugged.

"Don't do that. Shit." Lapis said over the phone. "You were supposed to go back to Florida, Ruthann. I should have known. Okay. Just go ahead to your grandson's home. You don't have to alert RC."

Ruthann covered the mouthpiece. "He says not to call RC," she told her daughter.

"You may work for the prick, but he's got no say about how you and me do our business with family. He met with RC yesterday. Tell him to fuck off!"

Ruthann unmuffled the phone. "RC's got a right to know, and besides, Virgil, he's the one makin' the arrangements and all."

"What time do you expect to be there?"

"Shuttle's droppin' us off at the bus depot and we're takin' a taxi from there. Figure, maybe noon." She looked at Charity, who nodded. This was at least two hours later than they anticipated.

* * *

Lapis hung up. He had checked out of his hotel hours ago—paid cash—and was surveilling the Plyer residence from the woods, where he had parked his car. He had been right, of course. Charity did the opposite of what he had commanded Ruthann.

Leaving his car hidden, Lapis checked his shoulder holster and patted his leg strap. He checked his jacket pocket, then walked with purpose through the woods, to the home of Jacob and Carmen. He knocked on the door. Carmen opened the door just enough for her to see who was there.

"Good morning, Lieutenant," Lapis said with a smile.

"Captain Lapis. ... this is .... this is unexpected. What can I do for you?"

"Actually, it's what I can do for you. I'm sure you know your mother-in-law is on her way here."

Carmen nodded as she suppressed a shiver. "It appears to be common knowledge."

"May I please come in and talk to you and Jacob? I'll not stay long."

"Yes ... of course. Please." She held the door open, and Lapis strode over the threshold.

She offered the soldier some coffee, which he politely accepted. "I'll tell Jacob you're here. I need to check on the baby."

"Of course. Take your time, Lieutenant."

She came out of the kitchen moments later with Jacob leaning on his high-tech metal cane. Pain etched his face. He sat down on the sofa opposite Lapis. Carmen brought coffee for them both. She turned away in a rush to tend to Emma.

"Seems you always get back to Dahlonega for my family tragedies, Captain."

"I take it, Corporal, you consider your mother's release from prison similar to the death of your brother."

Jacob shook his head vigorously. "Oh, they're both tragedies aw' right. But they ain't similar. The one tryin' to do some good, but instead his life gets taken from us. And the bad one bringing damage and destruction just keeps risin' like a vampire."

"I'm here to change that scenario, if I can."

"You? Don't see how you could make my whore mother disappear." Jacob chuckled at the thought.

Carmen appeared, standing at the entrance to the kitchen, bouncing Emma softly in her arms. "Please tell us. How would you go about helping us?" Carmen's eyes were lasers focused on her former commanding officer.

"You know as well as anyone, Lieutenant. Charity's real interest is recovering her drug business."

Jacob looked confused.

Carmen flushed and remained silent.

Lapis continued. "It's a shame she was paroled. She even got an early release. Only one day after the board approved her parole. Did RC tell you how she managed that sleight of hand? She said she had to come here and care for you. You had just OD'd and needed your mother."

"It was a fucking accident. Damn painkillers are fuckin' with my head! What are you talkin' about?"

"Particularly when they're not prescription-grade, am I right?"

Carmen asked, "Why are you here?"

Lapis smiled. "As I said, I'd like to help you. That's been the purpose of all my visits, hasn't it? Charity will have to agree to go to Florida."

"You sound just like RC. He's got a plan too. Seems like the two of you hate this woman as much as I do." Jacob sat forward. "I know why RC wants to get rid of her. She's been a pain to him since before I was born. But why you, Captain? What's your—"

A knock at the door interrupted Jacob. Lapis looked at his watch. It wasn't yet 9:00 a.m.

The voice on the other side of the door said, "Jacob, Carmen, it's Tina Spear."

"This isn't a good time, is it, Jacob?" Lapis said. "Ask her to come by, say, this afternoon. Or better yet, next week." Jacob stood up. His legs weren't steady. As he fell backward, he caught himself on the arm of his chair. Carmen put Emma in a highchair and rushed to Jacob's side.

"You know what she wants," Jacob said to Lapis.

"Of course. Now's not the time. Send her away, please."

Carmen walked to the front door and Jacob ambled behind her.

"Hello, Mrs. Spear," Carmen said, her voice quavering. "I'm afraid we can't have any visitors right now."

Tina saw Jacob behind Carmen. "Jacob, you're the only one who can give me the truth about your brother. How he died, why he died. I'm not leaving here until you share it with me. All of it. Please."

Jacob moved ahead of Carmen, into the doorway. "Look, ma'am, I know you were a good friend o' Ricky and all, but now is not—"

Tina walked past Jacob, who couldn't react fast enough to stop her. By the time Carmen realized what had happened, Tina was standing in the middle of the foyer. Virgil Lapis was sitting comfortably in an armchair. Tina shook her head to clear her vision, wondering what this visit could mean.

Lapis stood. "This is not a good time, Mrs. Spear. I advise you to go and come back later."

Facts and conjecture tumbled in Tina's mind. She moved into the house, ignoring the owners. "You. Captain Lapis. Why are you here? Why are you turning up in all these places that should have nothing to do with you?" Her thoughts continued to race. The warning issued from Tillyard leapt into her mind. *You don't want to become the loose end of a crime someone may be trying hard to cover up.*

"You have to leave now, Mrs. Spear," Jacob said, holding the door open.

"I'm staying, Jacob," she said without taking her eyes off Lapis. She took a seat.

"Look here. My ex-con mother and Gramma are going to be here this afternoon and I don't have—"

"Tell me what I want to know, and I'll be on my way."

Jacob looked at Lapis, who shook his head. Carmen took her baby out of the chair and into the kitchen.

Jacob said, "I'll just have to call RC over to haul you away, won't I?"

Lapis' eyes went wide. "It's so rare that I would even think of manhandling a woman, Mrs. Spear, so please don't make it necessary."

Why she didn't get up and run when every nerve in her body screamed for her to do just that, she never understood. When Lapis went to put his hands under her armpits, she slapped him. He shook it off and with a burst of strength lifted Tina out of the chair. She kneed him in the groin, loosening his grip, and ran to the center of the room and stood there panting. "Tell me what I want to know!" she screamed.

Jacob closed the front door.

"What a mess," Lapis said. "What a God-awful mess. It didn't have to be like this, you know." Reaching inside his jacket, Lapis unholstered a Heckler & Koch P7. From his pocket he pulled a silencer and screwed it into the pistol muzzle.

46

The Sheaves

Half a dozen cabs awaited the bus at the Dahlonega depot. Charity and Ruthann, each with one bag, disembarked and hailed one. Though the cabbie knew the road to Auraria, he missed the turnoff to Jacob's and had to turn around. Charity grumbled at him. The driver stopped at the bottom of the driveway to let the two women out.

"What the hell are you thinkin', huh?" Charity screamed. "We're older women here. We are not walking up this dirt and stone. You drive us all the way up."

The driver did as he was told, stopping the car about twenty feet from the front steps. "That's $8.50," he said.

"Pay the man, Ruthann," Charity said as she got out of the car. She gazed around her.

"What the …? Oh, good Christ," Ruthann muttered, fishing around in her bag for a small wad of bills. She peeled off a ten and threw it at the driver as she left the cab.

The driver backed up, spewing dust and dirt into the air, and sped away.

"Place looks nice," Ruthann chirped. "Kinda'in the woods. Private as all get-out."

Charity's head was swiveling. Her eyes and ears focused on the details, looking for something that wasn't right. "Bit quiet, don't you think? What's over there?" She pointed to the side of the hill, where she saw an Audi Cabriolet next to a pickup truck.

"Holy shit. Spear woman's here," Ruthann said.

Charity grabbed her mother's arm. "She's just wantin' the straight on Ricky, right? Shouldn't be a problem, long as Jacob comes clean with her. Or least gives her something she wants to believe. She don't wanna be around us any more than we want her around." She brushed her jeans and shook her shoulders. "Let's take a breath and go on in. Slowly. The less hassle, the better."

At the top of the stairs, Ruthann knocked.

The sputtering of wheels in gravel had alerted everyone in the house to a new arrival.

"Carmen, see if that's who we think it is," Lapis said.

She peered out the side window. "Ruthann and Charity are here."

"Hours ahead of schedule," Lapis said. "Well, well. The waiting is over, everyone." He got up and stood behind the door as Carmen opened it wide, head bowed and shaking.

"What's the matter, Carmen? You ain't happy to see us?" Ruthann said as she entered.

She saw Tina Spear sitting with her hands folded, looking at the wall. When Tina turned her face to the front door, Charity recognized the look. Terror. She pushed Ruthann into the house and tried to shut the door from the outside. Lapis swung around, and before Charity could flee down the steps, he grabbed her by the hair and dragged her into the house, shutting and locking the door.

He kicked Charity hard on her butt. She fell forward but turned around quickly to face her assailant.

Lapis knocked her down with a fist to her head, put his foot on her stomach, and pointed the gun at her face. "Five years in prison and you're still as predictable as when you went in."

"Fuck you, Virgil," Charity spat.

"Not for a while, Charity, and not ever again. Ruthann, why don't you take a seat next to Mrs. Spear over there."

"Captain," Jacob said, "this is way fucked-up. You can't do this shit in my house, with my family. You ..." He took a step toward Lapis.

"We're way past the point of no return, aren't we, Jacob? I mean, your brother got himself killed here not eight weeks ago."

Tina's mind broke through her panic at the mention of Ricky. "Did you kill him? Did you murder that innocent boy?" she said.

"Nothing quite so dramatic," Lapis said. "It was an accident."

Jacob took another step and spoke directly to Tina. "Ricky was ..." He swallowed hard. "He was thinkin' he was savin' my life when the captain, here, pointed my own gun at me."

"Remember who pulled the gun on whom, Jacob. You thought you could get out of the business, and so you're the one who threatened me. So unwise."

Jacob squared his shoulders as if to attack Lapis, but the captain lifted one hand from his pistol and waved it with a single finger raised. "Don't," he said.

Jacob looked at Tina. "When the captain took my gun away, Ricky jumped outta nowhere and grabbed the barrel. But he stumbled and the gun went off."

With his eyes still on Charity, Lapis said, "The boy should never have been here."

Tina's shoulders heaved. She felt both the horror of the truth and the euphoria of vindication as she stifled the scream mushrooming in her throat. Ricky had not committed suicide. He had committed an act of misplaced heroism. She put her hands to her face and let the tears flow.

"Now what's left is the hard work of the cleanup," Lapis said. "Ruthann, come over here, please. Lieutenant, do you have duct tape?"

Carmen nodded.

"Good. Please get it and give it to Ruthann. Do not try anything to upset this process. There are lives at stake."

Carmen fetched the roll of duct tape and handed it over.

"Good. Now, Ruthann, I want you to tape your daughter's leg to Mrs. Spear's leg and bind each of their hands together."

"What the fu …" Ruthann hesitated.

Lapis pointed the gun at her. "Let's not add to the body count, Ruthann."

Lapis pulled Tina from her chair and pushed her down next to Charity, who started kicking her mother. Until Lapis put the gun on Charity's forehead.

"What's your plan, Virgil? Gonna kill us, taped together like mules?"

"You two stand up slowly. Slowly. … Good. Now walk to the back of the house."

"Captain, you can't do this," Jacob said, taking another two steps toward him.

Lapis swiveled quickly, pointing his gun at Jacob. "Yes, I can, Corporal. I have my retirement to think about." Turning back to the two women, he said, "Keep walking, you two. We're going outside so these fine folks don't have to see what comes next."

"Virgil!" Jacob screamed. Before he could launch himself at Lapis, two quick rounds from the gun whizzed past Carmen and Ruthann, into the living room wall.

"That's the last warning any of you will receive. Let this unfold and all will be back to normal soon."

For Tina, now bound to a wretched, disgusting woman, this was too much. "You piece of shit, Charity Plyer. This is your fault. You sorry, pathetic woman. Now you've got me killed in your cyclone of filth."

"Oh, ain't them some words from a highbrow hag who ain't got sense to know when to stop hasslin' folks."

"Open the door, ladies," Lapis said from behind them.

They grabbed the doorknob at the same time, looked at each other with fire in their eyes, and fought for control.

"Enough!" With the gun pushed onto the back of Charity's head, Lapis said, "Mrs. Spear, please open the door."

They shuffled onto the landing of the back porch stairs and stopped. Going down the steps would require coordination to which neither woman was inclined.

"You first," Tina said.

"Hell you say, I ain't goin' first."

"Goddamn it! You are all about yourself, aren't you?"

"Like you're not, you stuck-up priss. Fuck you!"

"Fuck you too."

The two women started hitting each other with their bound hands.

Lapis took two steps forward to break up the brawl. When he did, Charity bent hard at the waist, pulling Tina with her. Suddenly, with all her strength she recoiled backward, smashing her head into Lapis's nose. He went down on one knee and started to rise. But Tina lost her balance, and the two women fell onto Lapis, knocking him flat on his back onto the porch. Though the gun was still in his hand, Lapis was trapped by the bodies of the two women he had so cleverly bound together.

Ruthann rushed out onto the porch and saw the gun in Lapis's hand. She stomped on it until he loosened his grip. She grabbed the gun and pointed it at Lapis. "Everybody just calm the fuck down. Right now! You hear? All of you!"

The three-body pile stopped writhing. Tina and Charity could see Ruthann had the pistol. It took them multiple tries to roll off Lapis. When they did, Ruthann took a step back and pointed the gun at the captain.

"Virgil, this ain't no way to settle whatever score you got with Charity. And killin' some innocent woman—lunatic and all she is—jus' gonna make everything worse. Stop this shit, okay?"

"Give me the gun, Ruthann," Lapis said, extending his hand that was red with blood from his nose. At the same time, he slid his other hand down his leg and gripped his second pistol. He repeated, "Give me the gun."

As Ruthann took another step back, Lapis pulled out the weapon and fired at Ruthann. The bullet hit her square in the chest, and she fell hard onto the porch, the gun plopping from her hand and onto the stairs.

Lapis turned over, aimed his weapon at the two bound women, and pulled the trigger.

47

Rendezvous

Detective Tillyard's call with the St. Augustine police couldn't take place until later in the afternoon, giving him the opportunity to meet Tina earlier than they had planned. Perhaps he could convince her, over coffee, of the danger she was courting. But if her husband's assault was not enough to dissuade her, Tillyard was pretty sure there would be no convincing Tina. There was no answer from phoning her room. He asked the front desk. Mrs. Spear had checked out thirty minutes ago.

"Damn that headstrong woman," Tillyard said out loud. He jumped into his squad car and drove to the Plyer residence. He thought to call her cell phone but knew it would be useless.

He pulled up next to Tina's Audi and walked toward the stairs, when he heard a shot ring out from the back of the house. His instincts and training ignited like a bottle rocket. Holding his Glock 37 in both hands, he ran to the back of the house. A second shot rang out as he turned the corner. A man on his back was pointing a weapon at two women rolling on the porch.

"Police! Drop it now!" Tillyard said.

The man ignored Tillyard and moved the weapon forward slightly.

"Stop now!" the detective called out and fired.

From the upward angle, the bullet crashed through Lapis's shoulder and into his neck. Tillyard rushed up the porch stairs. He kicked away the gun lying next to Lapis and knelt beside him. He had stopped breathing. From the two women he heard coughing and grunting. Carmen came out onto the porch.

"My God!" she said and bent down to look at the wounded women.

Tillyard cried out, "Mrs. Plyer, go call 911 now!"

Carmen ran into house.

Down two steps he saw Tina pinned under a woman who was taped to her. The other woman was bleeding from her side.

"Help," Tina cried. "Please help me."

Pulling a knife from his belt to cut the tape, Tillyard said, "Ms. Spear? Tina? Are you hurt?"

"I-I don't think so, but Charity's been shot."

Carmen rushed back onto the porch with rags and a bucket of water. She knelt by Ruthann and felt for her pulse. Finding none, she went to where Tillyard was still freeing Tina from Charity. She checked her former captain's pulse. Shaking her head, she moved over to Charity, compressing the area where the blood was gushing.

"Not dead yet," Charity wheezed.

"Not my fault," said Tina.

48

Make Mine a Double

PRESENT

RC was in his squad car, ahead of the emergency vehicle. He called Tillyard on the police band radio, but there was no answer. He dialed Tillyard's cell phone. "Talk to me, Detective."

"Jacob and family are shaken, but not hurt. Can't say the same for your ex, Boss. Though she's alive. Two others are gone. One is the army officer I met at the memorial service for Richard. The other, I'm guessing, is Charity's mom."

Tina nodded.

"I'll be there in two minutes."

"We're not going anywhere just yet." Tillyard hung up.

Jacob came out onto the porch and knelt next to Carmen, by his mother. "Is she going to make it?" he asked his wife.

"Can't say for certain. I'm doing what I can. The paramedics should be able to stabilize her at least until she can get to the hospital."

Charity lifted an arm slightly to touch her son. "Jacob, honey, I'm sorry."

Jacob shook his head. "You've always been sorry, Ma. Just hold on, will ya?"

"I mean I'm sorry about our son."

Jacob turned his head away. "Don't say another fuckin' thing, you hear me? You shut up and go to the hospital."

"I'm sorry," Charity said. She closed her eyes. Her breathing slowed but didn't stop.

Tina looked at Jacob, more confused than she had ever been. But only for a moment. "Oh my God. Jacob. You were Ricky's father. You were … I can't …" She held one hand to her mouth and gripped Detective Tillyard's arm with the other.

Jacob was a jumble of shaking limbs and clenched teeth as he tried to stand. Tina went to help him. He waved her off and managed to get stable on his own.

Tillyard went over to Ruthann's body to start reconstructing the events in his mind.

Tina said, "Jacob, I can't even imagine your agony, the sorrow—"

"I'm beggin' you, Mrs. Spear. Don't. Yeah, I was Ricky's dad and his brother. But you gotta understand. He was my best friend. My best—"

Jacob stopped talking and let Tina place a hand on his shoulder. He put his hand on top of hers momentarily and left her to go to the kitchen.

Sirens in the distance became louder until RC led the ambulance up the Plyer driveway.

Charity was taken to Lumpkin Hospital. Tina refused any treatment for the moment. RC made the call to the county coroner.

Tillyard and the chief worked the crime scene together while Carmen sat with Tina in the kitchen. Tillyard spoke with Jacob as he rested on the couch. The detective came outside to speak to RC.

"I finally get why you went out on a limb about Ricky's, quote, suicide, Boss," Tillyard said.

"Do you now? You must enlighten me. You know I have the county commission to explain all this to."

"Not sure my understanding will help. But I spoke to Jacob just now. He was having trouble keeping out of the captain's drug business. He was accepting lots more pills than he would ever use for his prescriptions. You weren't just protecting him emotionally. You were trying to keep him outta jail."

"Guilty on that one, Detective. A full-on investigation of Ricky's death would have led to Lapis, eventually, and Jacob would have gone down hard. As far as this mess goes, we'll complete the circle on Lapis, Charity, and Ruthann, then tie a big knot on the case and throw it into the crapper."

"There will still be unanswered questions, Boss."

"And they'll stay that way. You finish up with the coroner, will you? You and he should be good friends by now." RC turned and went to his son's side for a few moments before leaving. Tillyard took some water offered by Carmen and went to Tina. He sat next to her on the couch.

"Looks like we both got a lot more than we bargained for here," he said.

Tina looked at him. "You think? That's quite the understatement, even for you. But I admit your instincts on this were right. Knowing everything I know about Ricky, about Jacob, the drugs, all of it, I can't imagine I would have done anything differently. How could I?"

EPILOGUE

Two months later, the sunrise through Devon Tillyard's hotel window was brilliant, even through the gauze of the curtains and his translucent eyelids. His midnight arrival the night before at the DoubleTree Hotel in St. Augustine had been greeted with the hotel chain's famous cookies, a fitting dessert to his chicken sandwich and sweet tea from a rest stop on I-75. Up with a jump, he pulled on his gym shorts and running shoes and set into a jog down San Marco Avenue, toward St. Augustine's city center. When he looped back to his hotel, he noticed a cross in the distance peering over the trees, a sentinel, maybe, in prior times. Or perhaps a witness. He veered his run toward the cross, which towered over 200 feet above the grounds of the Mission Nombre de Dios and the site of the first European Catholic Mass on what would become US soil. He ran past the archeological dig, along the inland waterway, and back to his hotel while thinking of the time when the first Spanish settlers eked out a living so brutally sparse yet connected to this new unforgiving land. He thought of how far Western civilization had come in over four centuries since the first landing and of how far it still had to go.

After he showered and dressed, he looked at his watch. He made a call to Sergeant Wilmot and confirmed the start time for the trial of Cole Hart. With at least an hour before he had to appear as witness, Tillyard walked downstairs to the dining room, made himself a cup of coffee, Tillyard-style—cream and three sugars—and awaited his breakfast guest.

Tina Spear entered the hotel lobby and looked around. Seeing Tillyard at the far end of the restaurant, she glanced at her reflection in the floor-to-ceiling window, took a breath, and smiled.

Tillyard stood as she approached his table. She put her arms out and they hugged. She patted his back before taking a seat.

"Thanks for joining me, Tina. It's good to see you again. Particularly when you're not tracking or dodging criminals."

Tina smiled. "It's very nice to see you again, Detective. I'm particularly looking forward to showing you as much of St. Augustine as you have time for."

"I'll know later today how much time that will be. Probably only a couple of days. I'll have to be in court most of the time. But not all." He smiled.

"I'm looking forward to catching up more at dinner this evening. I suspect Dahlonega has returned to the sleepy northern Georgia cultural center it's always been. No longer a hub for drug trafficking?"

"We're doing our best. The Plyers had some information they used to keep themselves from prosecution. It's generated some additional investigations. Sleepy would be just fine for us in Dahlonega. Crime-wise, that is."

Tina laughed. "Okay. And for tonight, our dinner reservation is for seven at Michael's. They have a young chef there I know very well and she's fabulous. I'll plan to pick you up here, unless you call and tell me you're out having a beer with your new law enforcement buddies."

"Here is where I expect you'll find me. Do you know if your husband will testify?"

"His deposition could be enough, so he won't have to. But we won't know until just before the trial begins. He'll have to wait and see."

"How is your husband, if I can ask?"

"Walter has healed nicely from his injuries and is moving on with his life." She reached across the table and put her hand on Devon's. "And I'm moving on with mine."

About the Author

A former tech executive and Peace Corps country director with 20 years living and working on five continents, John E. Mooney is now writing full time. He has degrees in Literature, Mechanical Engineering and Business. His first novel, *The Siren of Good Intentions*, debuted in 2020. Although he grew up in Connecticut, he now calls himself 'a proud Florida Man, living in a sub-tropical wetland aviary with my remarkable wife, a few spoiled pets and friends that keep me young at heart."

Also by J. E. Mooney: The Siren of Good Intentions

Visit: http://www.jemooneybooks.com
Facebook: /jemooneybooks

Made in the USA
Las Vegas, NV
04 February 2023

66899049R00181